THE HARVEST SAGA

CASEY L. BOND

Reap
Copyright © 2014 by Casey L. Bond. All rights reserved.
First Edition.

This book is a work of fiction and does not represent any individual, living or dead. Names, characters, places and incidents either are products of the author's imagination or are used fictitiously. Scripture quotations taken from the Holy Bible, King James Version, Cambridge, 1769. All rights reserved.

Author photo taken by Sarah Dunlap.
Book cover designed by Casey L. Bond.
Professionally Edited by Anna Coy of AGC Editing and Services.
Paperback and E-book formatted by Nadege Richards of Inkstain Interior Book Designing.

Published in the United States of America.
ISBN-13: 978-1496046154
ISBN-10: 1496046153

dedication

THE LORD HAS BLESSED ME in unimaginable ways. I am thankful for each and every one. I'm thankful for my husband, Elton and our two beautiful daughters, Juliet and Eris. Watching them grow into beautiful young ladies is one of the best and most profound experiences of my life. I pray that I never take that blessing for granted.

I'm blessed with loving, supportive parents and grandparents, along with amazing extended family members. My friends and family mean the world to me. Some friends, I've had since childhood. I want to mention a few of those amazing chicks here. Heather Persinger, Erica Dixon and Tiffany Cabell have had my back since the sixth grade. They still do. My Church girls, Lisa Lovejoy, Tara Sansom, Emily Bond and Nikki Midkiff are beyond wonderful. They are uplifting and challenge me to be better.

Since my first book was published in October 2013, I've been on a wild ride. Sometimes it's been daunting and there have been several authors who have helped me trudge through and emerge on the other side of this adventure unscathed. I could fill a book with everyone who has helped me and I appreciate you all.

Just to mention a few, I want to thank my awesome friend Rachael Brownell. Her daily support and friendship has been such a blessing to me. She is my sister from another mister! I just love her. Delisa Lynn is another wonderful new friend. She is kind and sweet and incredibly supportive. Anna Coy has become more than just an editor, she's become my friend and for that I am grateful. She is hilarious, kind and a beautiful human being.

I want to mention the awesome authors who I'll get to meet at the Louisville Authors Event, UtopYA Con and anywhere else that will put up with me! I also love the Indie-pendents! You divas know who you are!

   To the readers: Thank you for reading what I spent so long writing. Without you, there would be no point in my dream. You give it wings. Thank you from the bottom of my heart.

Juliet & Eris:

DON'T EVER LET SOMEONE MAKE YOU FEEL LIKE
LESSER. YOU ARE GREAT. I LOVE YOU BOTH SO
VERY MUCH.

acknowledgements

—Anna Coy, I don't know what I'd do without you. You're an amazing editor, a wonderful person and have been such a great friend to me. Thank you for all that you do and for your love and support.

—Nadege has some amazing talent as a formatter and I am really excited to have been fortunate enough to work with her on Reap.

—To my awesome beta-readers: I want to thank you for taking the time to read over Reap in its infancy. I took all of your suggestions and observations into consideration and hope that you will also be proud of the final product. So, thank you, Mom (Sherry Bayless), Jill Holton, Rachael Brownell, Delisa Lynn, Anna Coy, Ericka Pasco, Megan Bracken-Bagley, Kristina Renee, Allyson Gottlieb, Cydney Lawson & Amy Miles. You are all very busy people and I appreciate the time you spent reading and helping me better Reap.

—I want to thank all of my UtopYA peeps for their encouragement and for sharing tips and advice on the boards.

—Thank you to everyone who spreads the word about my book, whether by mouth, on social media sites, or in the press. I appreciate you so very much. Thanks to all who attend my book signings or come to my booths at the local festivals and national conferences. I want to thank all of the amazing venues who have hosted book signings for me in the past, and those who might do so in the future. Thank you Eliot Parker for featuring me and my books on your television program, "Chapters." I hope my nervousness didn't freak you out. I'm outgoing, but am camera-shy. Thanks to the Herald-Dispatch for their recent coverage, and Cindy Martin / WV South magazine for its upcoming feature.

Prologue

LUELLA KELLEY—15 YEARS AGO

THE FEW MINUTES BEFORE DAWN were usually the most serene. Not today. Today, everything would change. Today, we would protect the future against the tyrants who ruled over us. The sky was lightening little by little, shedding the thick, dark blanket of night. Worn wooden planks creaked underfoot as I paced back and forth. Standing still wasn't an option. The platform of the village's train depot was empty. I'd made sure of it. So, my feet wore a path into the weathered wood as I silently prayed that everything would go smoothly, would go as planned.

My brother had gotten himself in trouble. Four years ago he'd been transferred from our village to work in the factories in Olympus, a Greater City. Two years ago, his lover had given birth to a baby girl. He was unable to marry her. He was a Lesser. She was a Greater. It was illegal for them to even speak. He wasn't even permitted to make eye contact with her. So, how they had met, fallen in love, and been intimate was beyond me.

A few generations ago, a great plague swept through The United States of America, what had until then, been a great and powerful country. The world had been connected in ways that I could hardly wrap my head around. It was said that people could ride great ships through the air, cross oceans in a matter of hours.

The plague spread from America to the other continents and countries, leaving nothing but death and sorrow in its wake. Ninety percent of the Earth's population was wiped out in a matter of only a few months. Certain technologies survived, along with a few of the experts who knew how to use them. Precautions against further spread of the disease were taken, and eventually, the plague was laid to rest along with its victims.

Those who had survived the disease, which affected everyone regardless of station, were tested. Those deemed to have superior genes, whose bodies could likely survive another onslaught of illness in the future, were separated from those whose genetics were less-than-ideal. And so began the separation of Greaters and Lessers.

The Lessers served the Greaters from small villages where their lives were consumed with producing raw materials that the Greaters needed. Over time, the divide between the two groups had formed into a deep, dangerous chasm. The Greaters had become power-hungry and oppressive, abusive of the power that they'd claimed.

So, I was shocked about my brother's news. He could be beheaded for consorting with the woman. I shuddered to think about what they might do if the Greaters discovered their child. She was a hybrid, a mix of both worlds. I had to help. I would hide her. Keep her safe. She was our future, the best of both Greater and Lesser, belonging to neither side, yet an equal and important part of both.

When the Greater woman had been questioned about the pregnancy, she had lied. She'd protected him. No doubt she loved him. But the baby had grown into a toddler and was now much more difficult to conceal. I knew this day would probably come, but had no idea what the urgency was. I'd received a communication from him, which was risky enough for both of us. If someone found it, we'd both be hanged, so I deleted it almost as quickly as I read it. The three needed a way out of Olympus, and the baby needed to be hidden. She needed a new home—a loving home. I was their only option. But having no children of my own, I would have to figure out how to provide that for her. I had no idea how to care for a toddler. But, I supposed we'd learn together.

The sky lightened further, lofty clouds streaked happily across the sky, tinged with oranges and yellows. The train would be here any minute. The smell of spring was everywhere; fresh and earthy. The fields were being fertilized. New ones were being sown. We would nurture and care for them until they bore their fruit in the fall. Our village was Orchard, and we grew apples for the Greaters who required the bounty of the Earth.

The loud horn of the train sounded in the distance, between two hills, further than I could see. Soon, puffs of gray smoke rose slowly and hung thickly in the valley beyond. Old and rusty, the wheels of the train screeched and squealed as the engineer applied his brake. Sparks flew from the contact with the rail in various places. The metal cars themselves were also rusted. It was a cargo train, the only kind that would be expected here in Orchard.

Car after car rattled past me. Third car from the back, I thought. That's where they were supposed to be. I knocked lightly on the steel door and then slid open the latch. It was hollow, with the exception of stacked wooden crates, buckets and bushels. I whispered for him. "Adam."

"Lulu?" A voice whispered in return.

"You have to hurry. The train is only supposed to stop for twenty minutes."

My brother stepped forward, carrying a child, whose head lolled limply on his shoulder. She was asleep and looked more peaceful than anything I'd ever seen before in my life. Drool pooled in the corner of her little mouth and her eyelashes fluttered lightly. Her curly brownish-red hair was stirred lightly by the breeze. My heart attached to her immediately. My niece.

A woman stepped out from behind Adam. He cleared his throat. "Lu, this is Kaia." He looked wearily from her to me. I stepped forward and offered her my hand.

"Hello, Kaia. I can't imagine how difficult this must be for you."

She nodded and tears cascaded from her greenish eyes, their pupils rimmed in Greater gold. It was an attribute they all bore, though the rings of some Greaters were more pronounced than others. "Does she have the ring?"

Adam swallowed and shifted his feet. "Yes. But it's very small. Almost unnoticeable. Will she be safe here?"

"I believe so. I have traveled out of the village a handful of times, but I'm the only one who has seen a Greater in years."

They both nodded. Tears welled in Adam's eyes as he peeled the child away from his torso and transferred her onto mine. She probably weighed 30 pounds. The little one stirred for a moment and then settled back down. "Please say goodbye quickly and hide yourselves again. This train will continue to Vesuvius. A man named Brock will meet you there and provide you with new identification."

"Thank you, Lulu. Please take care of her. If anyone finds out about her, please send word, or get her to safety."

"Why is this so urgent? What's happening in Olympus?"

A great burst of steam and smoke sizzled from the train's engine, several cars away.

Kaia jumped at the sound and huddled into Adam, who wrapped his arm around her lovingly. "I don't have time to explain. Just please keep her safe. No one can know she's a Greater, or part Greater, anyway."

"Luella?" The engineer called over my comm.

I depressed the button and answered. "Yes?"

"Are you finished? I need to pull out as soon as possible."

"Yes. Everything is secure. Please continue to your destination."

"Thank you. Preparing for departure."

"Have a safe trip."

His static-filled chuckle rang out. "Always. See you on the next pass-through."

Looking back at Adam and Kaia, my heart thundered in my chest. "Hide. I *will* keep her safe. I promise. I would give my life to keep that promise. It doesn't mean she'll be treated well here. Life is hard in Orchard, as in all Lesser villages, but I will give her a normal Lesser life."

My brother kissed my cheek and then brushed the child's hair back from her little face and kissed her, too. "Goodbye, Abby Blue."

"Abby Blue?"

"Yeah," he stroked her cheek. "Her name is Abigail Blue Kelley. I call her Abby Blue."

Kaia kissed her baby girl goodbye, and Adam had to pull her away and back onto the train car so that I could latch the door. As the wheels began to move them down the track and away from me, I could hear her cries. They echoed through the old metal car, fading into the cool morning air. I was certain that that sound would haunt me for the rest of my life.

Chapter 1

"THE FIELD OF THE POOR MAY YIELD MUCH FOOD,
BUT IT IS SWEPT AWAY THROUGH INJUSTICE." —
PROVERBS 13:23

I KISSED LULU GOODBYE AND rushed out the door pausing only for a moment to tie the lace of my left shoe. Most evenings I flung the shoes off, still tied, into the corner of my bedroom. They must have come undone. I valued my sleep and mornings weren't my thing, so even stopping to tie the stupid things wasn't normally an option. If I didn't run fast, I would be late and late wasn't tolerated. I wrapped my hair band around my wrist and ran—ran like the devil himself was on my heels.

The earth beneath me was parched despite the dew that hung heavy off of the grass and leaves around us, glittering coyly in the morning sunshine. Clouds of dust billowed up underfoot as I jumped over fallen logs and dodged ruts in the well-worn pathways of the village. Chest heaving and breath shallow, I finally spotted the whitewashed wooden fence surrounding the orchard. Running down the path and cutting the corner in the grass, I used the corner fence post to turn with so I wouldn't lose speed or momentum, and propelled myself forward.

I threw one leg over the bottom rail and ducked underneath the top one before taking off again, weaving my way through the thousands of rows that would lead me to my work for the day. A shrill scream stopped me in my tracks. The dust cloud that followed in my wake caught up with me. I coughed and swiped the air to get it away from my mouth, but I could still taste the earth on my tongue.

Another high-pitched scream. From the left. I jogged to the end of the row and saw her. Megan's trembling little body was backing quickly toward me. She shook her head fiercely, brown curls frantically bouncing to and fro. She turned to run toward me, but I caught her and turned her around to face me. Her eyes were wide with fear. "Megan? What's the matter?"

Swallowing thickly, she turned and looked behind her. My eyes followed hers. Norris stood nearby with his back leaning against one of the fence posts, an evil grin plastered on his face.

"Back to work. This isn't your business, Abigail."

Clenching my teeth, I ignored him. "Megan, what happened?"

Her trembling little voice shook when she explained. "I was so hungry. I just wanted one apple. I took it. I'm so sorry." Tears exploded from her eyes and her tiny arms and hands wrapped around my neck. I hugged her tight and shushed her.

Locking eyes with the disgusting man in front of me, I squared my shoulders, preparing for the fight I knew was inevitable now. "She was hungry. She won't steal again."

Chuckling, he grinned at us both, the scar on his face puckering and pulling his flesh. "You don't get any say in this, Abigail. She stole. You know the punishment for stealing. Don't you, girl?"

Megan nodded.

"If she's old enough to understand the consequences, she's old enough to know better than to steal. She gets five lashes." Before I even saw him flinch, he grabbed Megan from my arms and tucked her under his own. She kicked, screamed, and thrashed to get away. But, it was all in vain. Shrieking, she pleaded, "Please! Please, I promise I'll never take another apple. Please!"

Gritting my teeth, I ran after them and snatched her back from him. I set her on her feet and pushed her toward the sanctuary of the Orchard. "Run, Megan." She hesitated. I pointed into the orchard. "Find Kyan. Run!" Megan looked at Norris and then back to me. She took off as fast as her little legs could carry her and disappeared into the trees.

Barely able to breathe, I turned to face Norris. Judge, jury, and executioner all rolled into one fun package. That was Norris. Fear and adrenaline coursed through my body, shaking its very foundation. A sickening grin erupted on his face. "Looks like you're taking her punishment. You're old enough to be considered an adult now. You'll get the full fifteen."

There was no point in arguing. I was almost seventeen. And I'd learned the hard way more than once, that arguing with Norris always made things worse.

∞

A GUTTURAL SOUND ECHOED AROUND me. Sweat beaded heavily upon my brow and upper lip, before the droplets could no longer withstand the force of gravity, and carved their way down my face. I sank my teeth deep into the fullness of my bottom lip in a feeble attempt to draw attention away from the searing pain slicing through my back. A tangy, coppery taste flooded my mouth. I released my lip. Tried to lick away the blood.

"Shh. It's okay. I've got you. I'm taking you to the healer." He never paused, just carried me like a child, my legs wrapped around him hooking together by the ankles at the small of his back. I clung tight to him like a tick, choking his neck, afraid to let go. With each step, each jostle, the pieces of the torn flesh on my back separated ever so slightly further apart. But, the pain didn't feel slight at all. Another sound was ripped from my throat.

"Ky," I whimpered almost inaudibly, the words carried on an exhaled breath.

"Shh. Almost there." I forced my eyes open, allowing tears to escape in big pooling puddles that spread over the gray cotton of Ky's shirt and soaked in. The world bounced around me. Leaves that only hinted at the yellow that would soon overcome them, waved solemnly at me moved by the steady wind that blows constantly through the valley. Bile burned my throat. *My back. Oh, God.* I clamped them shut again.

A tree root dissected the path causing Kyan to stumble, a curse flew loud and free from his mouth. The sound of my scream echoed through the hills closing in around us. My back was tearing open and I was certain that this was the beginning of the end for me. I was dying, or would soon.

A sound like rushing water filled my ears just before black dots began to cloud my vision. He stepped up onto a porch covered end to end with planters in varying shapes and sizes, each overflowing with herbs. Medicines. I smelled mint, lavender, thyme, lemongrass with each step he took toward the door. This was the porch of the healer, I realized, just before everything faded to black. We were here.

Muffled sounds filled my ears. *Am I dead?* No. I could hear Ky's voice. And her's; Evelyn. Evelyn has been the healer in our village for longer than I could remember, even before I was born, or came to live here, anyway. I can picture her shriveled hands, the skin soft but paper-thin. The blue of her veins was visible through her delicate, translucent skin. But those hands. Those miraculous hands had healed and comforted so many through the years. And now, she was using them on me.

Lightning ripped through my back. Those hands were touching it. And, oh, how I prayed she would stop. But these wounds had cut deep. Into a place so deep, they would never heal, even if the flesh and muscle of my back ever did.

The muffled sound of whimpering filled my ears. *Who is that?* Confusion set in and I briefly wondered who else was in the room with me, until I realized that the sound had been my own. "Are you awake? If so, squeeze my hand." Her cool hand gripped mine and I concentrated hard, clenched my teeth and finally willed my fingers to tighten around hers. "Okay, dear. You're going to be in a lot of pain. I'm going to mix a special tea to take the edge off and Kyan is going to help you drink it while I tend to your wounds."

I squeezed her hand again in acknowledgement. A heavy sigh filled the room. A few minutes later, the sound of chair legs scooting across the rough wooden floor startled me and I opened my eyes. The lids were so heavy and it took so much energy just to try to keep them open.

I couldn't see his face, just his legs and stomach, but Ky was now seated beside the bed that I lay upon. He smelled like crisp leaves in the fall and sunshine all year long. And I would know that smell anywhere. He lifted my head slightly and positioned the porcelain mug at my lips. "Drink."

His voice sounded thick, gruff. *He must be angry at me.* I was angry. Not because of what I did. I would do it again in a heartbeat. I was angry because I had to do it at all.

I sipped slowly, gingerly from the mug. The liquid was steaming hot and horribly bitter, but I drank it down, or tried to, anyway. Some of it dribbled down my chin, and Ky swiped it away before holding the mug back up for me again. I gulped the rest down quickly in an attempt to get some relief and to just get it over with.

I hissed as Evelyn spread something cold and slimy over my skin. "I'm sorry, dear. But, there's no other way. Your back is really mangled. It's going to take a while to heal properly. Packing the wounds with this poultice is the only way to jumpstart that process." She sighed deeply and I realized that she had been the one to release the sigh that had filled the room earlier.

She plopped more of the slime onto my back. It burned a bit, but at the same time, was cool and soothing. I relaxed, sinking my head further into the soft down pillow beneath it. My body became very heavy. My arms and legs felt strange, like someone was poking them with a thousand small needles, and I wasn't sure that I could lift them anymore, even if I wanted to. "Feeling tired?" she asked.

I nodded, as well as I could, into the pillow that my face was nestled. "Good. The medicine is working." *Her voice sounds funny.* My eyelids drifted shut. Before too long, sleep claimed me.

"WAKE UP, ABBY." THE DEEP timbre of Kyan's voice hovered close to my ear. "Time to get you home." I blinked slowly, purposefully. My eyelids were heavy. The rough, calluses on Kyan's hands scraped gently against my arms as he pulled me upright. "If there was any other way to carry you, I would, but neither Evelyn nor I can figure out an alternative that wouldn't hurt you worse."

I nodded as he positioned himself in front of me and then once again lifted me like a child. I held tight, trying to will the fuzziness clouding my mind and vision away. Ky, usually talkative, was quiet, which probably meant that he was mad. He carried me down the worn pathway through the sycamores and pines, splashed across the tiny creek, toward my house. I lived in my aunt Lulu's small cabin on the outskirts of Orchard Village, a Lesser settlement.

He never faltered while carrying my weight along with his own. My body felt like it weighed a ton. A few minutes later, Ky stepped onto my porch, through the front door and into my bedroom. He'd brought one of his big button-down shirts for me to wear. Though I was all but swimming in it, it was functional– loose and didn't cling to the wounds or bandages on my back.

The buttons would make it easy to put on and remove. He lowered me down, positioning me just in front of my bed. My feet found the floor and I held up my own weight, steadied by his hands upon my arms. "Norris came by." He cleared his throat of the thickness that hung onto his words.

I cringed. Just the sound of his name was enough to remind me of both the sound and feel of the sharp crack of his whip. "What did he want?"

"To hand down the rest of your punishment." Kyan's words dripped of contempt.

A bitter laugh escaped my mouth. "What more can he possibly do to me?"

"It can always get worse, Abs. You're banned from the orchards for now. You'll work this week and maybe next, as a servant." His words trailed away.

"What? What do you mean? I can work in the orchards."

He shook his head. "No. Right now you can't."

"You're siding with him? He's a monster!"

Ky grabbed my chin, with his forefinger and thumb, and gently forced my face upward. My eyes followed. *Traitors.*

"No." His deep brown eyes bore into mine. His hair had been cut. It was short and golden—a halo on my angelic best friend. He clenched his jaw, working the muscle in his cheek. "I don't agree with anything Norris does, but—"

I tried to turn away, but he refused to release my chin. "But, you need to heal. If serving in a house for a week or so allows you to do that, then I'm all for it."

Tears flooded my eyes, blurring him for a moment. "Don't cry, Abby." His voice softened and he pulled me against his chest, holding tight to my upper arms. He was being so careful not to touch my back, although I wished with everything in me that he could wrap his arms around me and squeeze me for all he was worth.

Kyan had been my best friend ever since I moved here to live with my aunt. He lived just across the hay field that stretched out gracefully between our homes. Long ago, a path was trodden through the center of it, worn by both his feet and mine.

"Where do I have to work?" His body tensed. This was bad. *Oh, no. Not Norris. Please, not him.* "The Preston's house."

"No. I won't do it. I'm not going anywhere near Norris again. Not if I can help it." Norris was Councilman Preston's henchman.

"You don't have a choice. You can't get lashed again. He'd kill you if you defied him again. He almost did this time."

"I didn't defy him. I stood up for Megan."

Confusion knitted his brow. "Megan? I thought you were punished for insubordination."

"Yes, Megan. Five-year-old Megan. He caught her picking apples in one of the trees that line the orchard. She was starving, Ky. He was going to drag her to the square. She was kicking and screaming, crying, and begging him to let her go. He pulled out that whip and I...I just couldn't let him do it. She's so little. He has no business whipping a child."

"So, you distracted him?"

"No. Well, sort of. I grabbed her from him, and told her to run and get you."

His jaw clenched again and he looked away from me. "You took her punishment." It wasn't a question. He knew me like no one else.

"Yes."

He pulled me close again and planted a soft kiss upon my temple. "I've gotta go. I'm supposed to be in the north orchard."

I pushed him back. "Go. He's looking for a reason to use that stupid whip any chance he gets. You'll be next."

He laughed dangerously. "He knows I'm here. But, I have to get back. I'll check on you tonight after I get home."

"Where's Lulu?"

"Not sure, but she won't be happy to find you in this state. She may take her shotgun after Norris."

I nodded in agreement. My aunt would not be happy about this. She just might get the old shotgun out. She's pulled the rusty thing out for less. Of course, I didn't think anyone could stop Norris. He'd made a deal with the devil, losing his soul long ago. I was sure of it. He'd been terrorizing this village for years. Since the fool who had been sheriff appointed him the job at least ten years ago.

Norris wasn't old, maybe thirty-eight or thirty-nine, but he was one sadistic, evil man. Anyone who would even consider raising a horse whip to the back of a five-year-old, starving little girl has more than a screw loose. And, he was intimidating. His hair was a dark brown and always hung long and greasy into his eyes. The scar he wore on his right cheek was jagged and warped his already pockmarked skin.

Children had made up stories for years about how he got it. But, I wasn't sure if anyone really knew the truth about how he got that scar.

I squeezed Kyan once more and then all but pushed him out my bedroom door, wincing when I raised my arms a bit too high. I slowly followed him to the front door, which was only a few more feet away, and watched him jump down off the porch and start toward the orchard. "I'll be back tonight. Go rest. You start work tomorrow," he yelled back at me.

"Great," I muttered as I watched his tall form crest the small hill and then disappear behind it. I closed the front door. It was made of old barn wood and you had to slam it to get it to close all the way. I stepped through our kitchen slash living area and retreated into my bedroom.

The bedrooms in the cabin were small, barely large enough for our tiny beds and small wooden wardrobes. The whole cabin was wood. Wooden walls led to wooden floors. Wooden beams and planks lined the ceiling that wasn't quite tall enough. I'd always felt smothered by it, like it was slowly creeping down on me, instead of me growing taller.

There were no windows in the bedrooms in an attempt to conserve heat in the winter. Unfortunately, the other nine months of the year in Orchard weren't cold. And, the heat got trapped then, too. In the summertime, I slept on the porch or on the living room couch with the front door propped wide open.

My back stung and some of the slashes began to throb. Suddenly thankful for my day's reprieve, I decided to rest. Retreating to my room, I lied down on my stomach and settled my head on my crossed arms. My back spread and was uncomfortable for a moment until I relaxed. Sleep came swiftly.

∞

A SLAM JOLTED ME OUT of my slumber. Another slam echoed in the front of the cabin and footsteps hurried to my door. I didn't know how long I'd slept or if it was still daylight, but I was still tired and just wanted to retreat back into the sweet abyss again. My door opened and I turned my head to see my aunt standing in the doorway.

"What happened, Abby?" She rushed over. I tried to push myself up, but my back was so stiff. The skin even felt stiff. How was that possible? I winced trying to get up. "Stay down. Let me see." She gingerly lifted the back of Ky's shirt and peeked underneath. The fabric slowly peeled away from my skin where the bandages that Evelyn had applied didn't quite reach, or had shifted, and it felt like part of the wounds tore open again. A hiss escaped from between my teeth at the same time a curse flew from her lips.

"Evelyn sent more salve. She said that your body would absorb part of it and that more would have to be packed in." Lulu helped me sit up and one by one, I unbuttoned the shirt and again peeled it away from my back. The only portion of my skin not torn to shreds from the fifteen lashes was the part that my bra had covered, although at the last lash, it only hung on by a thread.

"Evelyn came to the depot. She said you'd been injured and gave me the medicine and salve. I had no idea. Did Norris do this?" All I could do was nod.

Lulu took my shirt as I lie back down on my stomach and tried to remain as still as possible as Lulu packed my wounds. Having left the room, I could hear her banging around in the kitchen before she returns with a steaming mug containing more of the special tea. I gulped it down, hoping it helped numb the pain like it had before. When my head hit the pillow, I fell asleep almost immediately.

Something was touching my face, caressing my cheek. The skin that brushed mine was rough, hardened by the work we all share. *Am I dreaming?* I waited, trying to see if this was real or part of a dream. Whichever it was, it was nice, comforting.

Rough fingertips moved over the parts of my back that weren't split open and packed with gunk. I sucked in a breath and held it. This was real. I moved my head and saw his silhouette against the candlelight flickering in from the kitchen and living room. "Ky?" My voice was raspy and barely sounded like my own. Sleep and exhaustion filled every chord.

"Shh. I'm here." Suddenly, I was very aware that I was lying shirtless on my bed. Even though, I was on my stomach, that didn't help me feel any less naked in front of my best friend, who happened to be a member of the male species—a very fine male specimen according to my girlfriends.

I knew he was handsome. I wasn't blind. But, I didn't see him like that. He'd dated many of my friends and now was getting ready to marry Paige Winters in just a few weeks, after the harvest was complete and the orchards picked bare. His fingertips trace the in-tact skin between my shoulder blades and I tensed under his touch.

He'd kissed my head and temple and hugged me more times than I can count, but this was somehow different. This was more intimate. His touch was delicate, gentle compared to his normal strength and anything but playful. "Ky?"

He didn't answer. His fingers explored my back, careful not to stray too close to the wounds that streaked across my skin. "Kyan?"

"Shut up, Abby. Just let me... Just shut up." He'd never talked to me like this. His voice was raspy and he'd never, ever told me to shut up before. So I did. I wasn't sure why. He shouldn't have been touching my skin. Shouldn't have been caressing the good parts left of me, but sitting with me in the dark, he was doing exactly that and I was allowing it.

Paige would be furious if she saw us now. She'd always had a jealous streak, had always hated any girl who dated or flirted with Ky. Lately, she told anyone and everyone who will listen that Kyan was hers and that she hated me with a passion. She wasn't lying. She hated me. Rather, she hated my relationship with Ky. He was my best friend. I wasn't interested in him as anything more or anything else. I'd told her that. He'd told her that a million times. But, she refused to listen, adamant that I wanted him for myself, adamant that he wanted me.

I honestly didn't have those types of feelings for Kyan. I never have had them. Ever. And up until now, I'd always thought he felt the same. But feeling his fingers exploring my skin made even me question that sentiment. And it scared me to death.

I lie there in the dark, his caresses awakening my senses like nothing else ever has. Sure, I'd kissed a guy before, but nothing more than that. And, truthfully, it wasn't anything to write home about. Seth Avery had cornered me behind a tool shed and planted a sloppy wet kiss on my lips. I pushed him away and ran off to tell Lulu as fast as my gangly legs and knobby knees would carry me. I wasn't sure if that really counted as a kiss, now that I thought about it. I was eleven. And, it was forced upon me. I certainly didn't want Seth Avery's lips on mine. The thought still made me cringe.

Ky removed his fingers from my back. He stood and began pacing the floor. "Bastard!" he barked. I flinched at his tone. "Somebody needs to teach him a lesson. I swear…"

"Ky. Calm down. It's not gonna be you. You need to go home. You're tired and getting worked up over nothing."

"Over nothing? Abby, he sliced your back wide open. This isn't nothing. I've seen grown men walk away with shallower stripes than this. You've been flayed. He meant to torture you. Can't you see that?"

"Yes. But, I asked for it. He wanted to teach me a lesson. He wanted to hurt me and he did. But, in the end, I knew what I was getting myself into. It was my decision."

Ky stopped and stomped over to me, kneeling in front of my face, still pressed into my pillow. He gently pushed some hair behind my ear. "He has no right beating around on kids or women. He damn near peeled your flesh from your bones. Do you even get it? Do you understand how bad you're ripped open?"

"I understand. But, you need to lay low. We need you for the harvest and Paige needs you to be there for her now. Soon she'll be your wife. You'll be her husband. Don't do anything stupid to mess any of that up right now. Not for me."

He clenched his jaw and then spoke quietly. "I don't want to marry her." Ky had never admitted it. I knew it was true. But, the words hadn't passed his lips until now. His warm brown eyes searched my face. I knew he didn't want to, but his parents and hers had made the arrangement and there was no stopping it now. He had no say in the matter. His opinion wasn't taken into account. Any protests, even now, would fall upon deaf ears and invite nothing but trouble into his life.

I looked at him. "Doesn't matter. You have to deal with it."

"I don't love her." He pinned me with his stare.

"I know. But, you might as well learn to." I hated this. I hated that we had no control. From infancy we were taught two things. Work hard and obey. Any deviation at all and a swift, harsh punishment would immediately be handed down. Beat into submission. Ruled by fear. It wasn't just Norris, either. It was our parents and guardians, the village council, but most of all the Greaters in their grand cities.

Control was paramount to maintain order and peace. But, right now, I felt anything but peaceful. I felt mutinous, rebellious. I wanted to lash out, fight back, jump up and down, and scream. But, it would do no good. I'd be whipped, again—beaten within an inch of my life, again. The lashes on my back would look like child's play when they were through with me.

"I don't love her, Abby Blue. I love—"

My eyes stopped him before my words did. "Ky. Don't go there. Whatever you're about to say, just...don't. It won't change anything." He recoiled and stood abruptly, before marching out the door, slamming the rickety wood into the wall behind it. I blinked at the sound. *Does Ky love me?*

Chapter 2

MORNING CAME WAY TOO SOON. Lulu woke me up and helped me get ready. There was no way I could possibly wear a bra, so she cut an old sheet and made a wide strip of fabric with. She carefully wrapped my torso like a mummy, effectively binding my chest and the wounds on my back at the same time. It had relieved some of the pressure and I asked her to bind me again tonight after she slopped the goopy herbal concoction on me. She was happy to have given me some relief and chastised me for even asking for her help this evening.

She helped me shrug on one of Ky's button-down shirts. The hem tickled my knees, but I didn't care. I wanted and needed something loose, especially since I had to report for work at the Preston's today. The thought made me cringe. Every movement of my arms, every step, reminded me of my punishment—not just the wounds on my back, but the punishment of coming into contact with Zander Preston.

I hated Zander Preston with a fierce passion. He had always bullied and belittled me. Not only me, but anyone he felt was beneath him or could be a threat to him. His father held a position on the village council, contributing to this unhealthy obsession with entitlement. An obsession that allowed him to believe he had the right to treat everyone around him as if they were beneath him.

Every villager in Orchard was born a Lesser, deemed by those in the cities, to be something subhuman and only good for one thing–work. The citizens of those magnificent streets, with buildings rumored to scrap the sky were the Greaters. They believed themselves to be born better in every way than Lessers, the workers they controlled. We were fit to produce and prepare their food and the raw materials that the cities required to keep running, but for little else. So how Zander, a Lesser just like everyone else in Orchard, could somehow consider himself more, I did not understand. Maybe by putting everyone else down, he managed to somehow make himself feel better.

I didn't know. And, right now, as I gingerly slid my legs into my jeans, my feet into my socks and shoes, I didn't care. I just hoped that I would get there after Zander left for the orchards. In the kitchen, Lulu hugged me softly and kissed my cheek, handing me a small burlap bag with my lunch packed inside. "Behave, Abigail. I know how you feel about that Zander boy, but for God's sake, behave. You're in no shape to take another lashing."

"I will, Lulu. I promise." I squeezed her a bit tighter and appreciated her sweet, comforting scent. She had always smelled of fresh grass and morning dew–earthy and like home. I came to live with her when I was only two years old. I don't remember my parents. Lulu says they couldn't raise me, so they sent me to her. They were too young to have a child, her baby brother and my mother.

I often wondered who they were, what type of people they were now, if they were even still alive, and if they would recognize me if they saw me now that I was grown. Would I recognize them? Would I favor my father or mother more?

I was never unhappy here with Lulu. She had always been great, so supportive and loving. She'd been my parent for as long as I could remember and I wouldn't trade her for the world. I harbored no bitterness or anger toward my parents. If they couldn't raise me, at least they gave me Lulu, and along with her, they gave me the chance to be loved by someone who wanted and could care for me.

I pulled away from her and smiled, looking her over. She was only five foot three, but she had always been a spitfire. Her brown hair was streaked with gray now and pulled back in a small bun at the nape of her neck, her hair having thinned over the years. Her eyes were strange, but beautiful. Sometimes they looked brown, but today they looked almost green. They were hazel, but so much more, ever changing with their surroundings. Chameleon eyes. Big and round and beautiful.

She nudged me out the door toward the Preston's, and I trudged down the path that began in back of our house. I passed several other homes along the way to the

Preston's. Their home was a bigger than ours, bigger than any in our village, actually. *Goes along with their haughty egos.*

Cresting a small hill, the house rose mightily from the earth cleared around it. My heart began to beat rapidly. I really, really did not want to go into the Preston home. And, I desperately did not want to see Zander this morning. I promised Lulu I would behave. I would hate to break my promise. But with Zander, all bets were off. And, even Lulu knew that.

Their home had two floors. It had more than four bedrooms in total. With only three occupants, this truly was luxurious. Most houses in the village had two bedrooms. Those were usually shared. Children would pile into one room and parents into the other. A couple of homes had three bedrooms, but an extra was usually only added when no more children could be stuffed inside the spare, and only after the council had consulted with the Greaters and they approved of the addition.

The Preston house was opposing. The wood had been whitewashed and the porch was held up by enormous wooden beams, adding to its imposing grandeur. I squared my shoulders, climbed the six stairs to the porch's landing, and made my way to the door. It opened before I could even knock. I stood there, my hand raised into a fist, ready to pound on the wood. Looking back at me with his ever present signature smirk was none other than Zander Preston. *Crap.*

If he wasn't such a jerk, he would be attractive. Actually, that was an understatement. He would be amazingly handsome. But, his horrific attitude made him ugly. He smirked at me and swept his open palm inward, motioning me into his home. I stepped over the threshold and sucked in a deep breath.

His palm landed firmly on my back, and I flinched and whimpered before I could control it. He laughed, but thankfully removed his paw from my skin, which was now on fire thanks to his carelessness, or purposeful placement, rather. "Oh, sorry, Abigail. I must have forgotten about your back."

"Right. You forgot the reason that I'm here? Sure you did," I bit back. I was not about to let him bully me.

"Easy, tiger. I'm just your welcome wagon. I'm supposed to show you what to do today. My mother left a list for you. It's underwhelming to me. But, she argued that your back is still healing and that you mustn't be pushed too hard; too fast. She plans to keep you around for a while and we need you healthy."

Keep me around for a while? Whatever. As soon as I could raise my arms without flinching, I'd be back in the orchard. He grabbed my elbow and led me into the kitchen. There, on the counter, sat a list, written in perfect loopy handwriting. And, if the items that stretched down its length were short, so was I.

For the record, I stood five foot seven, fairly tall compared to the other girls around here. Zander left me for a moment to rifle around a nearby closet, emerging with a bucket, cleaner, scrub brushes, mop, and broom. His teeth were white against his sun-kissed skin. His hair was so blonde it was almost white in places where the sun has bleached it over the summer. He wasn't tall, but wasn't particularly short either, just average. Zander was neither scrawny nor muscular. Again, average. Perhaps his attitude was a poor attempt to compensate for his mediocrity. His averageness.

He dropped everything in a heap in the floor. "Well, Abigail. I'm off to the orchard. Get to work. I'll check your work when I get home, so you'd better be thorough. I'd hate for Norris to hear that you're slacking on the job." He smirked and sauntered out the front door. I had never happier to see a door slam closed in my entire life. I decided to start upstairs and work my way down, based upon the items on the list.

I was accustomed to hard work. I didn't fear it, but would normally welcome it. But, being here in the Preston household made me loathe it. Somehow they did manage to make me feel less than Lesser.

∞

MRS. PRESTON'S "SHORT LIST" HAD made for a very long day. My back ached and sharp pains shot like forked lightening up and down one of the deeper slices in particular in almost a zipper-like pain—the one that curled overtop my left shoulder and licked its way across my collar bone. Darkness descended in the valley and soon everyone would come home from a long day in the fields. I furiously tried to hurry and finish. I wanted to avoid seeing Zander again like the plague.

Sloshing soapy water over the kitchen floor, I realized that I still had half of it to finish before I could leave. My back had definitely slowed me down today. If not for the pain, I would have been done at least an hour ago. My knees ached as I crawled across the roughly hewn floor of their immaculate kitchen, but the Preston's floor was much smoother than mine and Lulu's, so I shouldn't complain.

I scrubbed. Hard. Back and forth, pressing the brush into the bubbles until I felt that it was clean enough to move along to the next portion, and then the next. The rhythm was nearly killing me, but I was desperate to finish this last chore on the list, and so I pressed on.

Unfortunately, my efforts weren't enough. I heard the door open. Councilman and Mrs. Preston entered the room and I quickly dried the floor that I'd been scrubbing. Mrs. Preston's eyes sharply took in everything in the room, including me, unfortunately. Her lip curled upward on one side and her pointed nose lifted a little higher into the air. She must have given Zander his blonde hair. Hers was perfectly curled and stiffly sprayed into submission.

Her sky blue dress was starched crisp and she was the only woman in this village who bothered or dared to wear high heels. I wasn't sure if she was crazy or if I should admire her tenacity. Her small dark brown eyes fixated on me as I stiffly stood up before her. I could feel them both watching as I rinsed out the sponges and returned the mop and broom to the closet.

I quickly bid them goodnight and rushed outside to dump the water out of the bucket. I decided to just leave it on the porch. I'd no doubt need it again tomorrow and would have to get some fresh water in the morning anyway, so I could just dump it in the creek then. The

Preston's would likely have a fit if I dumped dirty water onto their precious, freshly-cut lawn.

∞

THANKFULLY, THE NEXT WEEK PASSED with little interact-tion with Zander. My back healed well with the salves that Evelyn kept sending my way, and before long, I was able to finish the chores at the Preston house before any member of the family made it home. I dealt with Zander when I arrived as he presented his mother's list for the day, but other than his usual rude remarks, he didn't bother me too much. My back felt much better. Every night, Lulu rubbed more medicine into my wounds. Most were scabbed over and felt like tightly stretched stripes. Other areas felt numb or tingly.

Another evening ritual had been the evening visits with Kyan after his day in the orchards. I could tell from his expression and the way he held his shoulders that he was exhausted. Work in the fields was hard and frantic at best, and he was missing one member of his team—me.

The harvest was approaching quickly, and I was glad that my back had healed faster than Evelyn expected. I wanted to help in the orchards, help in the harvest, as I had done since Lulu had showed me how to run beneath the trees and scavenge for recently fallen apples that hadn't yet begun to rot.

The leaves on the trees were turning quickly. Half clung to the green for dear life, while others relinquished control and turned varying shades of gold, orange and my favorite, the blazing red-orange. The entire village was hard at work and I was itching to do my part, and to get outside of the Preston home during the daylight hours.

We were coming up on harvest time. A few villagers were ordered to work outside the orchards getting the required, but mundane tasks out of the way before the harvest; when all hands would be needed in and around the fields of apple trees that stretched as far as the eye could see. Some cut the hay that the animals would need for the winter, while others tended to the animals themselves. Some harvested vegetables from the community gardens, while others preserved that food and stored it away.

Most villagers worked in or around the orchards, now. The apples we grew would be sent to the cities. Their factories would process them or the fresh apples would be shipped to stores where the Greaters could purchase them. Eat them. They would be fed from the sweat of our brows and strength of our backs. We would nourish them. The Greaters would take and we would give. Not freely, but because we were forced, because we had no other choice than to obey, or suffer the punishment for dissidence. The punishment for treason was more than just a simple lashing. It was death; swiftly carried out and unmercifully final.

I finished my chores for the day. It was Saturday and tomorrow was a day of rest. Mr. Preston came home about an hour ago. He didn't work very late on Saturdays, apparently, but he retreated to his study and I hadn't seen him since, so I couldn't complain. Mrs. Preston wasn't home. I wasn't sure where she went or what she did all day, but she didn't work in or near the orchards. That was for sure. She was much too clean and put-together when she came home. Maybe she worked for the council–definitely an indoor kind of girl.

I checked the last item off of my list and placed the cleaning tools in the small closet before heading down to the creek again to dump the water, now tinged with dirt and dust mixed with the sweat from my brow. How the water came out so dirty today after I just cleaned the floors earlier in the week, was beyond me.

My tennis shoes carried me down the flattened path toward the creek. It looked so wonderful. I could hear the trickling of the water flowing over the rocks before I could even see it. I kicked my shoes and socks off and waded in, letting the lukewarm water flow over my feet. Soothing and calm. The sun was still strong at this time of year and the water had not yet turned cold. But, before long, the cool mornings and nights that were slowly creeping in would change all of that.

I rolled up the bottom cuffs of my jeans to my knees and the sleeves of my white and navy button-down shirt, or Ky's rather, to my elbows. I didn't need the shirt to ease my back anymore, but it was comfortable and easy to wash. Uneven brown stripes stained the back of it in places anyway and I assumed that he wouldn't want it back now anyway. I sat on the bank swishing my feet back and forth, leaning back on my palms, face aimed toward the sun, taking a moment to relax and enjoy the welcome warmth washing over my body. I would certainly enjoy spending the day with Lulu tomorrow.

A shadow fell over me, blocking the sun. Shielding my eyes, I looked up to see Zander standing beside me. His arms were folded across his chest and his oh-so-humble smirk sat upon his lips. "Go away, Zander." I closed my eyes and tried to pretend that he was already gone.

"Now, is that any way to speak to your boss?"

"*You* are not my boss."

He laughed. "Oh, I am. You think my mother and father are the ones who write your little lists? The first day, maybe. Who do you think talked Norris into having you come work for us?" His eyebrows raised along with the corners of his mouth.

"Whatever. Norris wouldn't listen to you."

"He did. In fact," he said as he sat down next to me. "He was perfectly content to let you heal at home for a week before sending you back into the orchards. But, I told him how delicate your flesh was and how deep your wounds. I told him that you'd be able to heal better and be more useful working in our house 'helping' my mother with the chores, where she could keep an eye on you, make sure you healed properly."

I sat up straight. My hands trembled as I held them back, clenching them hard. I wanted to choke the life out of him. I could almost feel the flesh of his neck. "Why?" It was the only thing I could grind out.

He lifted his hand and fingered a strand of my hair. The auburn, not quite red and not quite brown, looked strange in his hands. I smacked his hand away. "Don't touch me."

Zander looked at me for a moment and then laughed, shrugged and dropped my hair. "I wanted to see you."

"You wanted to see me?"

"Yes. I wanted to see you. Is that so hard to believe?"

I scoffed. "It is. Why on earth would you want to see me? Why would you ask Norris to make me serve in your house? Why do you have to look down your nose at everyone in the village? Do you enjoy keeping me under your foot?" I was getting more irate with each question.

His icy blue eyes flashed, turning cold and the smile dropped from his face. He snarled, "Under my foot? You are nowhere near under my foot, Abigail. But, I can make that happen."

"Zander, you've bullied me since I was a child. You still make jokes at my expense. All of your little followers snicker at me every time I walk by. Now you pull this crap with Norris? I am most definitely under your foot."

He leaned toward me and before I knew what was happening, his fingers wove their way into the hair on the back of my head. His face moved quickly to within a half inch of my own. "I pick on you for a reason."

I tried to pull my head away, but couldn't. "What reason?" My voice cracked.

"If I make you undesirable, no one else will want you."

Wait. What? "No one *else*?"

"No. One. Else." His warm breath mingled with my own. "My father will speak with your aunt. I plan to make you mine."

My eyes went wide. "What? You hate me! No! There is no way I will marry you."

"You will have no choice. Nor will your aunt. So, get used to the idea. I have plans for you." Smiling and with

36

that warning left hanging heavy in the air between us, he let go of me, stood and stalked away.

What just happened?

Chapter 3

I'D BEEN AVOIDING KYAN. I hated the thought of feeling awkward around him, but after the intimacy we shared, wasn't sure it could be avoided. He was getting married, and I didn't want him to go into his marriage with any doubts at all, especially about me. I wanted him to be happy. He has to marry Paige. He needed to accept that fact. He needed to accept her, and once they were married, he would have to forget about me and about our friendship, which would be virtually nonexistent.

I hadn't told him about Zander and his threat of marriage. And that's exactly what I considered it: a threat. I wanted nothing to do with him. Especially in the way a woman should want her husband. *Never going to happen.*

Another week had passed. My back was almost completely healed. I had ugly raised pink scars of tender flesh crisscrossing my back. Most of the time now, I could forget about them altogether. The harvest had begun without me. But, there would be plenty of work for me, for everyone, for many more weeks to come. It took our entire village several weeks to pluck all of the ripe apples from the trees.

They would be packed into crates and bushel baskets, driven by truck to the train tracks that rested a few miles away. Old trucks rumbled back and forth, to and from the depot all day and long into the night. Train horns sound loudly as they stop only long enough to receive their loads and then again as they pulled away toward the Greater cities.

There were five cities in all. Each was situated along the coast lines. Five cities spread out like fingers from the palm where we resided—one in the far northeast, southeast, northwest, southwest, and south center of the country; the bottom of the world as far as I knew. They said that the glass and metal of their boxy structures stretched as tall as the clouds, as far as the eye could see. I'd heard that some were so high, they would block out the sun completely, blanketing the earth below in perpetual shadow.

There were factories and stores for shopping. Sometimes the trains brought shipments to the village. Sometimes we received shoes, clothes, blankets, and vehicles. We also received shipments of food that we couldn't grow here, from other villages nestled in the heart of the land, from other Lessers, like us.

It was said that every child in the Greater cities received an education. Lessers did not. We were taught to read and write, to add and subtract. Taught the only skills necessary to properly account for the food we produced and provided the Greaters. And, we were taught to be meticulous record keepers, because as our bodies aged, we would relinquish the work of the fields to account for the crop.

Beyond the basic instruction, there was little room for further education. Even the days of children were filled with work. Our importance lay in the hard work we could provide our community. Pride in our efforts was established early, and rewarded. Laziness was punished. No excuses were allowed or accepted, and we learned quickly and early not to bother making them.

Sunday was our only day of rest, if you could call it that. In reality, it was our one day to tend to our own houses and crops. We still worked from dawn until dusk. The dawn this morning was angry and bruised purple and red. Lulu was on the front porch scrubbing the planks. I went to get fresh water from the stream that was about a quarter of a mile from our house. Some people were fortunate enough to have wells on their property, but the Kelley property was dry as a bone.

The bucket handle bit into my fingers and seemed to get heavier with each step, even though water sloshed out with each one, actually lightening the load. I'd switched hands a dozen times on my trip back. It's a trip made so often, I could make it in the dark. As I rounded the house and Lulu looked up at me and smiled, blowing some of the hair from her face. I hoisted the heavy wooden bucket up onto the porch and smiled back at her.

"Lulu, has anyone asked for my hand?" *Best to cut right to the chase.* She dropped her brush in the water and looked up at me from her hazel eyes. I'd imagine the inner roots of a strong deciduous tree to look this color, brown crusty outside, but vibrant green within, guardians of hidden secrets and a lifetime of wisdom. She was really quite young, or her personality made her seem so. Though older than her brother, my father, she was only forty-two. She sighed and the smile eased slowly from her face. The parentheses around her lips sank a bit deeper, along with the creases in her forehead.

"Well. I had an interesting conversation with a certain Councilman, but it seems as if you were expecting that. I thought you hated Zander."

"I do."

Confusion further knotted her brows together until one lifted higher than the other. "Then why on earth would he ask to marry you?"

"I have no idea, but I think he's up to something and I don't like it."

"Why do you think he's up to something?"

"He's a snake in the grass."

She laughed lightly. "My dear, he may be a snake in the grass, but snakes are not born blind. Snakes can see quite clearly."

"What's that supposed to mean, Lulu?" She laughed wholeheartedly, the skin in the corners of her eyes radiated outward happily.

"You've turned out to be quite a beauty. You've blossomed." My cheeks were on fire. Lulu never talked about the way that I looked. In fact, she often spoke against vanity, beauty.

"Abby. It's true. You have turned into a woman—a beautiful one. And sometimes, beauty is coveted by others. Perhaps, Zander feels that with you on his arm, he'll be more, somehow— made greater than his current station with you by his side."

"We are Lessers, Lu. He needs to accept it. And, I am no one's arm candy."

Lulu's eyes lit up and she burst into laughter. "No, baby girl. You're beautiful, but you're fierce. And, I cannot imagine that you would be happy as anyone's 'arm candy.' Above all things, I wish for you to be happy. I'll not consent to the pairing."

I exhaled deeply and felt the tension ease from my shoulders. "Thank you, Lulu."

"Don't look so relieved, child. I didn't say you'd marry for love, although that's what I'd give you if you could. But, I'll not force the likes of Zander Preston upon you."

I smiled lightly. Love. No one married for love. But if I were to marry Zander, my heart would be filled with such hatred that love would certainly never have a chance to blossom. If I were to be paired with someone more mild mannered, and well, normal, maybe love could grow in time. At the very least, there would be respect. And, I supposed I could live with that. Or learn to, anyway.

Lulu started scrubbing the muddy planks again. I took my own brush and start scrubbing opposite her so that we would meet in the middle. "No. I suppose if I wanted you to marry for love, I would have pushed to have you marry Kyan."

"What?"

She grinned up at me. "Kyan. That boy has loved you from the moment he laid eyes on you. He certainly doesn't love Paige. That girl's voice is enough to drive even a bobcat mad. Like metal on metal, I swear."

I giggled. She was right. Her voice was incredibly shrilly and very annoying. Poor Kyan. He would have to listen to her voice for the rest of his life. I did not envy him. But, would I want to marry Kyan? It wasn't an option. Not at all, now that the pairing has been made and announced. He was my best friend and we would get along. We would have fun. Could we be happy as man and wife? I didn't know. It wasn't so bad to have him stroke my back. It was strange and thrilling at the same time, but I wasn't not sure if it was because it was Kyan or because no one had ever touched me so intimately before.

"Kyan doesn't love me. I know he doesn't love Paige, but maybe he will one day. I want him to be happy. He's my best friend, but he'll never be more, even if he would want to be."

It was as plain and simple as that. Lulu just nodded and continued with her work. She knew I was right. It didn't matter now and wasn't worth discussing any further. Dwelling on it wouldn't help. Neither will worry. And I was almost as worried about Kyan's marriage to Paige as I was about the lingering feeling that I hadn't heard the end of the Zander Preston proposal.

Chapter 4

MONDAY MORNING, LULU SHOOK ME awake. I was a mess. I was exhausted, but I'd always slept like the dead. On mornings that I was particularly difficult to wake, she even put a cold, wet towel on my face to rouse me. I hated that. So much. I dragged myself out of bed and wipe a cold rag over my face. It was different when I did it myself.

I pulled on my nearly worn-out jeans. A ragged hole revealed the skin my left kneecap and another, a portion of the skin on my right thigh. The cuffs were tattered and pieces of fabric and thread tickled the skin on the top of my feet and trailed behind my heels. I pulled on a hunter green V-neck tee, a pair of clean socks, and my dusty, trusty tennis shoes.

Running out of my room, I weaved my long wavy hair into a braid and tied it with a small red and white gingham fabric scrap. Lulu met me just before I reached the front door and finished tying it off for me. "Head to the main hall. You need to be back in the orchards, but Councilman Preston has to release you."

I pulled back from her. "Why? I'm fine."

"I know that, but it's just how it is. You're his charge and only he can release you to work the orchard."

"Great," I muttered.

"He'll send you back. They need help. They're so desperate they've requested reinforcements."

"Reinforcements?"

"From other villages. They've asked for help from those who aren't preparing their own harvests right now, or whose harvests have already taken place. The able from at least three other villages should join us in the next day or so. The Greaters have approved of their assistance and are moving the workers by train."

"Wow. I don't remember that ever happening."

She laughed. "That's because it hasn't. We've always been able to shoulder the load. But, the trees have produced more this year than they ever have before. There's quite the bounty and more than we can handle without help. Else, the apples will spoil on the trees, or on the ground. The Greaters aren't about to let that happen. You know how they feel about waste."

Lulu's eyes sparkled when she smiled. It was amazing how just looking in the eyes of someone you love could take you home. Made you feel comfort and love unimaginable anywhere else. I hugged her tight and kissed her temple before trudging to battle. I wasn't sure why I felt like I was marching into one, but I did.

Cutting through the woods toward the center of town, and the main hall, I crossed paths with none other than

CASEY L. BOND

Paige Winters and her best friend, Dawn. I nodded in an attempt to avoid speaking with them, but of course, Paige would have none of that. "Well, if it isn't Miss Martyr."

"Excuse me?" She wanted to rile me up. *Congratulations, Paige*. She'd just succeeded.

I whipped around. Her long pin-straight black hair shone in the early morning sun. Paige's nose turned up on the end slightly, but she emphasized the feature by keeping her nose pointed to the sky. She was much like Mrs. Preston, always looking down on everyone else. Especially me, because of my proximity to her fiancé. She huffed and put one hand on her hip, rolling her eyes. I wanted to scratch them out. If only I didn't bite my nails. Claws would come in handy in this kind of cat fight.

"You heard me. Miss Martyr. Had to step in and save the day."

"I did no such thing. But, call me what you want. You wouldn't have stepped up for that little girl." She made no attempt to deny it.

"Nope." She popped her 'P.' "There's no way any man would want a woman with a mangled back. Especially Kyan. He wouldn't want something tainted and ugly. Something scarred."

I really should have bitten my tongue. I knew it, but I couldn't help what came out of my mouth next. "Well, when he rubbed his fingers across the parts that weren't ripped open the other night, he certainly didn't complain." She stiffened and nearly growled at me. "You're lying. He would never lay a finger on a piece trash like you."

I just smirked. Kyan was going to kill me. "Well, maybe you should just ask him about it then. Maybe he likes

46

martyrs better than stuck-up bitches." And, with that, I turned on my heel making my way toward the main hall once more. The shocked expression on her face was enough to put more than a little pep in my step.

Dawn's dirty blonde hair whipped around as I passed them by, her mouth gaped open. Had no one ever stood up to them? Good grief. Paige Winters should marry Zander Preston. It would be a match made in wannabe Greater heaven.

∞

As was customary, I waited on the porch of the main hall until beckoned by Mary, the woman who really ran the place. I followed her inside the old building. It was the only one in the village constructed mostly of stone, highlighted only with accents of wood.

All resident dwellings were entirely made of wood, our most abundant resource. Those closest to the density of the forest were often ravaged by woodpeckers and termites. A few were so thoroughly consumed, that only the remnants of their thickest structural pieces remained. Skeletal reminders of the harshness and determination of even the tiniest predators.

Mary limped ahead of me. Her left leg was her strongest, and she pushed off of it in order propel herself forward. Her right was no help at all, but seemed rather to serve as a crutch. She was broad in the hip, but had shrunken shorter and shorter over the past few years. At one point, her eyes had been level with mine, but now were several inches below. A high bun crowned her head, thin white hair stretched backwards toward the whirlpool of white. Deep lines sunk into her forehead and parenthesed her mouth.

Her eyes were green-gray and she smiled with them even more so than with her thin lips, which from which delicate lines radiated as well. I followed to the last door on the left. My fingertips grazed the cold, gritty stone wall beside me. She knocked.

"Yes?" A gruff voice called out.

She opened the door slightly and stuck her head in. "Councilman Preston, Miss Abigail Kelley is here to see you."

"Send her in."

She swept her hand forward. My legs felt like the wall. Heavy stones. Hard to lift. I propelled myself forward, passing Mary and stepped into one of the largest open spaces I've ever seen. The walls were made of stacked stones, like the rest of the structure, but the ceiling was so tall, outlined with enormous beams of stained dark wood. Iron sconces were evenly spaced around the walls, a pristine, white candle in each, just begged to be lit.

Two windows were spaced perfectly apart on the wall to my left. Two more were behind Councilman Preston's desk. With all the light behind him, his face remained in shadow. Sitting silently, his fingers tented together in front of him. I moved forward slowly, taking in the grandeur, before settling into one of the wooden chairs in front of his desk.

Even his desk was enormous and was stained the same dark color as the beams that loomed overhead. I swallowed nervously and clasped my hands together in my lap. Dust motes floated and flew whimsically in the early morning sunlight beaming its way into the room through the windows.

Mr. Preston cleared his throat. His once-blonde hair was peppered with gray and white and had begun thinning on top. "You wanted to see me, Abigail?"

"Yes, Sir." I filled my voice with a confidence mocked by my quaking knees. "I'd like to return to the orchards for the harvest."

His eyes narrowed. "Your back?"

"Mostly healed now, Sir."

He shifted in his seat, intertwining his fingers. I couldn't see his eyes because of the lighting, but could feel his appraisal. "Abby, I know you're anxious to help with the harvest, but you must heal. If you aren't healed properly, you could be a danger to those around you. If you were to falter, and others had to take care of you, it would take others away from their work. Do you under-stand?"

"Yes, Sir."

"Let's compromise. You may work for two hours in the orchards during the morning tomorrow, and then will report to my home to complete your chores for the remainder of the day. If you handle that well for a few days, we will increase your time in the orchards, and decrease your work as our servant. Is that acceptable to you?"

I beamed a smile. "Yes, Sir. Thank you. It's more than fair."

He sat back and his high cheekbones pulled up. I couldn't tell with the lighting, but I thought he was smiling. "I would like to discuss another matter with you, Abigail."

I sat back in the chair. "Okay."

"My son has informed me of his intention to marry you. Are you aware of this?"

"He mentioned it one day, Sir. But, I wasn't sure that he was serious. He and I have never...seen eye to eye." I swallowed.

"Rest assured that his affections for you are both present and strong. I spoke with your Aunt about the pairing, but she was reluctant to agree. It seems that she is aware that the two of you have not, as you put it, 'seen eye to eye,' and so she will not approve of the match."

I was not really sure how to respond. I wished that I could be honest and tell him that I hated his son and that Zander would be the last man on this Earth I could be persuaded to marry. I wanted to squeeze Aunt Lulu for having declined his offer, for standing up to the Preston's when anyone else in this village would have cowered and bowed to their request.

"Abigail, I intend to speak with Lulu again. Zander was devastated with the news that she had denied him your hand. What say you on the matter?"

His eyes, though shaded bore into me. "Would you appreciate an honest answer, Sir?"

"Yes."

"I do not wish to marry Zander."

"I see." He inhaled deeply and then sighed. "Is it the boy you're always with? Kyan?"

"No. Kyan is to marry Paige Winters at the harvest festival."

"Do you love Kyan, his betrothal aside?"

I shook my head. "No. He's my best friend. I don't see him in a romantic way."

"Then my son is the problem?"

"I don't think we would be a good match. I don't love him."

Hearty laughter booms out from him. "Love? Oh, child. If only we were able to marry for love. We marry to procreate and produce more responsible citizens. To continue our traditions and values, but not for love." His laughter trailed off. "Don't get me wrong. Sometimes paired couples do find that after a time, love develops, along with respect. But, it's rare. I wish it were possible for you to find love, but sometimes, you have to think with your head instead of your heart, dear."

I nodded, feeling like a scolded child. Unfortunately, I knew he was right.

"I will try once again to persuade her. No doubt my effort will be in vain. It seems your Aunt values your opinion, Abigail. You're lucky. Most young women aren't so fortunate. Most aren't even consulted on their matches, but are simply told who they will marry and when. But, I promised my son I would try again. I don't break my promises, Miss Kelley." He stood and extended his hand and I did the same. His hand was frigid, his handshake like steel.

I nodded and stood to leave.

∞

THE NEXT MORNING, LULU WOKE me before dawn. I tugged on a green and white plaid shirt, jeans and my worn, brown leather boots. My tennis shoes were still drying by the fire after I'd washed them the evening before. Lulu plaited my hair in an intricate braid, pulling it up and away from my face. She quickly pinned it into place and placed my burlap lunch sack in my hand. My cheeks hurt from smiling so much. I was off to the orchard—for a couple of hours, at least.

The morning air was chilly and the grass blades damp with dew. Patches of spider webs dotted the tall grass. The sun had not risen above the horizon yet, but the sky was beginning to turn from deep sapphire. It faded toward the east to a lighter blue, smeared with royal purples, and brilliantly lit oranges and gold, as if touched with the strokes of a painter's delicate hand.

I turned down the pathway toward the orchards, following the white wooden plank fence that lined the great fields of fruit-bearing trees. I could smell the ripe apples, the supple earth. The leaves even had a distinct scent. Crisp, like the fruit they bore. I closed my eyes and inhaled deeply. Sweet, succulent fruit, freshly cut grass, wood and the lingering acrid smell of smoke permeated the air. I was home—as free as I ever had been.

"Hey!" Laney Adams raced up and paced her steps with mine. "It's good to see you back!" She smiled sweetly, her spiraled blonde hair bouncing in time with our feet like little golden springs. Her milk chocolate eyes twinkled.

"Thanks, Laney. It's good to be back."

Laney and I had been friends since childhood. She was the closest female friend I had. The smile drifted off of her lips. "How do you feel about Kyan and Paige?" She slowed her pace and I follow suit.

"If they're happy, so am I." I shrugged and looked back toward the orchard. Our entrance lay just up ahead. Laney was very petite. She could climb a tree faster than anyone in Orchard. Thus, her nickname: Sprite. "Have you set *your* eyes on any man candy, Sprite?" Her cheeks turned nearly as scarlet as the apples on the trees.

She giggled and shook her head. "No, but some workers from other villages are supposed to arrive today. Maybe you and I will find someone worthy among all the fresh meat!"

"Fresh meat?" We laughed together through the white fence's entrance. "See you later, Lane!"

"Enjoy your freedom while it lasts!" She waved before disappearing down another row into the dense blanket of fog that had settled into the valley, over the orchard itself.

Each apple plucked had a tiny part of me inside. A tiny part of all of those from Orchard Village, prepared the soil, planted new seeds, nurtured the delicate saplings, a part of those who fertilized and watered, and who now climbed and harvested, packed and delivered. I wondered if the Greaters knew of the backbreaking work, and love that Lessers poured into the care of the food that nourished their bodies. I doubted it.

I walked through the ghostly mist to the section of trees that I'd last worked in before the incident. It was a place to start. I had to find Kyan, my team leader, so that he could tell me where to begin and assign my position. I was surprised to see that the harvest hadn't taken our team very far. Kyan was pouring his bucket into a large barrel several trees away, an apparition in this thick mist shrouding us. I kept walking toward him, and though I doubted he could hear me, he turned around, his eyes crashing into mine. I smiled. I'd missed him. Missed this. Soon he would no longer be my team leader. He would be placed as an overseer, manager of the team leaders. Everyone knew he was already being groomed for the position. He would still work alongside us, but would also guide the teams and would become responsible for a portion of the orchard. It would be his duty as a married male member of our village to accept the position offered to him. A way to grant him more responsibility and respect for his new status in society.

"Ky." Inwardly, I cringed a little, thinking about what I had said to Paige on the trail yesterday and how I'd been pushing him away.

An angry look slid over his previously peaceful countenance. "What are you doing here, Abby?"

"I spoke with Councilman Preston yesterday and he's allowing me to work in the mornings for two hours before reporting to his residence for my chores. He wants to ease me into work in the orchards." I looked at my feet. Last night when he stopped by, I asked Lulu to tell him I was already asleep.

"You should still be resting."

"I'm fine. My back is almost completely healed." I hated arguing with Kyan.

He shook his head. "Paige said you ran into her yesterday." I peeked up at him from beneath my lashes, expecting to see anger and betrayal, but was met with a crooked smile. Even his warm brown eyes smiled back at me.

"What's so funny?" I cocked my head.

"You should've seen her. Heard her. She was madder than a hornet. Ranting and raving about how you were this and you were that and she was, well, her. You definitely ruffled her feathers."

"Well, you don't seem too upset by it."

"Upset? No. I'm glad you finally stood up to her. I was glad to take the hit for you. Anything for you, Abby Blue."

I grinned at him. "Where do I start, boss?"

He pulled me in for a hug, wrapped his big arm around my shoulders, and walked me to my first tree.

Chapter 5

I WAS UTTERLY EXHAUSTED. NOT that I was going to admit that to anyone. They would pull me out of the orchards so fast, I wouldn't know what had hit me. Mrs. Preston's list lengthened as my day at her house shortened. But I refused to let them win. I worked at breakneck speed and pushed hard to get everything done as thoroughly and quickly as I could. And my muscles screamed louder than the angry welts traversing my back. It was a good type of pain. My body was young and fit, and I had pushed it. And on some deep level, it was rewarding.

I pushed the front door open only to nearly be tackled to the floor by Lulu. "Have you seen Kyan?"

"Not since this morning. Why?" Even my voice sounded tired compared to her perky, hyper one.

"He stopped here after work and said he needed to see you. You're supposed to meet him at his house. He thought he might be able to meet you on your way home, but I guess that didn't happen. So, off you go." She attempted to shoo me back out the door, but I shouldered my way inside.

"I don't want to see him tonight. It's late."

"No. He said it was urgent. You really need to go, dear."

I sighed. "Lulu, I smell. Really bad. I just want to head to the creek to wash off and then have supper and head to bed."

Her eyes narrowed and her index finger flicked toward me. "I knew it. It's too much. You went back to the orchard too soon."

"No!" I chirped quickly, trying to hide the weariness in my voice. "It's not that. It's just that it's already dark, and I want to settle in because all of the workers from the other villages are coming tomorrow and I want to be ready." It wasn't a lie. The train was supposed to arrive overnight and the workers arriving were supposed to help in the orchards tomorrow. It was one of the reasons for Mrs. Preston's oppressively long list of chores.

Though some of those workers would be housed in the train cars themselves, others would be hosted by village families for the duration of their stay. Since the Preston's had such abundant space in their home, only using two of their four bedrooms, their house was being prepared for guests. Lulu already mentioned that the two of us may have to share her room and offer mine if someone needed it.

She narrowed her chameleon eyes. Tonight, they looked like the brown of an acorn freshly dropped from its tree. "You're avoiding him." It wasn't a question.

I rolled my eyes. "Yes. I'm avoiding him. Is that what you want to hear?"

She pulled me in for a hug. "Abby, look at me. Don't push him away, when you have so little time left with him. Enjoy it for all it's worth. Don't waste it." Her eyes and slight smile lovingly implored me to listen to her closely—to listen with my heart and not my stubborn head.

I sighed deeply. If only it were that simple. I wanted to scream out about how unfair it was to lose my best friend, especially to a woman like Paige Winters. "Okay. I'll go wash up and then head over to Ky's." Lulu grabbed my cheeks and pulled me toward her, and then kissed my forehead. Then, she proceeded to shove a bag of clean clothes at me and turn me around, all the while pushing me out the door. The woman should herd cattle.

Well, at least I was clean. I'd washed up at the creek behind our cabin and changed my clothes. My feet crunched the hay as I crossed the field to Kyan's. Candles flickered in the window sills of his house, which was settled down in the valley below. It was beyond dark, but the sky was clear. Every star imaginable winked down at me. The moon was blue and rounded more with each passing night. It even appeared larger than normal somehow.

A dark figure sat still on Kyan's porch. "Hey, Ky."

"About time."

"No 'thank goodness you made it dear,' or 'I was so worried. You could've been eaten by bears'?"

"Bears? Is that the best you can do?" I settled in beside him, my outer thigh pressed against his.

"Yes. At this time of night it is." I sighed.

He threw a piece of the grass he'd been picking at, his lips quirked up into a lop-sided grin. "It's not that late. Besides, I want to show you something." He stood and held out a hand, that mine automatically slipped into.

I chastised myself internally. As I held on, I knew I needed to let him go. This familiarity could not go on. And soon, neither would our friendship. Paige would see to that, but propriety and village expectations would also dictate our actions as soon as they were wed.

We walked through the darkness in comfortable silence. The air was crisp and the leaves were dipped in the signature colors of autumn. Smoke from the hearths of cabins dotted through this valley haunted the sky. When we passed by the familiar places from our childhood, I looked up and over at him. He just smiled and urged me on, giving my hand a gentle squeeze. He still hadn't let it go.

We left the heart of the village and headed quickly out on a very well-worn, wide trail–one that I only traveled under rare circumstances. The area was restricted. Lulu was our village's supply coordinator. If someone needed something, anything, they would tell her and she would make sure that all requested items were on the next supply train from the cities.

The city we dealt with the most frequently, most intimately was Olympus, the crown jewel of the southeast. I'd only seen the trains a handful of times. Lines of rusty rectangles would stretch from the depot as far as the eye could see. Though Lulu said that some trains were only six or seven cars long. Lulu coordinated with the Greaters as to the time of the supply drop-offs, as well as when they would pick up goods from our village. All of the interactions with the trains and the Greater City of Olympus were highly guarded and meticulously regulated.

Kyan remained silent, but looked over at me, pressing a finger against his pursed lips. I nodded. We slipped off the trail and wound through the woods. Pine needles blanketed the forest floor muffling the sound of our steps. We startled a deer, which leapt away at breakneck speed crashing into the forest beyond. I stifled a laugh, as we stepped through the underbrush. Then, I saw it, and my breath fled my body. Kyan's eyes widened as he took it in, as if for the first time.

The railway was lit up. Bright lights cut sharply through the darkness illuminating the small wooden train depot and tracks that stretched out in front of it. I'd never seen electric lights before, though I'd heard of them. That wasn't even what was so unbelievable.

I'd seen train cars before. Rusted metal or wood, loud clanking and grating boxes that rumbled atop stressed wheels. But, this was different. This was amazing. My mouth gaped open. My hand flew to cover it on its own volition, as I sucked in a deep breath. On the track sat a sleek, silver metallic chain of train cars whose head was seated just beyond the depot and whose tail stretched off down the track and into the darkness as far as the eye could see. A sleek silver serpent lying in wait.

I whispered. "It's so shiny. Is it real?"

Kyan nodded. It was real.

"What is it?"

"Passenger cars. It just rolled in. It's from Olympus. I guess the Greaters are letting the villages use their train to transport all of the workers from the various villages. The harvest is important, but I've never seen this before. This is just...crazy." He raised a brow.

It *was* crazy. I'd never seen anything that looked so new and clean. Polished and sleek. Perfect. When I was a child, Lulu told me stories that her parents told her, about great sleek ships that took men to outer space, to the moon. Until now, I'd always believed that the stories had been made up—great tales to entertain children, wide-eyed and gullible.

The windows of the train cars were lit from within, shadows occasionally moving in front of them, dimming their unnatural light momentarily. A few men stood along the wooden platform of the depot, barking orders to those still aboard. It was a buzz of activity.

We watched the scene in front of us for several moments. The awestruck feeling I had upon seeing the train has morphed into a feeling of unease, an apprehension of things to come. I had a feeling that Olympus and the Greaters were making our business, our harvest, their own, and that could not be a good thing.

Chapter 6

I WALKED QUICKLY TOWARD THE orchard. It was a clear, cool morning. The air was wet and the grass saturated with cool dew. Crickets chirped happily. A deep blue-gray unfolded overhead. Only the eastern horizon hinted at the dawn to come. I didn't even register the fact that someone had fallen into step beside me until he reached out and grabbed my elbow, roughly. I stopped and turned to face Zander Preston. *Crap.*

"Zander."

"Do you think your aunt can stop me from getting what I want?" He stepped toward me.

"Ever hear of personal space?" I backed up a few more paces into the dewy grass. Did that stop him? No. He kept moving forward, his face as hard as his icy blue eyes—eyes that almost glowed, even in the near darkness.

"She won't stop this. My father said that she refused our union. I will marry you, Abigail."

I shook my head. "Don't you get it? I don't want to marry you, Zander." He kept moving toward me and I kept walking backward until my back made contact with the wooden fence behind me, preventing further retreat. I gripped the top post for support.

"I don't care what you want." He grabbed my upper arm and squeezed tight.

"Zander, you're hurting me. Let go." I tried to wrench my arm away from him, but he wouldn't budge.

"Tell her you've changed your mind."

"No."

His jaw clenched along with his grip on my arm. I shoved him hard on his chest with my free hand, but it barely moved him. He lowered his face toward mine, and I twisted as far away from him as I could go.

"Get off her. Now," a rich, deep voice ordered. Zander, with his eyes trained on mine, backed away slowly, finally releasing my arm, which ached in the wake of his grip. I wouldn't rub it. He wouldn't get the satisfaction of knowing that he'd hurt me.

Zander pinned me with his eyes. "This isn't over, Abby," he said so low that only I could hear. He gave the stranger a hard stare and stomped away. I told him I didn't want to marry him. Lulu told his father the same thing. Why couldn't he just accept it? *What the heck is he thinking?*

"Hello?" A hand waved in front of my face.

"What?" I asked, still confused by Zander's actions.

"Are you okay?" That voice. It pulled me toward him. His eyes were the first thing I noticed. And, they were the most beautiful eyes that I'd ever seen. Honey-colored, and only outlined by a hint of warm, golden brown. Streaked gold radiated from the pupil outward. It was stunning. His sable hair was worn longer than what was considered proper in our village. It brushed his brow and curled around his ears, and at the nape of his neck, it flipped out. He was tall, at least as tall as Kyan. "Miss?"

"Yes." I finally breathed. "I'm okay."

He watched me for a moment and then relaxed. "Did he hurt you? I saw how he was holding your arm."

I rubbed it absentmindedly. "I'm fine. Thanks for helping, by the way." I looked down.

"No problem. Can I ask a favor from you? Two, actually."

I nodded, looking at those eyes again. "One. Try not to get caught alone with him again." He ticked his head in the direction Zander had fled.

"Easier said than done. I don't see him alone often, but I am often alone, so if he's determined to find me, he will. Two?"

"Do you know where I can find Kyan Marks?"

"That one is much easier. Ky's my best friend, and my team leader. I'll take you to him." I smiled, took a few steps and waved for him to follow.

"Kyan is a male," he stated, though it sounded more like a question.

"Yes." I drawled.

"Women and men are allowed to socialize here?" His eyebrows raised.

"Of course. We all work together in the orchards and some are friends."

A look of confusion knitted his brow, my face mirroring his own. "Which village are you from?"

"Cotton."

"And, are girls not allowed to speak with guys in your village?"

He blushed, a ruddy color filling his pale white cheeks. "Only on special occasions. They divide the fields by gender to prevent fraternization. Occasionally they have a banquet dinner or dance in which all can attend and socialize. Other than that..."

We walked into the orchard and down one of its many rows. "How strange. I wonder why the rules in your village differ so much from our own."

He shrugged. His white t-shirt clung to his biceps and his jeans hung perfectly from his body. The work boots he wore were barely scuffed, the warm brown leather pristine. Weird. We never received new shoes. Only worn ones recycled from other villages. Sometimes the soles were worn through when we got them.

He caught me looking at his shoes, turned red again and quickened his pace. "I got lucky. This pair came in our shipment about a week ago. It looks like they'd barely been worn and they were my size, so I grabbed them before anyone else did." He smiled.

"You're lucky."

He nodded.

"Hey, what's your name?" I asked.

"Crew."

"Well, Crew. It sure was nice to meet you this morning. Thank you again," I put my hand out to shake his and he looked unsure. Finally his hand met my own, his warm and soft. It wasn't calloused like Kyan's, or even mine, from working in the orchards. Very strange. He pulled his hand back and cleared his throat, looking uneasy at me from the corner of his eyes.

Kyan appeared from around a tree. "Hey, Abby." He hugged me lightly and placed a small kiss upon my temple. He'd done this a thousand times, but somehow, with Crew watching, it felt strange and I pulled away from him quickly, awkwardly. My face was on fire. Kyan was rattled by my abrupt withdrawal. I could tell. I knew he'd been angry that I've been pulling away from him in general, but physically doing so was something else. Something between us had changed. He looked past me to Crew.

"Ky, this is Crew. He's been assigned to your team."

"Oh, hey man. Welcome and thanks for your help with our harvest." The two locked hands and sized each other up the way guys do, each straightening up to full height. Crew was taller than Kyan, but only by an inch or so. I rolled my eyes and crossed my arms. *Really, guys?*

"Sure, man. Show me where to get started."

Despite my obvious reluctance, Ky pulled me in for another quick hug and then said, "Abs, can you start right down there with Laney?" I could see her blonde hair contrasting against the some of the still green leaves about 10 trees down. I nodded and waved to Kyan and Crew, making my way toward Laney.

"Remember the favor you owe me," Crew called out behind me. I looked back and smiled, and then saw Kyan. His face hardened as he looked from me to the newest member of our team. I just hoped he didn't go all 'big brother' on me.

"I will." I shouted back, hurrying to Laney's tree.

∞

"LANE, I'VE GOT TO REPORT for prison duty."

She laughed. "Prison duty? The Preston Prison. I like it. Hey, who was that hottie you were with this morning?"

I rolled my eyes. "His name is Crew. He's from Cotton." I wasn't sure why her question annoyed me, but it did.

"Is he available?"

"I'm not sure. I didn't ask. I figure he'll only be here for a few weeks max. Sorry."

She giggled. "It's fine. I was just wondering. Not for me." She holds up her hand, "He was looking at you like you were already his. If his eyes could have claimed you as his intended, you'd be married already!"

"What? Whatever. That's ridiculous."

"Abby, you should have seen him and Kyan from a distance. I thought they were going to come to blows over you. They went all caveman. My female. No, my female," she grunted, strutting around like she actually had muscles to fill out her tiny arms.

"Uga, uga." I laughed. "Later!" I yelled. I took my last bushel to the end of the row and started toward the Preston house. Mrs. Preston met me at the door. "Oh, Abigail. I'm so glad you're here." Her plump lips puckered dramatically.

She grabbed both of my forearms and jerked me inside. "This house must be spotless. Perfect. We are hosting a very important family from Cotton. So," she pulled out a piece of paper. I cringed. The list was twice as long as I'd ever seen it and I had two fewer hours to complete the tasks that it contained. "Here is your list. And, they will arrive at 4:00pm on the dot, so you must finish early." I was pretty sure a fly just flew into my mouth and back out. She didn't even look back at me, just swished her skirt and heels right out the front door. Heels? Really? Even she had to walk the dirty pathways.

I grumbled as I started but pushed hard and was finishing the kitchen floor at 4:00pm, 'on the dot.' Sure enough, Mr. Preston entered, as I was replacing the mop and cleaning items in the small closet, followed by another gentleman approximately his age. The newcomer had sharp, strong features. His jaw was chiseled and square, clean-shaven. Hair the color of midnight was peppered with gray along the temples, his skin pale and clear. He was tall and broad of shoulder and even though older, his body was well maintained.

That wasn't what was so different about him, though. His eyes. They were streaked with honey, like Crew's, but surrounded with deep brown, almost black. His eyes pinned me to the floor, like a bug. When I was a child, I knew a boy who used to pin bugs to pieces of paper or bark, or anything he could find, really. It had been disturbing then. It was equally as disturbing now, especially as I felt like the bug and not the pinner.

"Never mind the girl. She's a servant in our home at present." Mr. Preston tried to steer the stranger further into the house, and away from me. Preston glared at me, but my feet wouldn't move.

"Your name?" The stranger's voice was thunderous and I flinched at his sudden demand.

"Abigail, Sir."

"Abigail." It was as if he was pondering my name and its match with my face. "You look very familiar. Forgive me," his eyes softened, slightly, and he extended a hand to me. I took it and shook quickly. Mr. Preston cleared his throat and nodded toward the door. I took my leave as quickly as my feet would carry me. But not before I heard the stranger say, "It seems your village has a secret, Councilman." *What secret?*

After dumping the contents of yet another bucket of dirty water, peppered with soaked dust clumps, I started in the direction of home. Darkness hadn't fallen, so no one would have been dismissed from the orchard and for a moment, I almost turned in that direction, but decided against it. Kyan would get angry. Lulu as well. As I stepped out of the hayfield and into the outer edge of the woods that surrounded our cabin, I saw them.

Zander smirked at me as he approached with Crew at his side. Crew looked anything but happy. His jaw clenched and his hands were tucked in his front pockets. "Good afternoon, Abigail."

"Crew." I acknowledge first with a smile and a nod, although he wasn't the one who had addressed me.

"Abigail. Really? You can't ignore me. Besides, I have wonderful news. Crew and his family will be staying at our house for the duration of their visit."

Crew glanced angrily at Zander, who chuckled and looked back at me. "Crew, Abby is our current...help. She cleans our home."

"It's temporary." I barked.

Crew stood quiet, taking us both in.

"If you say so." Zander shrugged. "Do you think my Mother will want to go back to cleaning it now that she has you? Why do you think Father won't put you back in the orchards full time now, during harvest time, of all times? It has nothing to do with your...injury."

"Injury?" Crew questioned.

"Shut up, Zander. I got hurt and was taken out of the orchards, temporarily." I made sure to emphasize that last part. "So, I have to work at the Preston's house until I can return full-time. His father allows me to work the harvest for two hours in the morning, before I have to report to their house." I shifted my weight.

Zander grinned, feasting happily on my discomfort. He loved to put people in their place–beneath him and his perfect family. And, he knew he had just put me in mine. In front of Crew. The look on Crew's face bothered me, though. He looked at Zander, at our surroundings, but refused to make eye contact with me. *Does he think I'm beneath him now, too?* How in the hell did a Lesser manage to become less than their lowered designation? I'm not sure, but I think I just did.

"Oh," Zander's eyebrows raised. "And, Abby, you should reconsider my proposal. Lulu's not here to shield you anymore."

"What? What do you mean?" She's not here to shield me? Then it dawned on me. No smoke was rising from the direction of our cabin. She wasn't home. She was always home before me, cooking dinner and buzzing around the house.

"What happened to her?" I tried to push by them, tears clouding my vision. Rough hands clamped around my upper arms.

"Abigail. Calm down. Nothing happened to her. She's just been sent to Olympus on some official business," he paused. "Indefinitely."

I began to shake and blinked to release the tears that pooled heavily in my eyes. Those pools nearly turned red with rage. "Indefinitely? And, let me guess, you and your father had nothing to do with it?"

"Oh, we had everything to do with it. Like I said, you should really reconsider. She would want to see your wedding ceremony."

I ripped my arms away from him. "I will never marry you. One minute you treat me like scum on your shoe and the next you threaten me? Unbelievable, even for you Zander."

He grabbed me again. Big mistake. "Let me go."

Crew stepped in. "Release her, now. You've had your fun with her, now let's go. Surely you're joking, anyway. Why would you take a servant as your wife when you could have any female in this village?" He clapped Zander's shoulder and nodded for them to continue on their way.

"True. I could have any other girl in the village, or in yours," he released my arms. "But, there's fun in the challenge of breaking something so strong. Don't you think, Crew?" His fingers slithered into my hair.

"Get off me," I shoved him as hard as I could and he stumbled but didn't fall. He and Crew laughed as they walked off toward the Preston house. If I had been paying attention, I might have noticed Crew looking back at me as I fled. I seethed toward home, knowing now I would find it empty.

Chapter 7

SITTING IN THE DARK, THE old rocking chair creaked and groaned with every motion. Back and forth. Back and forth. Creak, squall. Creak, groan. I was on the porch when Kyan came running toward the house. Somehow, he saw me. Maybe it was the motion of the rocking chair that caught his eye. He scooped me up and held me tight. Tears had been flowing from my eyes all afternoon, but when Kyan showed me that he loved me, in whatever capacity this was, the real crying began in earnest.

"They took her," I sobbed and knotted the fabric of his shirt, dragging him even closer.

"I heard she had to leave and wanted to see if you were okay."

I shook my head. "They made her leave. Sent her away."

"Who?" He pushed me back, just enough to look at my eyes.

"The Preston's. They want me to agree to accept Zander or they won't bring her back. I'm not even sure if they'll bring her back even if I *do* accept his hand."

"You're not marrying Zander Preston."

"I don't want to. But, what am I supposed to do? Lulu is in Olympus. I can't just leave her there."

"Has she ever been sent to the city before?"

"Yes."

"Maybe this is one of those times. Maybe Preston's capitalizing on her trip to trick you into agreeing to marry Zander?"

I shrugged. It didn't matter. Lulu was all I had. And they took her. I needed to get her back. Kyan didn't leave me. He guided me inside, lit all of the candles and fixed dinner for us. I could barely eat, and though he noticed, he kept silent on the matter.

He went to the creek for water so that I could wash up before bed and then took Lulu's bed for himself. Though a wall separated us, I felt like we could see right through it, see each other. Right into one another's eyes—one another's souls.

∞

THE NEXT MORNING, THE SUN was working overtime. The air was hot and dry. Apples were baking on the branches and falling to the ground. They were rotting faster than we could pick them. The children were busy. Running in and out of the trees, they plucked the rotten fruit from the ground and placed them in buckets. Some squealed happily until scolded by their caretakers or parents. Their buckets were filled quickly and by the day's end a huge pile of rotten apples lay at the end of the orchard.

Kyan grinned and nodded his head at the pyramid of steamy, spongy fruit. Gnats and bees were busy buzzing around the pyramid of rot, making the most of the feast. Laney grabbed my hand and I told Crew to hang back with us for a while if he had nothing better to do. He did.

When the adults and supervisors were gone, and dusk had settled into the valley, we paired off into teams. Kyan and me versus Crew and Laney. "What do we do exactly?" Crew asked nervously. I decided a demonstration was the best explanation. I picked up a browning, wilted apple and chucked it at him. It was so hot and gross that it exploded when it hit his thigh.

For a moment, he looked stunned, but that only lasted a minute before he narrowed his eyes and grabbed an apple of his own. I tried to run but was too slow. His apple hit me directly in the calf. It was on. Apples flew everywhere. Their sweet smell and our laughter floated into the evening air. Laney tried to hide behind the pile, so I knocked the whole thing over onto her. She squealed and laughed, running away from the apple-anch.

Crew and Kyan exchanged blows. Kyan had perfected his strategy over the years. He launched multiple apples at once. But, Crew's aim was more precise. I ducked behind a nearby tree and barely avoided one of his stinging blows. We laughed and threw until we ran out of breath and collapsed on the ground in gasping giggles. It was one of the best evenings I'd had in a long time.

When we were spent, we all took off in different directions, but somehow, Crew had gotten lost. His trail connected with mine. "You took a wrong turn back at the old dead tree."

Shaking his head, he grinned. "I'll never figure out this maze of trails."

"You will. Maybe. I mean, you won't be here long, right?"

He stared at me. "Right. Well, thanks Abby. You could have let me wander around."

He turned to leave and I remembered how he'd treated me when I met him and Zander on the trail. Perhaps I should have given him bad directions after all.

∞

THE NEXT FEW DAYS PASSED in a blur, but on Friday morning, a fierce red-streaked sky greeted me on the way to the orchards. My eyes were trained on the bleeding sky the whole way there. I passed Crew before heading toward Laney, and his eyes fell on mine and then sunk to the ground. He didn't even want to look at me now. I guess Zander had done his job well. Crew and his family were staying at the Preston's so I was sure Zander had divulged all sorts of information about our village. And, apparently about me.

His skin was raw, bright red where it had been pale. And, I wasn't the only one who noticed. Ky slapped him on the back. "You're baked, dude."

Crew smiled back and then pinched the bridge of his nose. "I know, man."

"How do you pick cotton in the sun all day without frying to a crisp?"

Crew's smile dropped. He shifted his feet. I looked at Laney and she nodded back at the pair. "I...our healer mixes this lotion using a local bark that blocks the rays of the sun so we don't get burnt. I'm one of the palest in our settlement, so I use most of the lotion she makes, though." He smiled sheepishly.

"Wow. I wish we had some for you. Looks painful. Here's a hat, though." He took the hat off of his head and tossed it to Crew. Crew put it on backwards, exactly how Ky had been wearing it. He looked up to see Laney and me looking at him and then quickly corrected the cap, the bill shading his face. But, I was pretty sure his neck turned a deeper shade of crimson for a few moments.

"Did he seriously not know how to wear a ball cap? Cottons are so weird." Laney looked at me from her perch in the tree, dropping the apples into my wire basket. "I heard Lulu had to take a trip to Olympus. Are you okay in the house by yourself?"

"Sure." I shrugged like it's no big deal. "She has to go every so often. It's not the first time I've stayed by myself." I wasn't about to tell her that Kyan had been staying in Lulu's room overnight. Paige Winters would have me whipped within an inch of my life and Norris would no doubt be grinning as my blood spurted across his sickening face. I cringed at the thought.

"Oh! You're coming tomorrow night, right?" I looked at her blankly. "Oh, maybe I forgot to tell you. We're having a bonfire party for those from the other villages who are helping." She leaned down and dropped her voice conspiratorially. But her voice was so loud, I was sure everyone within a ten tree radius heard our conversation. "It's going to be so much fun. It's at the old park after dark tomorrow." Her blonde curls bounced with her excitement as she clapped her hands together.

"I don't think I—"

"Oh, no. No. No. No. You *are* coming with me, Miss Abby. Don't even think about weaseling out of this. We never get visitors here and we are going to be most hospitable." An evil grin erupted on her face and I suddenly wondered just how friendly she intended to get with these people.

"Fine. I'll go."

Laney squealed and climbed the tree a bit higher.

"Abby?" Kyan called.

I ducked around the tree and approached him. Crew was standing beside him, barely making eye contact with me again. There was no lukewarm with him. He was either friendly or avoided me completely. "I need you in the trees until you have to leave. We're behind on our quotas. Crew will go between and help both you and Laney."

I nodded and began climbing the tree beside my strangely silent-normally bubbly-blonde friend. My back stretched painfully as I maneuvered into the tree. The limbs were close together and some of the knotted bark scraped me as I moved past making me wince. I went straight to work, settling myself in a comfortable spot and began picking. "Crew, may I have a bushel please?"

He passed me the small woven basket and our fingers brushed. I felt a jolt of electricity from the contact and broke it immediately. He jumped back, too, releasing the basket so that I jerked harshly back against the trunk. His lip snarled accusingly.

I rolled my eyes. As if I had done anything on purpose. I didn't even know what had passed between us. It was strange, like a spark of static electricity without the physical zap—only the shocking feeling left behind.

I quickly filled the bushel and handed it down to him, making sure to avoid touching his hand again. The hour passed quickly and I was pushing it. I wanted to stay and help, but knew I had to get to the Preston's house.

Reluctantly, I handed Crew the final bushel and began my descent. I had positioned my sneaker on the final tree joint and shifted my weight. The worn rubber on the bottom of my shoe couldn't grip the tree's bark like it used to. It slipped and so did I. I wasn't that high up, but felt the wind in my hair as I began to fall, clawing at the small branches beside my hands, though I knew they couldn't hold my weight if I did grab hold of them. I closed my eyes. This was going to hurt. My back didn't hit the ground. Instead, two strong arms folded around me, one under my back and one under my knees. I clung to him, out of breath.

I couldn't move. Beneath my bandages, I could feel the wetness soaking in. Some of the just barely healed gashes had just been torn open again and were bleeding. I panicked and began kicking and scooting away from him. Crew. He reluctantly let me go.

"Are you okay?"

His eyes searched mine, before they moved over my body. I winced as I stood up and began backing away. "I'm fine. Just shaken up. Thank you. Thanks, Crew. I...I have to go...to the Preston's. Tell Kyan for me?"

He pushed himself to his feet, eyeing me warily. "Are you sure you're okay? You're not hurt?"

"No. I just can't be late. Thanks, though. Seriously. I owe you one."

He muttered something under his breath as I ducked into the next row and quickly began walking toward the dreaded part of my day. I couldn't let him see my back.

∞

THAT EVENING I WAS SORE from the fall, or the landing, though it had been better than landing on the ground. I was sweaty and needed to be clean. The only one place I could think of that would both soothe my skin let me get clean: the lake. A swim sounded amazing. I grabbed some clothes to change into and a bar of soap and took off down the trail that into the woods beyond. The sun had set and crickets were serenading the evening. The tall grasses along the pathway brushed my bare legs. I'd rolled my jeans up earlier in the afternoon. It had been a hot, sunny day.

Crew's bright red skin flashed into my mind and I smiled. I could smell the wild onions that thickened along the lake shore, made lush by the plentiful water and sunlight. My favorite spot was along the eastern side of the water, where a large flat rock jutted into the lapping waves. No one else was here tonight. Some nights I had to wait to clean up. Most villagers, male and female alike, had lost their sense of modesty long ago due to necessity, but like my clothes, it was something I'd never been able to shed.

I undressed quickly, hung my clothes on a nearby tree branch and grabbed my soap bar. Lulu had made it with a rope sticking out of each end so we could secure it to our wrists when bathing and wouldn't lose so many bars. It took a while to make soap, so each bar was a commodity. She and I both hated that job with a passion. I missed her. Exhaling, I gingerly sat on the end of the rock, dipping my toes in to test the temperature of the water. It was perfect. The sun had warmed it today, but only just enough. The cool nights had tempered it nicely. This was going to feel great. I unwrapped my bandages and peeled them away. Some were stuck to me, bonded with the dried blood from earlier. It hurt, but I ripped the fabric away. Best to do it quickly.

I slipped off the rock into the water and adjusted to it for a moment before swimming several yards out into the lake. I made the trip out and back at a leisurely pace several times. Approaching the rock again, someone was standing nearby undressing. Oh my...no! It was Crew! I grasped my mouth with one hand and my breasts with the other and then decided to swim back out and wait for him to wash up and leave.

My plan backfired. He didn't just wash and leave. He stripped and then began swimming laps, straight toward me. And he was fast, a damn good swimmer. I couldn't swim well because of my back and though I was comfortable, I'd never seen anyone with so perfect a stroke in my life. I dodged to the side and began swimming horizontally away from him. His head was down. Surely he would miss me. When he was right across from me, something slimy touched my leg and I let out a screech. He popped up from the water and looked right at me. I covered my important lady bits.

"Abby?" He shook the water from his hair and used his hand to clear it from his eyes. "What are you doing here? And why are you screaming?"

"I'm swimming and was going to bathe. What are you doing here?" I accused. The water rippled down his skin in tiny torrents. Holy hotness without a shirt on. The boys from Cotton shouldn't be so selfish. They should never wear shirts. They should conserve raw materials and go shirtless all the time. Because it was nice. Very nice. And, very, very hot.

Freaking out internally, I treaded water and tried to cover myself. He grinned as he looked at me, and his smile widened as his eyes drooped lower than my own. I gritted my teeth together, my cheeks hot as fire. "Hey! I asked you what you were doing here! This is my spot."

"The lake is your spot? I'm swimming and going to clean up, too. Not like there's running..." He shook his head.

"Not like there's running what?"

"Nothing. Forget it. Why were you screaming like you were dying?" He splashed some water at me.

I splashed back at him with my free hand. "I was screaming like some slimy fish brushed my leg, which was exactly what happened. It's probably your fault. You probably scared it toward me. You were swimming like someone was after you." He didn't respond, just grinned. He was so beautiful. If a man could be considered beautiful, he was exactly that. It was time for me to leave. He stared at me intently, silence drowning out the sounds of the night swirling around us. "Well, I'm going to go. Can you stay out here for a few minutes?"

"Yeah. Sure." He was treading water with both arms extended and I couldn't help but look at him again. His dark hair glistened in the moonlight and I could still tell his skin was pink. He smirked when he caught me ogling him, and I rolled my eyes and started to the shore sideways, one arm covering myself and the other paddling. The movement concealed my back. If it wasn't mangled, I would have faced away from him and used both arms. He chuckled as I struggled toward the shore.

"Maybe we can skinny-dip together tomorrow, Abigail!" he yelled from behind me.

"I was not skinny-dipping with you. I was bathing!"

"Sure. Whatever." I looked back at him and felt like roaring, but he was grinning back at me. I kicked my feet and hoped the splash shut him up. He started laughing. Before I exited the water, I looked at him. He was openly staring, waiting for me to climb out. "Turn around, Crew!" My voice had risen an octave.

"Fine." He grumbled something else and then raised his hands out of the water in surrender and then turned around. I jumped onto the rock and ran to the tree where my clothing hung. Snatching it up, I ran into the woods and quickly dressed. "You're so bashful, Abby! Not what I expected from tough as nails Kelley."

I wasn't proud of what I did next. Oh, who was I kidding? I was proud. Very proud. I sauntered back to the rock and found his discarded clothing. "Hey, what are you doing with my clothes?"

"We'll see who the bashful one is, now!" I walked away giggling, his clothes neatly bundled under my arm.

"Come on, Abby. Leave my clothes! Come on!" He splashed the water with both hands. His pleas faded into the darkness the closer to home I strode.

Chapter 8

SATURDAY EVENING AFTER I COMPLETED the dreaded list from Mrs. Preston, or Mr. Preston or Zander—whoever wrote it, I hurried home to meet Laney. She was staying with me tonight and somehow I needed to let Kyan know. He'd been sleeping in Lulu's room since she left. But, that was not going to happen tonight. Laney would freak if he climbed into bed with her. He was going to the bonfire, so I would have to try to steal a moment with him later. Discreetly. I knew Paige and her cronies would be there as well.

Laney burst through my front door seconds after I had entered it myself. She nearly tackled me in a hug, squealing and then jumped up and down. "This is going to be so much fun. I'm so excited." She squeezed my neck.

"I can tell," I eked out.

"Oh, sorry." She released my neck. In hardly any time, she squeezed me into a pair of her jeans, which were a little too tight for my taste, but she said made my butt look amazing. I was tucked into one of her button up flannel shirts, red and navy cross their ways across my body. Her shirt was a bit tight, too. But, she insisted and I had nothing clean anyway, so I relented.

She tugged on an off-the-shoulder brown sweater which made her hair and eyes look amazing and a tight jean skirt that flirted delicately with her knees. She finger-combed her curls into submission and brushed my hair until it shone in all its mahogany glory. Before I knew it, Laney had painted my lips red and lashes black.

She squealed in excitement taking me all in, making me do a twirl. I felt stupid, but I could tell it meant a lot to her. She painted her face on as well and then pulled me into the night, laughing happily. Freely. I even laughed, too. Something I hadn't done since Lulu had been sent away.

Crickets chirped happily in the tall hay beside us as we curved our way through the hayfields and thicker forest, away from the village. The park, as we called it, was just that. A forgotten relic that somehow still survived, hidden in the middle of the forest not too far from the village. It had been a childhood rite of passage to go there, to be scared out of your mind there. Dares had centered completely on the skeletal remains that the forest hid just beyond our reach.

The moon was high and shone on the lake, like million silver fish scales dancing in the dark. The first trace of the park came along with that lake, complete with half sunken giant plastic swans, their eyes masked in faded black, contrasting with their once stark white bodies, now cov-

ered with algae and mold. One swan remained upright.
One solitary swan.

It had been that way since I was a child. Situated right
at the shoreline, ensuring that it would probably remain
upright until I was long gone. If one looked closely, the
trails of snails and slugs carving through the green-gray
algae glistened. Laney chattered on about how hot the
guys from Cotton, Wheat, and Coal might be. I had to
agree. Crew was the only male I had met from the other
villages. If he was an example of what they all looked like,
then they most certainly were hot. They would be
different and somehow, that alone was appealing. New.

Most of the girls kept to their usual cliques from home.
They would wave and smile but rarely attempted to
converse. Laney spoke with disappointment that the few
guys she had seen had been guarded by the females from
their villages like hellacious she-cats. But, their relation-
ships were built on years of trust and familiarity. No doubt
some were intended, betrothed, and excited to be joined
together as one.

It was announced yesterday morning by team leaders,
by Kyan, that all couples in attendance who were already
intended would be joined in marriage at the harvest
festival in approximately one week's time.

Kyan's eyes had found mine during this announcement. They were hard. He was steeling himself for what
lay just around the bend. For Paige. The words he had
uttered to me kept screaming through my mind, "I don't
love her..."

We passed by the fun house. Inside, fastened to the
walls, among the leaves, dead branches and creeping

things, were mirrors that could make you look extremely tall and thin, short and round, or as if your body had no bones at all. The reflection would wave back and forth distorting reality. Bottles that once contained sweet apple wine littered the corner of the room, remnants of the fun of youth.

Many times, Laney had dragged me out here with her to partake in the festivities. Sure, it was a bit on the macabre side as far as entertainment was concerned. But, it was ours. Away from prying village eyes sat our strange, long forgotten place of refuge. And, it was exactly that. The Greaters didn't even know it existed.

A game booth, its wooden counter sunken and rotting in the middle, sat next to the fun house. Dry rotted teddy bear pelts were still tacked to its walls, prizes that would have delighted any child passing by. One could still see the faded, peeling remnants of the vibrant colors that once coated it, that had once coaxed passersby to stop by and enjoy a little bit of fun and excitement.

A structure with little cars, the backs of which had long poles that connected to the ceiling with small swiveled wheels, sat to our left. Several more ghostly booths and stands lined the familiar concrete pathway. Sunken basketballs and dry rotted nets hung from their rusted metal, bent hoops pointed down or to the sides at odd angles.

A spinning prize wheel creaked eerily when the breeze took hold and teetered it. Freak show oddities with promises to delight and astound, were shouted out in lettering that was once bold and must have been quite a sight to behold when new.

The pathway diverged. To the left, I could see it. A giant steel and wooden loop stretched into the sky, in the middle of the forest. The steep hill that led to it had been a pathway into adulthood. Many a boy would be turned into a man attempting to climb those hills and defy gravity on a dangerous but important dare. But, Laney hooked her elbow with mine and steered me to the right.

A Ferris wheel, its cars dangling precariously, rusted and hollow, unoccupied, filled my vision. The metal, once red, was now rust. Vines wound their way up to some of the lower cars, as if anchoring the structure to the ground, or swallowing it up from below. Reclaiming it to the earth. Dust to Dust.

The dancing firelight illuminated the structure and laughter, whoops, and hollers lift into the night sky, like embers from a fire. A good time was being had by all. Clusters of people, some sticking to their village friends scattered around the fire, bottles of apple wine everywhere. I wondered where and who had been able to get their hands on a shipment this big. Surely, someone would notice such a supply decrease. My palms began to sweat and I felt like running away.

Laney must have sensed my tension, because she looked my way, pinning me with her eyes, shaking her head. "No way. We're here to have fun. Not to think. Let's get a drink and loosen you up, hmm?"

I nodded. She was right. We found the crates of wine and grabbed one to share. Many greeted us with nods, waves and smiles. We made our way to our usual spot–a stone bench under one of the maple trees nearby and began to laugh with one another about this and that. With each sweet swallow of wine, I felt myself relax a little more.

Paige pulled Kyan into my line of sight and all but tackled him to the ground as she plastered herself onto him. She smirked at me and then kissed him full on the lips, pushing into his chest, moaning loudly. I looked away. What she and Kyan did privately was their own business. I just wished she understood what privacy and discretion were all about. Kyan pushed her away after a moment and then followed her line of sight, still pinpointed on me, before pulling her away. He looked angrily back at me before following Paige into the shadows.

"What was that?" Laney gaped.

"What?"

"You know what!" she whisper-yelled.

"Paige molesting her future-husband? She has every right."

Laney rolled her eyes and took another sip of wine. "How about her making sure you were watching or the smoldering look Kyan just gave you before following her off like a whipped little puppy."

I laughed. "Whipped little puppy?"

She snickered. "Yep. Argue all you want, but that boy is in love with you. Not his intended."

It wasn't long before my nightmare showed up, dressed in a dark blue button down, his golden hair illuminated like a halo by the fire. I couldn't help wondering if his halo was held up by horns. Zander sauntered to a bench nearby and set down a box. Music. He has his father's music machine. He hit a few buttons, a blue screen illuminating the features of his face. He really would be hot if his personality wasn't so awful. Maybe that was the apple wine talking, though.

A sultry beat filled the air and before long, bodies began to part off, male and female, and sway together. A hand landed in front of me, and I looked up to find Zander its owner. "Dance with me?" He smiled sweetly, which sent red flags flapping wildly in my mind.

Laney looked at me with wide eyes, before smiling and pushing me up toward him. I glared at her and she giggled and shrugged a shoulder. Zander's friend, Eli showed up and asked Laney to dance with him. Eli had always been quiet. I wasn't really sure why he was friends with Zander other than the fact that his father also sat upon the village council. Eli's hair was dark brown and his eyes are deep and dark, too. He had that look that clung to boyhood for dear life, but was now mostly man. Freckles even splashed across his nose. He wore thin silver wire glasses, a green button-down shirt and jeans. Laney placed her hand in his and let him lead her closer to the fire and music. Zander led me over near them as well.

He always wanted to be seen, so he chose a prime location and led me into a dance. I couldn't make out all of the lyrics, but they dripped with sensuality, of sex. It felt weird dancing with Zander to a song like this. I didn't feel any sort of attraction to him. None. The way his icy eyes looked me up and down, made me sigh in frustration. The other day he humiliated me and bathed in the discomfort he'd caused me and today he was sweetly swaying me to the hypnotic beat while his lips seem to be inching closer. Laney was so going to get an ear-full later.

His right hand warmed the small of my back and his left held mine on his chest. I looked up at him and he smiled. I smelled it. He was already drunk. Now, I took him in. His eyes were a bit glassy. He smiled a lot, which was out of character. His steps were smooth, though. When the song ended, I pulled away, but he wouldn't allow it.

He just smiled and pulled me back into him. Ky and Paige had reappeared and swayed together nearby. Kyan nodded toward Zander, his eyes questioning. I shook my head. I knew he wanted to help, but Zander was behaving so far, so I decided to go along with it, for now. A few songs later, another slow, sultry sound emanates from the music machine. The smell of sweet apple wine filled the air tangling with the bonfire smoke.

"I've wanted to dance with you forever," Zander admitted, his breath warming my neck just below my ear.

"I call bullshit."

He pulled back a little. "Why would you say that Abigail?"

"You go out of your way to humiliate me, to make sure I know just how beneath you I am, so there is no way that you've wanted to dance with me, or do anything else with me, forever. Where is this all coming from? One minute you hate me, the next you want to dance with me. What is this, Zander?"

His eyes pierced mine. "This," he pulled me flush to his body. "This is me getting familiar with my future bride."

I huffed. "I'm not marrying you. I've already made that perfectly clear."

He laughed. "You and I will be joined at the harvest festival, my dear. It's all being arranged. My mother has even chosen your dress. It's hanging in her closet."

I started to argue, but he put his finger over my lips. "Shh. Yours will be the best, the most beautiful in the village. Our house will be built, bigger than my parents'. You and I will rule the council. It all makes sense. *We* make sense, Abby."

I shook my head. *Why doesn't he get it?* "I don't love you."

"I don't care." His voice turned cold, distant. His hands clawed me closer. "You're mine." Zander's teeth grazed my ear. I inhaled sharply and tried to pull away from him.

"I'm not yours, Zander. Choose someone who actually wants you." He growled. Literally growled, before pulling me away from the crowd into the shadows, then into the darkness. He all but dragged me down the walkway and into the fun house. I dug my feet into the dry leaves just outside, but he nearly pulled my arms out of socket.

I was jerked forward and landed with my body against his. His lips slammed into mine, bruising, punishing. He wrenched me further into him, his fingers laced their way into my hair. He yanked hard. My mouth burst open in a silent scream and he used it to his advantage. Zander pushed me hard against one of the mirrors that line the walls, and thrust his tongue into my mouth. I tried to get me knee up enough to damage him, but he sensed or felt what I was trying to do and bit down on my bottom lip, hard.

I screamed and jerked back hitting my head on the mirror. A fissure began to creep down the mirror from the circular indention left by my head. It stopped at the mirror's edge. The coppery, salty taste of blood filled my mouth. "You bit me. You jerk!"

My fingers came away, stained crimson. He grabbed my upper arms and slammed me against the mirror again. "You bitch. Who do you think you're talking to? Huh?" Slam. The back of my head throbbed. I screamed with rage and pushed him away.

"Get off me, Zander." My hands and body shook violently. I was scared, angry and hurt. And, alone in a dilapidated fun house with a psycho. I was a caged animal, backed into a corner.

He looked at me for a moment, jaw clenching, fists tightening, and then his demeanor completely changed. He laughed and smirked at me, throwing up his hands in defeat. "Fine. I can get laid by anyone in this village tonight. I don't need you until after the wedding. Maybe not even then."

"If you think I'd marry a maggot like you, something is seriously wrong with you."

"Maggot? I think we both know who the maggot is in this relationship." He motioned back and forth between the two of us, turned, and stalked out the door.

I sank to the floor, trying to make sense of what just happened. The back of my head throbbed. One thing was for certain, Zander was seriously disturbed.

Beams of light stretched out long, crossing the room, only impeded by the debris in the floor. Zander had forgotten the flashlight. Thank goodness. The beam bounced off a mirror and into the room, illuminating the creepiness of this playhouse, of this park that had filled my childhood with nightmares and fantasies of monsters and all things creepy.

My lip finally stopped bleeding, but I wasn't sure if I had blood on me now or not. The distortion of the mirror showed a bit just beneath the corner of my lower lip. Licking my fingertips, I swiped it away and tried to straighten my hair and clothing. Poufy and a bit swollen, my bottom lip was split on the right side, but thank goodness wasn't too bad. Forcing some deep breaths to calm down my beating heart, I grabbed the flashlight and headed back toward the bonfire. I just wanted to grab Laney and go home.

Yellow-orange haze up ahead beckoned me on. Someone grabbed hold of my elbow, and a hand covered my mouth, stifling the scream I had been about to release. "Shh." My heart was trying to thump its way out of my chest. "It's me. Calm down. I saw Zander take you this way and was looking for you." I would recognize that voice anywhere.

Crew's breathing nearly matched my own. "If I let go, will you please calm down and refrain from screaming?"

I nodded, my breaths evening out. His hand uncurled, releasing my mouth and then my arm. "You scared me!" I accused in a whisper yell.

"Are you okay? I saw you guys take off and then Zander came back looking pretty angry and was slamming back the liquor. I just wanted to make sure you were alright."

I snorted. "As alright as I ever am with him. I don't see why you care anyway. I'm just a servant, right?"

He stared at me for a long moment. Most of his face, and I'm now sure most of mine was bathed in shadow.

Probably a good thing given the current state of my lip. He grabbed hold of my hand, leading me back toward the bonfire. After a few paces, he slowed and looked down at our joined hands. Mine trembled horribly and he'd noticed. His dark brows drew together. "That's not just from me sneaking up on you, is it?"

I licked the split in my lip and shook my head. A curse tore from his lips and he dropped my hand and squeezed the bridge of his nose. "I'm sorry."

"You have nothing to apologize for, Crew. I appreciate your concern. Thank you for coming to get me. I just wish you'd showed up a few minutes earlier, although, I'm not sure what good it would have done. It's not like you're going to go against Zander Preston. He's your friend. Not only that, but his family is very powerful in Orchard."

He grabbed my hand again, rubbing slow circles on the back of it with his soft thumbs. His skin, though sunburned was still so pale in the light of the three-quarter full moon drifted down upon us. It was almost otherworldly. A pained expression crosses his ethereal face and he looked over at me. "I was going to take you back, but..." He blew out a harsh breath. "Come and talk with me?"

I nodded. "Okay."

He led me away from the fire, back past the not-so-fun house and all of the rotting games, toward the lake. We walked out onto a solitary small wooden dock and sat just a few feet down from the algae-swirled swan sentinel. "It's kind of creepy here."

I grinned. It was. But, it was fun, too. "I need to apologize to you, Abigail."

"For what?"

"For two things, really. The first apology is for how I behaved the other day on the trail with Zander. By allowing him to put you down, I contributed to your embarrassment and shame. For that I apologize."

I nodded. "Forgiven."

"Just like that?" His honey eyes almost glowed amber in the blackness that surrounded us.

"Yep."

Silence fell over of us. Even the crickets hushed their song. "Besides," I continued. "You didn't say those things."

"I didn't refute them."

"True. Why did you go along with it?"

Crew took a deep breath. "You know we are guests at his house, my father, mother, and I?"

"Yeah. So, you didn't want to rock the boat with your roomy?"

He laughed, deep and rich.

"No. I wanted to know what his problem is with you. One minute he acts as though you walk on water. The next as if you are nothing. I just wanted to see what his deal was. I needed him to trust me."

"You're playing him?"

He grinned wide, revealing sparkling white teeth. "You could say that."

My brows lifted. Impressive. "Well, have you learned anything on your reconnaissance mission?"

His smirk dropped into a frown. "Yes." He cleared his throat. "I think that Zander Preston has a superiority complex. It's a shield. His father berates him endlessly."

"I had no idea. They try to project the image of the perfect family. Although," I folded my legs underneath me, "I can definitely see where Councilman Preston can be intimidating."

"He can be."

"So, I understand why he treats me poorly, but why does he keep saying things about marrying me. Is it all some sort of joke? Is he just trying to point out that I'm beneath him?"

He snorted and then nudged my shoulder with his. "He definitely wants you beneath him."

"Ha. Ha."

"No. In all honesty. He does want to marry you. In fact, his father and mother are making arrangements for the same. There is an enormous, atrocious dress in the guest bedroom for you. I'm sure it cost a small fortune to have had made, but the Preston's are all about appearances."

"Can they really do this? Force me into this?"

He released a long breath. "I'd like to tell you no, but with your aunt gone, I'm not sure. The Council holds such power in this village. It is possible, it seems."

"In this village? Doesn't the Council in Cotton hold as much influence over its residents?"

He shifted uncomfortably. "Of course. I just mean... yes. They do. But, Preston has more influence than others. His reach even extends to the some of the lower leadership in Olympus."

"Olympus?" What? The Preston's are friendly with the Greaters in Olympus?

He nodded, looking out over the water. "From what I've gathered, yes," his words barely a whisper.

"How do I get out of this mess?"

He grabbed my hand in his. "Don't worry. We'll come up with something."

"We will?"

He nodded and moved closer, ticking his head for me to follow suit. I inched closer. His warm breath brushed softly over my ear as he moved my hair back from my face. "Don't worry about Zander. And don't worry about my allegiances from now on either. I will support you in all things from this point forward."

"Thanks. You know, Cotton is really different. You speak so formally, so proper."

A breath escaped me just before his mouth crashed onto mine. His lips were full and soft. They moved over mine softly, slowly. Soon it wasn't enough. My hands wound into his dark, soft hair. He smelled like some sort of exotic spice.

His hands found my waist and reeled me in. I was basically sitting in his lap, my legs stretching off to his side. The kiss grew more urgent, hungry. When his fingertips grazed the skin just below the hem of my shirt, I gasped. It felt as if fire had been rubbed along my skin. A blaze left in the wake of his touch. My surprise allowed him to sweep his tongue along my broken bottom lip and into my mouth. We kissed like this for what seemed like hours. When people started filtering home from the fire, crossing our path, we parted, both out of breath and panting for the sacred oxygen our lungs required.

He pulled me to my feet and brushed another soft, chaste kiss over my lips, holding me tight to him, the slight stubble from his chin raking across my forehead. I could hear the thundering of his heart, which I was sure matched the beating of my own.

"Hey, you said you owed me two apologies. What was the second apology for?"

"For scaring you at the lake. I didn't mean to frighten you or cause you discomfort."

"It was a little uncomfortable. But, you were right. I had no claim on the lake. Everyone has to get clean." I cringed a bit before I said, "Besides, I think I'm the one who owes you the apology for that night. Sorry for taking your clothes."

He laughed. "The brisk air definitely made me do a little soul-searching. It's fun here in Orchard."

I gasped. "What? You think it's fun here? You must have a really distorted image of what fun is, Crew."

He smiled lightly. "Yes. Perhaps, I do."

We walked hand in hand back toward the pathway and it wasn't long before Laney comes stumbling along with a group of people. One of those people was Zander Preston. He glared at the pair of us, at our hands that were still intertwined and molded together. Seething doesn't even begin to describe it.

Laney was drunk. Obviously drunk. She stumbled crookedly over to me and hooked her arm around mine, needing the support. I glanced back and smiled at Crew before guiding Laney in the direction of our cabin. He smiled back, until Zander walked over and shouldered into him from behind. "Time to go home, buddy," he spat. I could see the anger ripple through Crew as he stalked off, trailing a few steps behind one very fuming Zander Preston.

REAP

Chapter 9

SUNDAY MORNING, I ROLLED OUT of bed before dawn. Laney's soft snoring echoed from Lulu's room. My heart clenched. I missed her. On a normal day, she would already be up and buzzing about the kitchen, vying for some early morning coffee. The smell of the rich ground beans would fill the house as it brewed. She would greet me with a smile, a hug and a kiss on the cheek.

I wanted her back, needed her. I'd been so selfish. If I would have just agreed to accept Zander when he offered, or again when his father pressed Lulu for my hand, she would be here with me. Instead, she was in Olympus–indefinitely–and I was alone. Something I couldn't bear to be.

Marrying Zander would secure a prosperous future for us here in the village. His family was prestigious. No doubt, he was being groomed for the council, to follow in the footsteps of his father. I would be given everything I need, everything I could ever want. He would be able to provide a nice home and all of the necessities it requires. Maybe even some luxuries that others cannot even imagine, perks from being on the council.

I could learn to be a help to him instead of a hindrance. I could be a good wife. I had always been a hard worker. Cooking, cleaning, and basic chores came easy to me. I'd helped Lulu run the house since I was a child. She would give me chores appropriate to my age and maturity. Over time, they increased and I learned different things about properly running a household.

The only thing lacking in the relationship with Zander was any sort of love or affection. I definitely didn't love him, didn't even like him. Not at all. The thought of being with him physically, as man and wife, made me sick.

My fingers drifted over the now scabbed over slice dissecting my bottom lip on the right side. A sore reminder of how messed up our relationship would be, if this marriage was allowed to take place. I could put up with a great many things, but being belittled or beaten by someone who was supposed to love me, or at the very least respect and provide for me, was where I drew the line. I had to get Lulu back, though. I didn't know what was happening to her while so far away. A shiver crawled up my spine.

I returned to my room and tugged on a pair of jeans, long sleeved emerald green t-shirt and my trusty tennis-shoes. I needed fresh air and there was much to be done today. Lulu and I usually worked all day to get the household chores done. Now that she was gone, the work was mine alone. I grabbed our large wooden bucket and headed to the creek. Smoke rose lazily from Kyan's chimney. His mother, no doubt, was cooking breakfast and heating water. I would be doing the same shortly.

The creek water was cool and clear. I could see the mud and algae settled upon the bottom of the bed and the smooth, flattened rocks that sat beneath the surface. The water clouded for a moment, disturbed by my bucket's intrusion, before settling back into a comfortable position. Would I be the same way? I was disturbed right now. My life is in a state of upheaval with Lulu being sent away and the Preston's forcing me into marriage with their son. Abusive jerk that he is. Would I ever be able to settle and be comfortable again?

Laney stirred just as I finished building and lighting the logs and kindling in the fireplace, and hung the bucket of water on the hanger, flames licking its sides hungrily. She stumbled into the room, hair matted on one side and sticking straight up on the other, yawning and stretching her back. "My head is going to explode." She plopped down hard on a nearby chair, and rubbed circles into her temples.

"I'll make some coffee. You're gonna need it."

She just nodded, groaned and kept rubbing her temples.

"Apple wine is the devil." I just laughed. "Shh. Not too loud." She groaned and covered her head with the pillow.

Poor Laney. It was going to be a long Sunday for her. She still had to go home and would certainly have chores there waiting for her. A few cups of strong brew and she gathered her things and left for home, waving back at me as she crested the small hill along the pathway.

I waved back and went back to washing the clothes on the porch, sudsy water sloshing onto the wooden planks every so often. Rainbow swirled bubbles landed happily for a moment, before that happiness burst into nothingness. I thought, hard. I need Lulu. I'll do anything to get her back. Anything. Even marry Zander Preston. The image of Crew's moonlit face flashed through my mind.

∞

USUALLY KYAN VISITED ON SUNDAY, but he didn't yesterday. I hadn't seen him since Saturday night. Not since he had returned to the bonfire with Paige in tow. Perhaps he loved her, or would grow to in time. There was definitely something going on between them Saturday night. The tension was palpable, thick as bonfire smoke hanging in the cool valley air.

The days were growing darker. Night clung to the sky when I arrived at the orchard on Monday morning. It was hanging on tighter each morning, as the sun relinquished control to the moon.

I stepped through the white wooden gate and walked down the aisles of carefully planted trees until I came to the area that I stopped working Saturday morning. I wasn't sure how far the team got after I had to leave, but I could find them from here. It was eerily quiet. Laney usually beat me here. So did Kyan. But, I saw no one. I stepped into the next row and scared some crows into the air. They cawed in protest and flapped into the steely blue sky that was only now beginning to lighten, ever so slightly, slowly.

No one. I stepped into the next row, and the one beyond that, until finally, I saw Kyan arranging wooden crates. Pickers used the flexible bushel baskets. They were lightweight and easier to haul up into the trees when needed, but to ship the fruit to the cities without bruising it and ultimately damaging it.

The apples would be neatly packed into crates and loaded onto the trains. During harvest, the train left daily or every other day with our shipment. I assumed it also collected the goods and produce from other villages before traveling to the ultimate destination of Olympus or whatever Greater City requires our goods.

Those unable to labor in the orchards, the elderly or injured, were charged with packing. They packed the crates carefully. Our village had a job for everyone. It was Lulu's job to assign the tasks in the village, to ensure everything ran properly.

The entire village worked at harvest time. It was how we were able to produce such a crop of apples. Rows of trees stretched as far as the eye could see from any position in the village. Move to the outer edge of your vision and stand there. The fields stretched further. An endless ocean of fields, rows and succulent fruit.

In the off-season, there were greenhouses to tend. Winter vegetables for village consumption, soil to fertilize for the next planting season, seeds to sort, food to preserve and store, we were nothing if not hard workers. Those who weren't able to walk to the orchards, tended local gardens for village consumption.

We were forbidden to eat the fruit we grew in the Greater orchards, though we were allowed to have our own fruit trees on our properties. That's why Megan had broken the rule and would have been punished by Norris. That's why I made her run away.

In Orchard, there was always something for someone to do. Often, there was too much for even all of us working together, to accomplish. There were always pathways to clear, repairs to be made on dwellings and community buildings, animals to feed and care for. No idle hands here.

Cold and eerily quiet, the morning stretched out across the heavens. For a moment it felt like I was the only person on earth. That moment, however, was fleeting. Soon, people began drifting in, ready to start their day. We'd made significant progress with all of the help and for the first time, I could actually imagine us meeting the harvest deadline of a Friday finish.

Kyan walked toward me with Laney at his side. A few girls from Wheat tagged along behind them. That was one thing I had taken notice of since the bonfire, since working in the orchards again, even if only for a short time each day. Most of the help, with the exception of Crew and a few others were female. Could the males not be spared?

Kyan's hair was shorter, golden brown shone in the early morning sun that peeked over the hills to the east. His brown eyes locked on mine. Laney made eye contact with me and then jerked her eyes toward Kyan. I knew this silent warning. Kyan was in a bad mood. I nodded very slightly.

She passed me and traveled about 20 trees down the row and readied her ladder. The other three girls fanned out around her readying bushel baskets and rolling up their sleeves. One pulled her long golden hair back, securing it with a long ribbon.

Kyan stepped up to me, his face like steel. "Abigail."

What? I ticked my head back. "Abigail?"

"That is your name," he scoffed.

"You never use my formal name." I narrowed my eyes. *What was his problem?*

His jaw clenched. "Things change."

"What changed, Ky? Paige finally lay down the law about our friendship?" Goading him was wrong, but I couldn't stand it when Kyan acted this way. It was rare, but bothersome.

"This has nothing to do with Paige and you know it." I crossed my arms. "Actually, I have no idea what your problem is. So, either enlighten me or back off."

"I saw you with him." A chill ran up my spine. He saw Zander.

"Zander?" He looked taken aback. His eyes harden along with his jaw.

"No. Crew." *Oh. Oh, no.* He saw me with Crew. He must have seen us kissing. Crap.

"I'm not apologizing. I wanted to kiss him. He wanted to kiss me and so we did. It's not like you and Paige didn't have some special alone time."

"I don't like him. Something's off. I don't know what it is, but you should stay away from him. And, you certainly shouldn't be kissing him. He's leaving soon. You'll get hurt."

A bitter laugh left my throat. "I know he's leaving. I know I shouldn't have kissed him, but it happened. I can't take it back. Not that I regret it. It was amazing. But, it's not going to matter after the festival."

"He's got to leave sometime. I'm sure there's plenty of work waiting for him and the others back in Cotton." "It's not that. Zander is pretty much forcing me to marry him. I want Lulu back, so..."

"You cannot be serious." He nudged my chin up so that my eyes followed. "You can't be serious. You can't marry him. He's such a bastard. He'll make you miserable. And not just for a little while; he will make you miserable for the rest of your life."

I nodded. He had spoken the truth. But I had to do something. From the corner of my eye, I saw movement. Crew was standing a few trees away, Paige by his side. If looks could kill, her caramel eyes would have burned a hole through my heart and I'd be lying in a heap on the ground.

"Isn't this cozy?" she screeched. "Kyan, I need a word with you." Her hands were folded over her chest and her plump lips were pinched tightly together. "Now!"

He rolled his eyes and escorted her away to a private spot. Not that their conversation was kept private. Her whiny screeches could be heard by anyone within a two mile radius. I looked at Crew and then decided it best to leave it alone. We kissed. I liked it. He liked it. But, it had to end here. So, I turned away and joined the girls in the trees. I could feel his eyes burning into my back as I began to work.

Two hours flew by, and in that time the earth around us warmed. The dew evaporated away, the leaves and grass once again became crunchy underfoot. Lifting my final bushel onto my shoulder, I walked to the ladies waiting at the orchard's exit.

Kyan's mother and Miss Evelyn, our village healer, sat together happily chatting while keeping a watchful eye on the laughing children who ran around gathering the rotten apples from beneath the trees. They raced one another, taking the brown, soft apples to a large barrel, dumping two or three in at a time, screaming and giggling in triumph. Girls with golden curls and dark haired boys made work play, and I prayed they enjoy it while it lasted.

∞

THE PRESTON'S HOUSE WAS EMPTY. I called out for Mrs. Preston and then Mister but was greeted with silence. No list awaited me on the counter, or on the long wooden table. The pounding of hooves echoed outside. Stepping onto the porch, I was met with the man who still haunted my nights.

Norris dismounted an enormous black stallion, which whinnied and grunted, rearing as Norris subdued him secured the beast to one of the porch railings. I wasn't sure that the porch would actually stand a chance against such an enormous animal. Norris pushed his greasy long hair back behind his ears and smiled at me. It was the most frightening of his smiles, the one that didn't reach his eyes. He stalked forward and I felt like an animal caught in a snare, thrashing around as it saw its fate in the eyes of its hunter.

"Why aren't you in the orchards?" His voice was rough, harsh as the scar dissecting the flesh on his cheek. The shiny raised slash lifted and puckered as he smirked at me. It wasn't the scar that scared me. It was him. I knew others with scars. Their kindness mitigated their injuries. Norris didn't know what kindness was.

"I'm supposed to work for the Preston's. I only work two hours in the orchards, then report here."

"Well, allow me to be the first to inform you of your schedule change. You're to report back to the orchards and then back here after you clean up this evening. Mr. and Mrs. Preston have invited you here for dinner this evening. A formal dinner."

"As a server, or—"

"No. You're apparently the guest of honor." He laughed harshly, revealing the yellow grit around his teeth.

"Okay. Thanks for the message." I quickly started toward the orchards once more. The last person I wanted to spend any time with was Norris Jones.

"Ah, ah, ah. I'm to deliver you. In fact, I'm to pay *extra* close attention to you for the rest of the week. Seems you're marrying Councilman Preston's son. Can't have you doing anything to embarrass your new fiancé or his family, can we?"

Anger tore through me. "So they sent you, huh? Gonna stripe my back? You better tell Mrs. Preston to get a high-backed gown to hide it. Though, the blood might seep through onto the pretty white fabric." In an instant, he was in front of me, his nose nearly touching mine. Rancid, hot breath fanned my face, but I stood my ground in a stupid attempt at false bravery. Inwardly, I trembled.

"Mr. Preston gave strict orders *not* to stripe you." He slid his leather riding crop across my jaw, up my cheek and rested it under my eye. "But don't worry. I can get *very* creative with my punishments. Some won't leave any marks upon the body at all."

"I'm sure Zander will object to your creativity. I'll have to tell him about your threat."

Laughing, he stepped back a few feet and I finally released the breath I'd been holding. "Who do you think suggested that I handle you *differently?*"

He nodded toward his horse. I was almost as afraid of it as I was of him. Norris mounted the midnight stallion and once it calmed down, reached down for my arm. I pulled myself up and sat in front of him, scooting as far away from him as was possible in the small saddle. Norris's arms withered around my stomach as he clenched the reins. He whipped the horse and we took off, a tall trail of dust in our wake.

The ride was fast. I was back with my team in no time. Kyan all but ran over me as Norris dismounted and then clenched my waist, harshly yanking me off of his devil horse. The horse was wild. It almost threw us twice on the short trip over. Even now, it whinnied and snorted like the maniac it was. I'd always liked horses until now.

"What's going on?" Kyan addressed Norris, not once looking at me.

"She's been cleared for full duty." The two eyed one another for a moment, tension thickening the now unseasonably warm air.

"Abigail, go work with Laney." He pointed down the row and I could see her signature blonde spirals beneath a tree. She was discreetly watching what was unfolding. But, I knew her, she'd heard every word. She never missed anything. For someone who spoke so loudly, she could be still as a statue when she wanted to be. I walked toward her and her eyes grew big.

She mouthed the word, "Norris," and her light chocolate eyes glistened as she jerks them to the spot where I'd left the two men standing. I quietly shushed her and we began to work. Norris walked to the end of the orchard nearest us and secured his horse to the split rail wooden fence, giving it a few apples to eat. Devil beast. I figured it ate babies.

While he was out of earshot and probably couldn't even see us too well, Kyan came over, crouching down beside me and Laney. "What the hell, Abs?"

"I know. It's the Preston's. They want me to marry Zander. They know that Crew and I kissed and now they've ordered Norris on me to 'keep an eye on me' until the festival." What began as a whisper had transformed to a yell.

"Shh. Calm down." Kyan scrubbed the back of his neck roughly. "This is not good, Abby."

"I know! He said I have to attend dinner at the Preston house this evening and that Councilman Preston and Zander have told him that he can't whip me, but that he can get creative in his punishments. He can punish me so long as my body isn't marked. What does that mean?" I was nearly in panic mode.

Kyan trained his dark brown eyes on mine. "I don't know. But he's one evil son of a—"

Laney interrupted. "Shh. Here he comes."

Throughout the rest of the day, Norris never let me out of his sight. When I went to relieve myself, I thought he might follow. Luckily, Kyan intercepted him and kept him busy for a few minutes. At lunch, he disappeared for a while and I was able to talk to Laney a bit. She was every bit as afraid of Norris as I was and as I was working with her, his very presence put her in danger.

But, being the awesome friend she was, she told me to come to her house after we finished in the orchard. She offered to help me get ready for this sure to be awful dinner. Mrs. Preston would die if I showed up in my normal jeans and plaid shirt. I had few clothes. Lulu had never been much of a seamstress and neither am I. Laney on the other hand, was amazingly talented. Give her a needle, scraps of fabric and she could fashion beautiful ensembles. Like spinning gold from straw like the little story Lulu used to tell me as a child.

With half an hour left in the day, the wind whipped our hair and thrashed our clothing. Thick gray clouds smothered the sunlight. The branches on the trees twisted and fought against the onslaught, scraping our exposed skin. Everyone rushed around to get the full bushels to the packers and from them onto the trucks and wagons. From there, the apples would be packed onto the train cars. Everyone had a job and rushed to finish before the storm hit. When their job was complete, they helped someone else complete theirs, until all was finished.

Soon thunder boomed in the distance. And, a few minutes later, lightning made its appearance. The warning whistles began filling the air. I heard the shrill pitch of Kyan's whistle slice through the howling wind.

Laney and I grabbed the last bushels we had and ran toward the end of the orchard. Her foot caught on an uplifted tree root in our path. Apples tumbled over the earth around her. As thunder crashed overhead, and rain began to sprinkle down upon us, she grabbed her right ankle and cried out in pain. Her face contorted in pain, a silent scream.

"Laney! Can you walk?" The wind whipped my hair around my face. The leaves were ripped from their branches and rained down around us.

"I think I sprained it. I don't know if I can walk." Tears formed in her eyes.

Crouching down, I tucked her arm around my neck, wrapped mine around her back under her arm and lifted her up. "Easy. We can do this. Let's just take it slow. I'll be your crutch." I tried to smile and make it look genuine, but even I was scared of the storm at this point.

She nodded and we started hopping down the row. The rest of our team was gone, gathered with Kyan as protocol dictated. If we didn't make it to him soon, he would come find us and help. He would come. Thunder crashed against the angry gray sky and lightning flashed brightly. It was closer. Right upon us.

"What about the apples?" she screamed above the wind.

"I'll come back for them. Don't worry." All apples must leave the fields before the laborers. A Greater Rule. We were expendable, their crop was not. Simple as that.

She nodded again. The row seemed longer with each step, the end of it getting further and further away. Then, we saw it and both squealed in happiness, as we clung tight to one another. Headlights of the old blue work truck shone down the aisle in front of us. We waved our free arms frantically. Kyan stopped six feet ahead of us and jumped out of the truck.

"What happened?" The rain pelted his face.

"Laney fell and hurt her ankle. Take her to Evelyn."

"I've got her," and with that statement, Ky scooped Laney up as if she weighed nothing at all and ran toward the truck, placing her in the passenger seat.

I turned back to get the bushels that she dropped and I had abandoned. If we didn't bring this bushel out of the orchard, we would all three be punished. Grasping frantically for apples that scattered away from the overturned baskets, my knees ground into the earth below.

A strange surge filled the air. The hair on arms and then the rest of my body stood on end. A low vibration hummed from the earth around me. I looked around frantically through whipping hair and tree limbs for the source of the strange feeling. Nothing. I couldn't see anything unusual. The sky barked loudly right above me and then quieted. Eerily.

A loud crack and a flash of light fell, connecting with the apple tree beside me. The smell of burnt wood filled my senses and I barely had time to cover my head with my arms and curl up before one of the large branches gave up the ghost and fell toward me. My arms and back were battered by the branches and leaves as it crashes down. A scream was torn from my chest. I wasn't not sure if the whole tree hit me or if it just felt that way.

A string of curses flew from a familiar voice and another as they counted in unison, "On three! One! Two! Three!" The weight of the large section of tree and its minions were lifted from my back. I looked up to see Kyan and Crew moving the once healthy tree half to the side. I uncurled and took note of my arms. Aside from blood pooling up from a few scratches, I was okay. Probably bruised, but I would take it. I could easily have been killed.

Kyan rushed to me, looking me over from head to toe. "Can you get up?"

I took his offered hand and pulled myself up. "We need to get out of here. Fast!" I nodded. The sky opened up. Rivulets of rain running into my eyes, down my face. Crew followed close behind us. The three of us crowd into the cab of the rusted out pickup with Laney. Kyan punched the gas to the floor board. Soon, we were out of the orchard, and in front of Evelyn's cabin. Crew helped Laney into the house as Kyan came around to the passenger side where I sat.

"I'm fine."

"Abs, she needs to look at you and make sure."

I shook my head. "I'm scraped up and will probably have a few bruises but I'm fine." He shook his head in protest before opening his mouth to do the same. But I stopped him, "This is nothing. I have to get home and get ready. I have to be at the Preston's for dinner. If I don't show up, you *will* have to carry me back here."

He muttered something and looked up at me with pleading eyes. "You know I'm right. Norris is all over me. All they need is one reason. One slip up...and I'm in deep trouble. Deeper than any lashing Norris can dish out. This goes far beyond him for some reason."

"Why does Zander even want you?" His anger flared but his words cut me.

"I don't know, Kyan. Why would anyone want me?" I crossed my arms in defense.

"That's not what I mean, Abs." He grabbed my elbow. "I mean, he could pretty much pick any girl in the village, and half of them swoon over him anyway. He could pick someone who wants him. You don't but he's still forcing you into this. I just don't get it and I...I hate it...for you."

"Part of me thinks he just wants me because I don't want him. Like it's part of some twisted game to him. But, I can't let him win Kyan. I won't. I just don't know what else to do. The Preston's are much more powerful than I had ever imagined. They sent Lulu away. What will they do to my friends, to the people I love, if I don't submit to their demands? Laney..." My voice broke. "Laney is scared to death. Norris has been watching us both all day. One slip up and it isn't just my back on the line anymore. Something is going on. I don't know what and I don't understand, but this is beyond just me and Zander." I shook my head and let out a pent up frustration laced breath.

Kyan looked at me, jaw clenching for a long moment and then finally said, "Let's get you home."

I checked on Laney quickly. Crew was seated at her side, waiting patiently as Evelyn taped her ankle. She whispered in my ear and I nodded, turning to leave.

"You'll help her get home?" I asked Crew.

"Of course."

In the cab of the truck, a couple of feet between me and Kyan, tension separated us once again. "Ky, can you stop by Laney's house for a minute. I need to pick something up."

Chapter 10

LOOKING IN THE SMALL MIRROR that sat atop Lulu's dresser, the now familiar pang of regret crept into my heart and mind. I should've just agreed to this marriage to begin with. It was always going to happen, regardless of protest. Zander would get his way. Now Lulu was in Olympus. I didn't know what was happening to her there. What I did know was that my heart hurt without her.

She would've helped me get ready for this night. I bathed, careful to clean the fresh abrasions. My hair had been washed with the lavender soap we kept hidden away for special occasions. It had been brushed, braided and coiled tightly at the nape of my neck. Pins held it into place. The dress Laney told me to get out of her bureau hung delicately across my curves.

I'd never felt more like a woman than right then. The dress was exquisite. Its capped sleeves delicately skimmed my shoulders, while the beaded square neckline emphasized the swells of my breasts tastefully, revealing neither too much nor too little. The bottom layer was emerald colored silk, while the top layer was gauzy and swished over the top delicately as I walked.

It was the single most beautiful garment I'd ever seen and I was scared to death to wear it. What if I ruined it? Split a seam or accidently spilled something on it. Laney would kill me and I would be mortified, would die of embarrassment in front of everyone. What if it was too fancy for this particular dinner? Was I overdressed? Underdressed? I couldn't imagine being underdressed for anything in such a divine piece.

I tilted the mirror up and down, moving back and forth in front of it. Nothing seemed bunched or pulled. Hair looked good and I pinched my cheeks for some color. Before I left her at Evelyn's, Laney had insisted that I take her lipstick. I wasn't even sure where or how she got all of this stuff. Makeup and fine fabric weren't things you often saw in the village

The black flat dress shoes that Laney let me borrow squished my toes, but I took a deep breath and started walking slowly toward the Preston's. The storm had blown over and the dark clouds had given way to sporadic billows that punctuated a sky that faded from gray blue to gold across the horizon.

Walking toward the sunset, I silently hoped that all would go well with dinner. I felt as though I was walking into a den of hungry wolves, fangs bared, frothing at the mouth, gnashing and snarling menacingly. The image of Mrs. Preston's toothy, straight, white smile popped into my head.

As I crested the last knoll before the Preston estate, the sound of music stopped me in my tracks. Beautiful classical music poured from its direction and I followed it like a sailor to a siren, blissfully ignorant to its danger.

Before I could knock on the door and was greeted by a smiling Zander Preston, who offered his elbow and ushered me inside. He grinned and leaned down to my ear. "You look ravishing. Perhaps I will get to do some of that later." He winked and I had to stop myself from vomiting a refusal. I was in the den and must survive.

Scattered among the couches were Mr. and Mrs. Preston, Mr. Harrison Cole-Crew's father, Crew, and a stunningly beautiful woman, seated between the two. Everyone stood. Mr. Preston's suit was dark gray, as was Zander's. They had probably been made from the same fabric. Cut from the same cloth. Most people in the village had matching things. We could not waste what we were given by the Greater cities.

Introductions were made again, though I had met everyone but Mrs. Cole. She was dressed in a deep red gown, cut into a 'v' at the neckline. It was tight and silky, and clung to her like a second skin. I'd never seen anyone wear anything so revealing and yet be covered from neck to toe. I shook their hands and smiled when appropriate. *Survive.*

"Abigail. It's a pleasure to see you again." Mr. Cole extended his hand and I took it as well. "You know my son, Crew." I nodded and accepted his formal handshake as well. "This beautiful creature is my lovely wife, Alyce. Her dark brown hair loosely curled down her back, a small piece pinned back on one side with an ornate piece of hair jewelry.

Her face was covered in makeup which made her face look flawless and beautiful. Full lips were painted the color of a blood red rose to match her gown, which I noticed up close was covered in small glass beads and stretched to the ground, where a small train pooled behind her feet. Her eyes were mostly brown, but there is a honey colored circle surrounding the pupil, the honey pooled and spilled out further into the brown on the outsides, reminding me of a spotted butterfly. How did this family get such unique eyes? And from both parents?

"Abigail." Her eyes lit up excitedly. "I've heard so much about you. It's wonderful to meet you, my dear." She clasped my hand inside of both of hers. I swallowed. *Who had been talking about me?*

"Thank you."

An awkward moment of silence hung in the air until Marjorie, a village cook, popped her head into the room and announced dinner. I couldn't miss how her eyes widened as she took me in and then shifted between me and Zander.

Mr. and Mrs. Preston led the way into the dining room. This was the only house in the village that boasted a separate room housing only a long wooden table and chairs. Zander ushered me inside, his hand upon the small of my back. Crew followed directly behind us. His parents and the Preston's claimed seats around the table. Crew's suit was made of different material than his father's. Small gray stripes streaked along the fabric of his, while his father's was solid in color. The Cole's had the finest clothes I'd ever seen.

On the table, bowls and platters of steaming food surrounded an enormous turkey, its skin golden-brown. The aroma from the bounty on this table alone, made me salivate with anticipation. I'd never in my life eaten a meal so grand. This much food would feed a dozen families if divided right.

Mr. Preston settled into the chair at the table's head, with Mrs. Preston to his left. Crew settled in the seat to her left. Mr. Cole sat opposite of Councilman Preston. I sat to his left, and to my left was Zander. Crew, seated directly across the table stared unabashedly at me. Averting my eyes, I tried to get him to look away, but felt the warmth from his gaze on my anyway. He couldn't do this. I'd pay dearly and given that they already took Lulu away, was scared of what they might do next.

Kicking his shin, I looked at him in warning and he finally relented. No one seemed to have noticed. Not even Zander. Marjorie filled our plates, which was strange. I'd always served myself, never been served by another. She rushed around filling glasses with apple wine and water.

Darkness crept in through the window. The candles glowed as warm as the food in my stomach. Crew didn't stare at me anymore during dinner. The time and meal were passed in awkward silence. Awkward for me, anyway. Lulu and I, along with Kyan if he joined us, would always laugh and discuss our day during dinner. It was eerily quiet, save for the clinking of silverware upon porcelain and glass bottoms upon the wooden table.

When all silverware was abandoned, all plates and glasses empty, Marjorie cleared the table in front of us. All of our plates, the serving bowls, even the turkey was whisked away into the kitchen. Like a whirlwind, she sat small plates and new forks in front of us and once we were all settled, brought out a beautifully decorated square cake with two layers, the bottom one larger than the top. Small flowers sculpted expertly from icing draped formally across the layers of cake. It was exquisite.

She carefully cut and served a piece of cake to each person. Mr. Preston cleared his throat and raised his glass. The Cole's and Mrs. Preston and Zander follow suit and so I raised my glass of sweet apple wine as well. "Thank you for attending dinner with us this evening. I do hope you have enjoyed the bounty that Orchard Village provides. This cake was made in celebration of a momentous occasion in the life of our only son. He has certainly made us proud to be his parents and even more so by picking such a lovely young lady to join with him in marriage."

I swallowed hard. *Oh, crap.* Crew's eyes met mine and I quickly looked away. Zander glanced over at me, smirking. "I cannot imagine a better match for our son. And, so with this dinner and beautiful dessert creation, we welcome you to the Preston family, Abigail Kelley." He took a deep sip from his glass and everyone followed suit. Crew trained his eyes on mine just as he took a small sip. I gulped the rest of my half-full glass down. I felt nearly as empty as that glass as I swallowed it down, trying to accept my fate.

I'd never been more eager to return home in my life. Being treated like royalty wasn't something I wanted, or something I enjoyed, apparently. So, when the Councilman suggested that the 'young people' retire for the evening to rest up for a hard day's work ahead, I was quick to find the door. I accepted hugs and offered goodbyes to everyone mechanically and stepped onto the porch.

Zander stepped across the porch to meet me. Everyone's eyes were on us. "Until tomorrow, my love." He leaned before I could even protest, and kissed me full on the lips. I wanted to cringe. I wanted to smack him, to hear the satisfying sound of my hand making contact with his deceitful face, but I valued my skin and the skin of those I love and so I allowed it. Bile rose in my throat. I disgusted myself.

I broke contact first and looked over. Mr. and Mrs. Preston smiled menacingly. Mr. Cole stood back in quiet appraisal, while Mrs. Cole looked as if she'd just seen a puppy lick the cheek of a child. Crew looked off into the woods. I stepped off the porch and onto the pathway and started walking home, thinking what a big mess this situation, my life, was at the moment. Tears burned my eyes.

Someone grabbed my elbow. I turned around to find Crew looking down at me. "Here. Wear my jacket home. You can bring it back to me tomorrow." Without another look, he helped me shrug his dark suit jacket on, turned and walked quickly back to the porch. "Thanks," I muttered. Not that it mattered.

I walked into the darkness down the trail that led into the woods, through the fields of hay. The smell of wild onions surrounded me, but even they couldn't drown out the masculine, crisp smell that was Crew, emanating from the warm jacket wrapped around me. In the woods, the chirps of crickets and scurried steps of small animals could be heard. Shivering, I tucked my hands into the pockets of Crew's jacket. *What is that?* I eased the object out just enough so that I could see what it was. It was a piece of paper, folded up into a tight square. When I got home, I locked the door behind me, lit the candles and examined the paper with the firelight. It was a note from Crew.

MEET ME AT THE SWANS AT MIDNIGHT.
—YOURS, CREW

Chapter 11

BEFORE I COULD EVEN START a fire, footsteps fell heavy on the porch. The front door ricocheted off the wooden wall behind it and Kyan stepped in, his face cloaked in shadows. In four strides, he stood in front of me. "Are you okay? Did they hurt you?" His eyes raked over my face and then over my body. He stiffened and stepped back, still clasping my shoulders. "Wow. You look amazing."

"Don't sound so shocked, Kyan. It's a blow to my ego."

"No. It's not that. I've never seen a dress like this before and you...-wear it well." Suddenly, I was once again aware of the way the dress accentuated my chest and if his gaze was any indication, he was aware now, too.

I cleared my throat. "Eyes up here, big guy," I teased.

He grinned and makes eye contact again. I debated whether to tell him about Crew and decide against it. He wasn't very happy after seeing the two of us at the dock the last time. "I wanted to make sure you were okay. I was scared for you." Ky's eyes darted around nervously, which was unusual, for him. *Is he nervous?*

"I'm fine. Actually, it was really weird. They were very nice and oh my goodness, Ky. You should have seen the amount of food they served. It was obscene. It would have fed a dozen families. There was a turkey, green beans, corn on the cob, potatoes, yeast rolls, ham. Then, for dessert, there was an enormous two-layer cake with icing roses! It was so pretty..."

"What?"

"The cake. Councilman Preston said the cake and dinner were held to welcome me into their family."

My breaths became shallow and I couldn't catch hold of the air I needed. I needed a distraction. I threw another log into the fireplace and stuffed some kindling beneath. My hands shook so badly that I couldn't strike the flint. Couldn't make a spark.

Ky crouched down next to me and took the knife and flint stone from my hand. In a couple of strikes, he has sparked the kindling cupped in his hands, coaxing a flame with gentle breath. He tucked the small bundle under the split wood awaiting its warmth. The flame grew ravenous and licked and lapped at the firewood above, seeking more of something, anything.

Ky pressed his lips together in a sort of smile and helped me up. I glanced at the small clock on the mantle. Ten o'clock. Dinner took the entire evening. And, now I had only a couple of hours before I needed to meet Crew. The angel on my shoulder was begging me to stay home, to avoid Norris at all costs. But, the little devil that sat opposite her won, whispering that this may be my last opportunity to talk to Crew alone before he leaves and I marry. There was no telling when they would load up the trains with our help and cart them back home. I may never again feel the softness of his lips upon mine, or his hands around my waist. And, I needed this. I needed him, even if only for one night.

His eyes darted around again, as if searching for something to grab hold of. "You know I'll always take care of you, right?" Kyan cleared his throat. "I need to tell you something."

"Ky, don't. It's okay. Whatever it is."

The look in his eyes made me weary and I stepped back from him. The soft orange light highlighted his hair softly and caressed his face, softening the hard angles that had formed recently, erasing any trace of boy from his visage.

He growled in frustration, swallowed and scrubbed the back of his neck. "I don't know how to tell you this." He looked at me, blinking away tears.

Kyan did not cry. Ever. I'd been his best friend for years and have never seen it. Even when he fell from a tree when he was eight and broke his forearm. "Ky? What is it?"

"I..." His voice broke.

"Kyan. You're scaring me. Please just say it. Whatever it is, spit it out."

He blinked and twin tears carved paths down the skin of his cheeks. And, then it hit me. It wasn't him. It wasn't about him or his family. He was crying for me. Dread coiled like a snake in the pit of my stomach. The only thing that would upset him this much and mattered to me was...

I croaked, "Lulu?"

He nodded and pulled me tightly into a hug. *No.*

"No!" I pushed him away, but he hauled me back to him.

"I'm so sorry, Abby." Tears filled his words, thickening with grief. He loved her, too.

"NO!!!" I roared. "She's fine. She's in Olympus! That's what the Preston's said! She's there!"

He shook his head. "Yes, she is! She is, Kyan!" I pushed him backwards. How dare he lie to me like this?!

He shook his head again. "They found her today. They had to bury her right away because...-because her body was decomposed so badly. But, it was her, Abby. I was there. I helped them take care of her. I put her into the grave, Abs. It was Lulu. I promise." He hugged me tight. "It was her. I promise."

Numbness. Tears streaked down my face. I couldn't move. "They killed her."

"Shh." He pulled me in and his warm breath tickled my ear. "Don't say it. If they did this to *her*..."

"Okay." I got it. If they murdered Lulu, they wouldn't hesitate to get rid of me as well.

"The Preston's don't know we found her. But, they will soon. Probably tonight. Norris was there."

Red flashed before me. "Norris? He probably killed her! You didn't let him touch her did you, Ky? He didn't touch her, did he? Please tell me he didn't...touch...her." Sobs erupted from my soul.

"No, shh. He didn't touch her. I wouldn't let him touch her. He was just called there because it's his job to report village deaths. You know that. Shh." Kyan's strong arms led me to the couch and settled me down. He rocked me as I cried. I knew something was wrong. From the moment they had told me that Lulu had been sent to Olympus, I knew. She would have found a way to contact me, before she left or as soon as she was safe in the City of Greaters. Lulu was smart and resourceful. She would have found a way or made one herself. I knew it. On some level, my very soul recognized that hers was gone.

Kyan rocked me for what seemed like an eternity, but the last place I wanted to be was out of the comfort of his arms. But, finally, he pulled away and went into the darkness of my bedroom. I could hear him shuffling around in my dresser. He pulled me into the room, lighting the candles along the walls. He'd laid out clothes for me to change into. I nodded and he stepped out. I carefully slipped out of Laney's dress and hung it in my closet, separate from all of my other clothes–the ones that will never be good enough to hang in its vicinity.

Automatically I dressed myself, removed the pins from my hair, and then loosened the braids, leaving a trail of flowing mahogany down my back. Kyan was pouring hot water that had been heating over the fire into a mug. The steam stretched long into the air above it before disappearing. My eyes were swollen and stung with each new tear that leaked out.

"To help you rest." Kyan extended the mug to me. The water was a warm yellow color and I knew it was from Evelyn. And, no doubt, it would help me rest. Testing the water with my upper lip, it was cool enough to sip. The bitter liquid slipped silkily down my throat. Before long, my eyelids began to slip shut on their own.

Kyan guided me to my room and helped me into bed before stretching the covers over me. I cuddled into them and sighed. The tears had finally stopped. But, the gaping hole in my chest still screamed out in pain. One thing was for certain, I would *not* marry Zander Preston. He could go to hell.

He didn't have anything to hold over my head anymore. Lulu was dead. Buried in a proper grave now. I didn't care if he killed me himself or had Norris do it for him. I wouldn't let them get away with Lulu's murder. I fell asleep thinking of Crew, how I wished things could be different. How I wish we had the freedom to choose our future.

∞

I WOKE LONG BEFORE MORNING and stepped out into the main room of the house. The fire still raged against the wood it furiously consumed. A white piece of paper sat atop the mantle.

I HAD TO LEAVE TO GET READY FOR WORK. PLEASE STAY HOME AND REST TODAY, ABBY. I'LL CHECK ON YOU WHEN THE DAY IS FINISHED.
—KY

He must have added wood to the fire before leaving. Its warmth didn't quite reach where I needed it to. I put the kettle over the flames to heat more water. A small white packet sat atop the wooden counter next to the mug

I used last night. It must contain Evelyn's sleeping mixture.

I refused to take more of it. I would not sleep the day away. Even the strong herbs couldn't ease the ache in my chest. I was going to the orchards. There was no way I would let the Preston's win this. They would not get away with it. I didn't care how powerful they were or might become. And Norris. If he did kill Lulu, he would live to regret it. I'd personally make sure of it.

I washed my face and plaited my hair carefully so that it curved around my head and draped over my shoulder. Donning a long sleeve black t-shirt and black and white plaid button-down over top, I shrugged on my jeans, tugged on my work boots, and chugged a hot cup of coffee before pouring the water over the fire. Steam angrily tried to escape up the chimney. I snuffed out the candles and strode toward the orchards.

My eyes searched for any sign of that serpent Norris, but he was nowhere to be found. No doubt the Preston's thought I would cower in my cabin today. Sorry, folks. Hated to disappoint them, but they would not win this fight. Zander was missing as well. I scoured the area for him, but he was conveniently missing. *Guilty, much?*

Kyan grabbed hold of my elbow. "What are you doing here? You need to go home, Abs."

"I won't crawl home. That's for damn sure."

He released me and stepped back, blowing out a pent-up breath. "Fine. But, you need to keep hold of your tongue. Don't go making accusations yet, and..." He stepped closer and whispered, "Don't say anything against

Norris. He won't hesitate to put you in your place. I don't want you hurt because your heart is broken. Okay?"

His brown eyes searched mine for lies. "Fine. I'll try." It was all I could promise. With a stern brow, he nodded.

"Laney is packing because of her ankle. Can you climb?"

"Yep."

"Get to it." He motioned for me to get started on a tree to my left. "Crew!" he yelled.

Crew stepped into the row a minute later, looking back and forth between me and Kyan before fixing his eyes on our team leader. "You're with Abigail today."

As I climbed up into the tree, I heard Kyan tell Crew, "Watch out for her today. I'm trusting you."

Crew nodded and walked beneath the tree I was climbing up in earnest. He grabbed a bushel and as I began to hand down the few apples I'd picked, our eyes met. Betrayal rested in his honey colored eyes. "Why didn't you show?" he asked softly.

"You don't know?" I felt my brows pinching together.

He shook his head, his eyes never leaving mine.

"They found my aunt's body yesterday evening. She'd been murdered and dumped into a shallow grave."

"But the Councilman said..."

"Yes. He did. He lied."

Realization washed over his strong features. The sun highlighted his sable hair and made his skin seem as pale as porcelain in the morning light.

"I'm sorry, Abigail. I thought you just decided not to meet me. I see that there are many secrets in the Preston household."

It was my turn to nod, gritting my teeth until my jaw hurt. Because if I opened my mouth, I would start crying all over again. And, I wasn't confident that I'd ever be able to stop this time.

Crew and Kyan watched me closely all day. I had worked like a woman possessed. Our team had carved through twice as many trees today as we did yesterday, even with Laney's nimble climbing and picking. I was nowhere near as graceful. Stubborn determination fueled every motion, making me swift and sure, efficient. After we stopped to take lunch, the sound of hooves digging into dirt came closer and closer to our position in the row. Norris.

The demonic stallion reared and Norris whipped the beast's flanks hard with the crop he had so disgustingly slid down my cheek. "Where is she?" he barked at Kyan.

"What do you want with her?"

In a flash, Norris dismounted and stood menacingly over Kyan. But, Kyan stood tall, didn't waver even for a second. "Are you refusing to give me information, boy?"

"No. I simply ask what you want with her. We are making amazing progress today and I would hate to report to my superiors that you're interfering with the numbers we're producing today." Kyan shrugged nonchalantly, but his eyes were fierce. I could see it all from my perch in the treetop above.

Norris stepped into Ky's personal space. "I don't like threats."

"No. You love them. You love to threaten hundred pound auburn headed girls. Are you brave enough to threaten a man? Huh? You're a sadistic bastard and you need to take your ass and your horse out of my orchard. Now! Unless you want me to drive straight to the Council and request an emergency meeting."

Norris stepped back and grabbed the horn of his saddle. "This isn't over. No one threatens me."

"Out. Now." Kyan barked, pointing in the direction of the orchard's exit. Norris mounted quickly and kicked the black beast in the belly, causing him to rear up in Kyan's direction. With a sneer on Norris's face, the beast galloped angrily away, a trail of light brown dust rose in his wake.

When he was out of sight, the dust settled on the leaves and ground all around us, Crew reached his hand up to me and I made my way down and out of the tree. Sweat dotted his brow and lip and I realized that I was sweating, too. It was in the mid-sixties outside, but a threat from Norris can cause anyone to sweat.

Kyan hadn't moved from the spot of the showdown. Hands on his hips, he looked over at Crew now towing me along behind him. He finally spoke. "Thanks for keeping quiet, Abs. I know it was hard for you."

His arms fell to his sides as he released a pent up breath. I nodded. It had been hard to keep my mouth shut. I wanted to scream at him. To stick my finger in his vile face and tell him that I knew. I knew he murdered Lulu, stuck her in a shallow grave because he was too damned lazy or stupid to dig a proper one. He'd probably enjoyed it, too. He reveled in the misery that he inflicted on others, whether physical or mental. I wanted to spit right on his scarred face and unleash hell on him.

Ky, Crew, and I agreed that Norris wouldn't be back this afternoon, but Crew offered to sneak away with me out a back orchard entrance before the official quit time is called. Kyan agreed. I could tell he wanted to escort me, but he would have been missed. It would have called attention to the plan.

And so, we worked. Climb. Pluck. Drop. Crew plucked and pulled all he could reach, took my baskets and emptied them, and loaded the bushels. Then two gangly teenaged boys assigned to us today came by and carried the bushels to the packers so that they could proceed with the rest of the process.

Chapter 12

"YOU CAN'T GO BACK HOME. Kyan told me to take you somewhere else. But, I'll admit, I'm not sure where to take you that would be safe from Norris or the Preston's," he spat their names just as I would have.

"The swans. It'll buy some time and maybe after they find my cabin empty, they'll leave me alone. Maybe they won't even bother looking for me again." I shrugged, not believing the words that had just leaked out of my mouth.

Crew lifted a brow and pinched his full lips together on the side. I rolled my eyes. "I know. They don't give up easily and now that Lulu's been found, they're going to want to cover their tracks."

He stopped and grabbed my hand. "I'm afraid of what that means for you."

I nodded. "So am I." It was the truth. There was nothing else they could take from me, except my life. I wasn't afraid of death, only the way I would leave the earth. I didn't want Norris's violence to usher me out of it.

In no time, we were on the outskirts of the park. The long standing swan had finally capsized, having finally relinquished control to gravity and fate. For some reason, my heart clenched at the sight. The dirty plastic had always, on some level, given me hope. Hope to fight against what plagued me. To keep standing up. Now, I felt like even that swan had given up on me.

We sat at the end of the small wooden dock, careful to avoid splintering wood that spiked up and the planks whose nails were pulling up from their anchors. The last thing I wanted to talk about was the mess that had become my life, so I did what I do best—I created a diversion.

"So, tell me about Cotton. Is it very different there from Orchard Village?"

He glanced sideways at me quickly and shifted uncomfortably. The thought crossed my mind that maybe it was even worse. Maybe he would divert as well.

"Uh, what do you want to know?"

"Are there a lot of people in your village?"

He cleared his throat and his voice deepened once more. "Yes. There are a lot of people. I live in a large village." Crew's honey eyes met mine briefly before he looked back at the lapping water surrounding us. Soft peaks rose and fell all over the lake. It was the largest and closest to our village. In the summer, we would all swim here in the evenings when we weren't working and on our day of rest.

"Are the girls in your village friendly?" I blushed. I hoped he knew what I was asking.

"Yes. They're nice enough." Crap. He didn't get it.

"Is there one in particular that is especially nice to you?" I nudged his knee with mine and smiled.

"Ahh. No. There is no one." His cheeks reddened against his pale skin. He shifted again. "I know that you're not interested in Zander. What about Kyan? You two are close."

"He's my best friend. We've been friends since I came here as a child. He thinks he harbors some sort of feelings for me, but mostly he's like my protector. I see him as a big brother. Nothing more." I pulled my tennis shoes and socks off and dipped my toes in the now-very-cool water. I shivered as my body adjusted to the cold.

He nudged my shoulder. "I think he might feel differently."

I shrugged a response. It didn't matter. I didn't see him that way. *Time to change the subject.* "When is your harvest?"

"At the end of summer. In late August or early September depending on the crop."

"Is that why your hands are so soft and your skin so pale?"

"I suppose so. Look, why don't we talk about something else. I'm enjoying my time away from my village. So, I don't really want to discuss it further." His voice hardened. I'd never heard Crew speak so sternly.

I nodded. We sat in silence for a few awkward moments. "You said you came here as a child? Where were you before?"

"With my parents. They decided after having me that they couldn't raise me, or didn't want to, so they sent me to live with Lulu. She raised me." My voice clogged with tears again and I tried in vain to blink them away.

Warm arms encircled me and pulled me in. I relented, much like the swan, and sank into the momentary comfort that Crew so freely offered.

"How old are you, Abby?"

"Seventeen. How old are you?"

"Twenty."

I looked up at him, surprised. "Twenty? How have you avoided getting married? " I thought about the Preston's. "Most of us are married by eighteen. It's rare for someone to be single at twenty."

"In my village, people marry later. Most everyone is permitted to choose their spouses, but village leaders sometimes use their children's unions to increase their power and influence. My family is no different. Unfortunately."

"Being the son of a Councilman must be difficult."

He nodded. "At times. I wish I had more freedom. Instead, my entire day, even the clothes I wear are usually dictated by my father or mother. In the village, I rarely see them, though. Maybe once a month, but their servants see that I wear, eat, and go where they tell me."

"Servants?"

He nodded and glanced at me quickly. "Yes. We have servants."

"Wow. You must think we...that I am very poor. The Preston's have people who help them occasionally, much like the woman who cooked and served dinner the other night, but no one on staff permanently. No servants." Even the word felt strange on my tongue.

We all worked hard, but not for one another usually, unless there was a special circumstance–my back was one of them. That was the only reason I had become a servant for a short time. We worked for the good of the village, for its prosperity, or rather for the prosperity of the Greaters for which it provided.

"Have you ever met anyone from Olympus, or any other Greater city?"

His golden eyes flashed at me. "No. Have you?"

"No. My aunt, when she was alive, was in charge of Village Supply. She arranged the shipment of raw materials from the Greaters. Of course, they would get the goods from other villages and send it to us, but she worked with them. She had to go to Olympus a few times. I wonder what the cities are like, what a Greater looks like. I can't even imagine how they live compared to us."

Crew didn't answer, but removed his shoes and socks, rolled up the legs of his jeans. His legs were muscular, but pale and dusted with sable hair matching his head. "I'm sure the Greater cities differ from our Lesser villages. It seems that even those differ from one another as well."

"I guess so." I swished my toes around in the water, making little ripples that fanned out across the surface.

"You're seventeen?"

I nodded. "Yes."

"When is your birthday?"

"In the village, we celebrate birthdays in the winter, out of the growing season."

Crew chuckled. "Okay. But when is your actual birthday?"

"I don't understand." I searched his eyes and his mouth opened.

"Your birthday. Mine is April 4th. When is yours?"

I stared at him. I had no idea of the date of my actual birth. Cotton certainly had strange customs. We had no time or supplies to waste celebrating birthdays individually.

He cocked his head back. "You don't know? You don't know your date of birth?"

I shook my head. "No. We celebrate together as one each year. To celebrate individual birthdays would deplete supplies that are hard for us to obtain from the Greaters in the first place. Not to mention that we are too busy working for most of the year for us to take time to celebrate birthdays for each person. It just doesn't happen. Cotton is so different. How do you celebrate your birthday on April 4th?"

His eyes lit up and his lips rose in a slight smile. "Well, my parents invite friends and neighbors to our home. Usually there is cake and sometimes even musicians. Dancing lasts into the night. Wine and food flow freely..." He trailed off.

"Wow. I know that your father is a councilman, but how does he do it? We barely have enough flour to make it through the month, let alone bake an extra cake or...I've never seen live music before. I can't imagine it. Zander usually brings his machine for parties, so I've heard recorded music, but never live. I bet it's amazing. I would love to see your birthday celebration one day. Of course, that will never happen, but..."

"Maybe you will one day."

Right. "You think they will let me leave my duties here to travel to Cotton so that I can attend your party. Your father is powerful, but even he can't move mountains, Crew."

"Of course. You're right." Defeat hung heavy with his words.

"So, you don't see your parents much back home, but do you have friends? Who do you hang out with?"

"Hang out?" He laughed heartily. "I hang out with my brother, Cam. He's eighteen, but will turn nineteen next month! And, he's fun. Where I am quiet, he's boisterous and loud. Where my hair is dark, his is nearly golden. We are almost opposites, but that's why I love him."

"Why isn't he here with you? Was he needed in Cotton?"

"Yes. Um. He was needed there. He was also just recently married, so..."

"He didn't want to leave her."

"Yes. He would have missed her greatly. Their marriage is one of love. As the second born son, he has less of a responsibility to my father and his position, and so is afforded the luxury of marrying the woman he has loved since we were children."

"Wow. I'm sorry, Crew."

He turned to me. "Why are you sorry?"

"I'm sorry you don't get to have that. That you don't get to marry for love, or choose someone you want for your forever."

"My forever?" I wasn't sure if it was a question or a statement. So, I nodded. I meant it. I felt as though he was as helpless in this aspect of his life as I had felt being pushed into marrying Zander. Of course, that was before he and his horrible family killed my aunt. Now he was the last man on earth I would marry. One second with him would be like an eternity in hell and I would rather die and face the tortures of hell, than give my hand to Zander Preston.

∞

FOOTSTEPS CRUNCHED THROUGH LEAVES THAT now littered the path a short distance away and we looked over to see Ky crest the small ridge. The footfalls that seemed large and determined, I can now see are frantic. He ran to us and stopped at the end of the small pier. "Get your shoes on. They're about to tear the village apart to find you. Norris told the Council that you have been kidnapped and are missing. It's just a rouse to flush you out. You have to hide. I've got to figure out a way to get you out of here." Ky breathed frantically.

"I can't let them hurt the village because of me. I'll go back."

Kyan shook his head and Crew launched to his feet and threw his socks and shoes on. I did the same. The hole in the toe of my ragged tennis shoe mocked me. Crew had servants and I had holes in my shoes and wore plaid shirts and jeans all of the time. I remembered how confident his parents looked in their eveningwear at the dinner party. They must consider me a real joke. Not that I cared what his parents thought. But, Crew's opinion did matter. I liked him, a lot.

Crew's eyes locked with mine as I stood up and started forward. "I don't think you should go. Kyan is right. We should try to get you out of this village. Are there other villages nearby? Somewhere we could take her? Hide her?"

Kyan shook his head. He knew it as well as I did. "No. The Orchards are extensive and though there are two more orchards in this region, we have no way to travel that far. The old pickup trucks are nearly dead and someone would notice them or an animal missing. Not to mention that there is little fuel left. Those who keep the livestock pay close attention. We wouldn't be able to take a horse without someone noticing. There's no way to sneak her onto the railway either. She's stuck." Kyan cursed and crossed his hands behind his head, as if trying to squeeze another idea out.

"No. It's my decision. They may be powerful, but they can't hide Lulu's murder. The village won't stand for it. And, I need to address the council. I need to speak my peace."

"This isn't a good idea. What if Preston has the council convinced that you're in danger, or are one. His roots run deep." Kyan paced.

Crew's hand brushed under my own and he intertwined his fingers with mine. "I agree. I don't think this is best." I began to protest, but he put his free hand up. "But...if you feel that you must do this, I will stand beside you. I'm sure Kyan will as well."

The two exchanged a heated look before Ky relented. "Of course I will. *I'm* her best friend." Tension and fear fueled our pace all the way back to the village, and into the center square where I sought out the council.

Chapter 13

FAMILIES WERE GATHERED IN FRONT of the main hall. Fear and anger molded each face. Mothers clutched their children, who held tight to their legs and waists. Fathers remained stoic, jaws clenched. Their houses were being ransacked as we walked into town. No doubt mine lay in shambles. Eyes widened as the three of us passed by. Kyan's hand was at the small of my back. He didn't guide me, but with that simple gesture, told the entire village that he stood with me.

Crew's fingers were still clamped between my own. His palm was sweaty and I knew it wasn't because of the unseasonable warmth hanging in the evening air. I knew what this means to him. To so publicly defy the Preston family would no doubt bring shame on his family, too. A shame, I was sure his father wouldn't let him soon forget. His mother, I couldn't read as well. She seemed almost kind, but I took her as a woman who wouldn't cross her husband under any circumstance.

The gathered crowd parted like a body of water as we made our way toward the main hall. The Councilmen were gathered, in crisp suits, on the front porch of the seat of their power. Boredom hung on their countenances, until Councilman Preston's eyes honed in on me. Like a hawk to its prey. He stood suddenly, stepped off the porch and rushed to stand in front of me. "The suspect has been found. Thank you Kyan and Crew for bringing her in to face the charges against her." His voice boomed into the night. Charges?

"What charges?" The words left my mouth before I could even think about them.

"Murder, Concealment of a body, for starters." He smirked. "You are aware that we have discovered the body of Luella Kelley, rotten in a shallow grave."

"Of course I know you found her. But I didn't murder her, and I certainly didn't conceal her body or put her in a shallow grave. You did! You and your pet, Norris, killed her! You just weren't smart enough to dig her deep enough!"

My entire body trembled with rage and I pulled away from Crew and Kyan. "You killed her!" I launched myself toward him, intending to remove his head from his body by force. I was jerked backwards by two sets of strong arms before I could connect. I wildly thrashed against them, mad as hell at their interference. "You'll pay for what you've done."

"How dare you accuse me of such things? I am a Councilman. An upstanding member of this village. I should see you beaten and then hanged." His face reddened and contorted in rage as he spat the last word.

"I wish to have an immediate audience in front of the council." I demanded.

The other councilmen had formed sort of a semi-circle around Mr. Preston and were staring at me, mouths agape. No one had ever challenged one of their own. The four other men looked at one another and nodded. From behind him four words cut through the tension hanging in the air that evening. "We grant your request."

"What?" Preston turned to face them, stunned that they would entertain me at all. Of course, he would prefer that I hang and that he not have to stand and atone for his dark deeds. Lulu's murder was most likely the last horrible offense he'd had a hand in, but I don't know if it was even the worst. But, this would end here. Now.

The Councilmen fell away leading our party into the Main Hall and into the judgment room. Preston was livid. His entire being shook worse than mine, but he followed obediently. "As Councilman Preston is involved in such matters, he will not be consulted on any decisions made. As four of us remain, and it is an even number, we must ensure that no decision is nullified and so I ask that one Councilman remove himself from the decision making process as well."

Councilman Regar stood up and moved aside. "I shall step aside from this decision, leaving three to determine the outcome." His tall, thin body limped to the side of the room, where he found a chair, still intent to watch from beneath the bushy white eyebrows that match the hair remaining on his head. He clasped his hands over his thin stomach, leaned back against the wall in his seat and watched sharply.

"Very well. Please tell us why you have accused our peer of such a despicable crime, Abigail Kelley." Councilman Ward asked before leaning forward to await my answer. His dark brown hair was evenly peppered with gray and he was short and rounded in the middle, where his dark brown suit stretched and puckered.

"I was approached by Zander Preston. He asked for my hand in marriage and I refused. Councilman Preston then asked my aunt, Lulu, I mean, Luella Kelley if she would give her blessing on the union. She refused. After working one day shortly after these occurrences, I came home to find her missing. She never came home. Zander and the Councilman informed me that she had been sent to Olympus on official village business. He and his wife and son then tried to force me into the marriage agreement, as my aunt was not here to thwart their efforts. I feared the worse when I didn't hear from her in such a time, but it wasn't until..." My voice cracked. "It wasn't until Kyan told me they found her body, that I knew she was dead. I didn't kill her. I had no reason to do so. I loved her. But, the Councilman needed her out of the way. He needed her blessing for this marriage and knew he wasn't going to get it. So, in my opinion, he got rid of the only thing blocking him: my aunt."

I wiped the tears from my cheeks. "Be seated."

"Councilman Preston. What say you to this accusation?"

Mr. Preston raised to his full height. His blonde-gray hair shone like a crown upon his head, glistening in the candle-light which was now mixed with the last light of day. He cleared his throat. "I did ask her aunt for permission for the two young people to wed. I will not deny it. But, I had nothing to do with her disappearance, death, or dishonorable burial. Nor is there any proof to that effect. I vehemently deny these charges against me. I am sorry for the young lady's loss and for her grief, which seems to be overwhelming her and clouding her judgment, but I deny her accusation. I had no hand in this. It would seem that the young lady was the last to see the victim, Luella Kelley, alive."

The three men before us looked at one another. They nodded, already knowing what they were going to say. I thought it was customary that they convened in private before issuing their decision.

Councilman Ward stood. "We will continue to investigate the murder of Luella Kelley. But, with no evidence to support your accusation, beyond the fact that the Councilman asked your aunt for her blessing in joining you with his son, we cannot in good faith say that he *is* indeed guilty of her murder."

The air had been sucked out of my lungs. I couldn't breathe. I fell on the hard wooden chair behind me. "You can't be serious," I muttered.

Ward continued. "We will get to the bottom of this, dear. And whomever is responsible for Luella Kelley's death will be punished. Rest assured of that." I nodded. What else could I do?

∞

I NUMBLY WALKED FROM THE room, down the hall and onto the porch. Crew stood with his parents. His father looked at me with a sharp eye and his mother stared at the ground. Kyan's hand found the small of my back again and he led me through the crowd, which once again parted for us. Councilman Ward stepped onto the porch, flanked by the other members and announced to the crowd the decision rendered. Gasps, a few claps and murmurs sounded out behind us. We were already on the way home.

"Kyan!" *Oh, no. Anyone but her, right now.* "Kyan, wait! You can't go with her. Didn't you just hear the council? She's crazy! She accused a Councilman of murder!"

Paige rushed up to us and grabbed Kyan's elbow, tearing his hand from my back. He shrugged away from her and I saw a flash in his brown eyes. "Get off, Paige. Not now."

"But, you're embarrassing me!" She brushed her black hair off her shoulder and pushed her lips out into a pout. *How disgusting? Does she think she's cute?*

"I can't do this." His words were low and deep. He pinched the bridge of his nose.

"What?" she asked. "I couldn't hear you, baby."

"I'm not your baby. I cannot do this!" he roared.

She shook her head and I stepped back from them. They obviously needed to have this argument in private and I didn't want to cause them any trouble. I started to walk on toward my house. "Abigail Blue. You will wait."

He ordered. Kyan never used that tone of voice with me. I stopped dead in my tracks.

"Paige. I cannot do this. I can't marry you. I don't love you. I know you don't love me, either. I'll make the announcement tomorrow. I'm dissolving our betrothal." His eyes darkened as if to invite her challenge.

"Dissolving our...? Because of her!" she screeched and pointed at me. Her face contorted with rage and she actually bared her teeth.

"Not because of her. Because of you. I don't love you. I can't spend the rest of my life listening to your voice. I hate it!" He paced. *Word. It was a horrific voice to have to listen to. I couldn't imagine hearing it for the rest of my days.*

"Look. You need to find someone who loves you and wants to be with you. I'm not that guy. I'm sorry. I tried to be. I know our parents want this, but I don't and we'll both be miserable if we go through with this. This has nothing to do with Abby. But the fact that my best friend on this planet embarrasses you, tells me that I shouldn't be with you. She *will* always be a part of my life, regardless of who I choose to spend it with. My future wife, will have to accept our friendship. It's as simple as that." He stopped in front of her. "I'm sorry. I'll talk to your parents and mine and then announce it tomorrow. I'll take the blame. You won't be shamed for this."

Smack! Her open hand connected with his cheek. "The hell I won't. I hate you, Kyan Marx!" And with that, she turned and stomped away. We both watched her retreat but stood quiet and still for a few moments. Could this day possibly get any worse?

Chapter 14

LIFE PASSED IN A BLUR for the next several hours and days. Friday evening swooped in like a thief in the night, having stolen the time it seemed it would take to get here. All teams had converged in the center of the orchard, plucking the last of the succulent fruit from the boughs. The smell of sweet apples and crisp leaves floated gently on the cool breeze. Days were now shortening and darkness came quickly in the evenings now.

I pulled the last apple that I could see from a branch above me and settled back into my spot where a large limb meets its lifeline, the backbone, and strength of the tree itself. The fruit itself this year was huge. My hand wouldn't even fit around it. I remember in scant years when I could easily wrap all my fingers around it and touch my palm on the other side. Those years had been dry and I had been smaller then than now, so I could imagine just how difficult it had been.

Swirls of red, light and bright green streak down the side of the shiny orb, the stem attached still held tight to one leaf for dear life–its last attempt to cling to its mother.

I hadn't seen Zander or his horrible family since the day of the hearing before the Council. Nor had I seen Norris and both of those facts had made the rest of the week just barely tolerable for me. The council had ordered her body exhumed to further the investigation into her death. They had banned the Preston's or Norris from being present during the examination, and during the re-interment. After Lulu was examined, she was laid to rest properly. As was customary, I wasn't allowed to be present while she was interred.

I had a feeling that as Lulu was once again committed to the earth, the secrets surrounding her death had died and been buried as well. When I was given permission, I visited her grave and placed a small bouquet of the remaining wildflowers on top of the earthen mound that now blanketed her. She always loved wildflowers, especially the bright bluish-purple ones that grew tall, whose edges were jagged and uneven. She said those were the strongest and in a world full of weeds, one had to be strong to survive. To avoid being smothered, they had to have deep roots with which to draw up water from the ground.

Crew's hand fell upon my own pulling me back to reality, grounding me. I needed it. I needed him. I knew he was leaving soon. Tomorrow would be our harvest festival and then he would be sent home, his help no longer required by our village, by the Greaters that brought him here. I wasn't sure I would be able to stand seeing him go.

Eyes of molten honey bore into me. I wondered if he felt the same way. Not that it really mattered. The Greaters, in one way or another, dictated every move we made, everything we did in our lives, however short or long they might be.

He took the last apple, placed it gently into the top of the almost overflowing bushel and hoisted it up, walking it to the bed of the rusty pickup, filled to the brim with the last of our crop. Cheers, sighs, and laughs of relief filled the air as the tension that had filled our days recently floats away on the clouds that race gently across the evening sky. They were bright orange and yellow, illuminated by the sun against a dull blue-gray sky.

Kyan approached and gave me his hand. I leapt from my perch above. "Finally," he breathed.

I nodded. "It's been quite a harvest this year."

"I've never seen the crop produce so much or such big fruit in my life."

"I know. The apples are enormous."

He smiled slightly. "Hey, I've got to stay. All the leaders do. Why don't you go home with Laney or hang out with Crew and I'll catch up with you later." Laney was busy packing, her ankle still swollen and bruised. She was able to walk but not climb, so her job there was safer and would help her heal more quickly. She giggled with Mary, a girl from Coal, with hair that matched her region's namesake. It was so black that it looked nearly blue in places. She was a very tall girl, nearly as tall as Kyan, and very pretty. Her lips were pouty and pink. Mary was loud and fun and reminded me a lot of Laney, so the two had become fast friends.

"I'll be fine, Ky."

He nodded. He left to meet up with the team leaders, who clapped him on the back and shoulder, and laughed heartily alongside him. He looked light, happy. I hadn't seen him smile in too long. The past couple of weeks had been hard on everyone. But, that was what made Kyan so great. He never complained.

Crew returned. He'd been partnered with me for the remainder of the harvest. Kyan's doing, of course, but I was thankful to have met him and to have been able to spend time with him in any capacity.

I ached for his kisses. I just wanted to feel the strength of his lips on mine one more time before he was taken away. As if he could read my thoughts, he clasped his hand in mine and pulled me away. We didn't speak, but walked together quickly toward our spot. People left the orchards and we passed Paige and her friend Dawn. Both sneered and whispered to one another, but there was no confrontation and for that small reprieve, I was thankful.

We passed a few others, two girls from Wheat and one from Dairy. All were friendly, smiled and greeted us giddily before resuming their conversations of what to wear to the Harvest Festival celebration tomorrow. Laney insisted that I wear the green gown that she'd let me borrow for dinner at the Preston's. Though I hated even thinking their name, the gown was beautiful and would be perfect. I had nothing else that would remotely be appropriate.

Lulu might have something in her closet, but I hadn't been able to bring myself to even step foot into her room. I didn't want to disturb her things. I knew Laney slept in there when she stayed with me, when we thought she was in Olympus, but now that she was gone, I just didn't want to be the one messing up the way she left things. It was her house after all. Without her there, I felt like an intruder.

Tall hay brushed against my jeans and tickled the tips of my fingers as we cut through a field. My heart pounded in my chest. Anticipation hung thick in the air. I just hoped he wanted the same thing I did. Time with him. Kissing him. Memorizing his face; the curve of his jaw and the strong angle of his nose. The way his lips felt against mine, the pressure of his large hands on the small of my back. We topped the last small knoll and the swans bobbed gently in the water just ahead of us. We didn't make it to them.

He stopped abruptly and reeled me in. "Tell me I can kiss you," he whispered against my lips. His breath was sweet and minty and I couldn't wait to taste him.

"Yes." I barely got word out before he crashed into me. His lips swept over mine baptizing me in their soft strength. I could feel his tongue brush my lips and parted my own, granting him access. We all but molded to one another.

When we parted, both of us gasped for breath. He pulled me along the trail, past the swans, past the games with decaying teddy bears, beyond the fun house full of contorted images and bad memories, and even further still. We ran by the spot where our bonfire had taken place.

He pulled me quickly, glancing over at me and smiling from time to time. We stopped at what once was a small train station and he backed me against the wooden wall, now rough from age and weather. Our lips and hands quickly found each other again. "I love to feel you against me," he heatedly whispered, before pushing my hair aside and kissing the spot just under my ear.

It was divine and I couldn't believe the sound that escaped my throat when he continued down to the spot where my shoulder and neck connect. His hands kept me pushed completely against him, enveloped in all that was Crew. I ran my hands through his sable hair, reveling in its softness against my fingertips. We kissed like this for what seemed like hours before he finally pulled back. Darkness had fallen. His eyes found mine, almost glowing from within, they were so bright and golden.

"We should get back. It's getting late."

"I don't want to leave." I admitted.

He brushed his lips over mine and the scruff now emerging along his jaw raked lightly along my skin. "I don't want to leave either." His eyes locked on my own. I knew he meant more than just leaving here tonight. He didn't want to leave Orchard. Maybe he didn't want to leave me. But, the Greaters never asked us what we wanted. Only what we could give them. They didn't care that Crew and I wanted to be with one another.

It dawned on me. I was falling hard for Crew Cole and I couldn't let that happen. I stepped back and my fingertips found my lips swollen from his attentions. "I think we should go."

"Don't." He ordered.

"Don't what?" I stepped back further.

He stepped forward to mitigate my retreat. "Don't pull away from me. Not now. I don't know how much longer I have left here. I want to spend it with you."

I nodded. "I want that, too. I just hate to think of you leaving." Tears flooded my eyes and then overflowed. I couldn't help it. I felt so alone in this world and Crew was now the only thing that made me feel remotely human.

"Don't think of it. We still have tomorrow."

"Tomorrow," I tried to smile. He pulled me in for a hug and then clasped my hand within his and we walked back toward my cabin. We found it empty. Kyan, Crew, and I had cleaned it and restored it after it had been ransacked. Crew built and lit the fire, while I lit all of the candles and oil lamps. A few of the candles in wrought iron sconces along the wall needed replaced, so I found the extras and tried to busy myself. I knew he had to leave. The Preston's and his parents would definitely object to his staying here.

As I lit the last candle along the wall in my bedroom, warm, strong hands fall on my waist and pulled me backwards. My back collided with Crew's warm chest. He tucked his head into the crook of my shoulder and sighed. The rough stubble along his jaw scratched me deliciously. "I have to go. They'll know where I am and I don't want to cause any trouble for you."

"I know." I tried to memorize how his arms felt wrapped tightly around me, how his warm breath tickled my ear. His scent. He smelled like spice, exotic and male, even after having worked outside all day in the orchard, he smelled divine.

I spun around, still in his arms and kissed him long and urgently on the lips before releasing him and stepping back. "Go. Before I decide to tie you up and keep you here."

He grinned. "Maybe I'd like that."

"You would. Trust me. I would personally see to your comfort and entertainment." I smirked.

Crew growled, prowling forward, "How am I supposed to leave now?"

I shrugged nonchalantly and smiled at him. "One foot in front of the other."

His eyes narrowed into tight slits and before he could move, I ran for it, laughing as I sprinted away. His arms caught me as I grasped for front door. Turning me around, Crew pushed me up against the wood. His knee parted mine and we were pressed flush against one another, molded together. He kissed me hard, hungrily before finally releasing me slowly. I wasn't sure if my bones had turned to mush, but was wobbling on my feet.

He stepped back, shrugged nonchalantly and said, "Guess I'll see you tomorrow," as if nothing had ever happened.

I giggled. "Touché, Crew!"

Laughing, he jumped off the porch and into the darkness beyond. As he crested the small hill, he yelled, "Kyan is going to check on you soon."

"He always does." I yelled back.

I thought I heard him mutter something, but couldn't make it out as he had disappeared into the obsidian.

∞

FAITHFULLY, AN HOUR LATER, A knock sounded at the door before Kyan eased it open and stepped inside. I'd made a pie on the woodstove yesterday and put some meat and vegetables into a pot leaving it to roast today while I was working. When Crew was here, I didn't notice any smell other than his spice. But, once he left, I realized how good the house smelled. The rich, smokiness of the cooked meat lingered. We rarely had beef, but with the festival, several cows had been slaughtered and each family was given a small portion as a reward for their hard work during harvest.

Kyan sniffed the air, long and deep and moaned. His hair was wet and shiny. "It smells so good in here. Mom smoked our meat to preserve it. This is so much better. This is how you enjoy a reward."

"I didn't get much because it's just me. So, I thought I'd make a roast. There are more veggies than meat, but it smells good. I made bread."

He laughed. "You never could eat roast without it."

Smiling at him I narrowed my eyes. "Shut up."

"Is that what I think it is?" He eyed the pastry a few feet away, its dough crisscrossing across the top, weaving a pattern of tasty goodness. I grinned in reply. Apple pie was Ky's favorite. And Lulu planted her own apple tree, so we could have apples of our own. They were nowhere near as big as those in the orchard, but they were sweet, juicy and wonderful for baking.

He moved closer to the pie. I kept my eye on him. "What's that?" He pointed to the stove.

Nothing was out of place. "What?"

I looked back and caught him. His finger was stuck into one of the lattice holes of my pie. "Kyan! Remove your finger from my pie, right now!" I yelled.

He grinned, took his finger out of the pie and licked it off. "Mmm." He literally moaned. "Your spices are the best, Abby Blue."

I ticked my head toward the stove. "Want some roast?"

Kyan chuckled as he pulled two bowls and two glasses from the cupboard. "Did you even have to ask?"

The dinner was like a feast. The meat was so tender it fell apart at the touch of my fork. The vegetables were cooked to perfection. Potatoes, carrots, and cabbage floated happily the beefy broth. We wasted no time devouring the contents of our bowl and then another. As I sliced the pie, Kyan watched me intently.

"Is that drool on your chin?" I teased.

"Probably. You make the best pie in the entire village." He seemed serious, though I know his mama made pie all the time and everyone liked their own mama's cooking. I loved Lulu's pies. She taught me how to make this one.

We ate our slices and talked. He told me about the numbers, the amount of apples harvested was more than any year before. Thousands and thousands of pounds were put onto trains during the harvest and sent to Olympus. He said that some would be sent to big buildings that house all sorts of different food. Residents could go pick out what they wanted to cook and the apples would be offered to them as an option.

Other apples would be sent to the Greater factories where they would be made into applesauce, apple butter, cakes, and pies that the Greaters could buy in the city.

Some of those products would be sent to the other Greater cities, too. It seems very complex, but organized.

"I can stay tonight, Abs."

"No. You need to go home and rest. The festival is tomorrow."

"I know." He sounded somber.

"Do you hate that you won't be getting married tomorrow?"

His rich brown eyes met mine. "Yes." His answer was so quiet, so unlike Kyan.

"I'm sorry. I didn't mean to come between you and Paige. Maybe you can talk to her, tell her how you feel and work it out before tomorrow."

He shook his head. "I didn't lie to Paige. I didn't want to marry her. I never did. Our parents pushed us into it."

"But you said you were upset that you weren't getting married tomorrow?"

"I am."

"Okay. I am confused. It's official." I pushed my plate away and leaned back in my chair, my stomach holding a very rare full feeling.

He laughed. "I wish I were getting married tomorrow. Just not to Paige Winters."

He cleared his throat. *I hope he isn't about to say what I think he is.* "Abby, I wish with all my heart I could marry tomorrow." He paused. "I wish I could marry you, tomorrow."

He said it and now I can feel the air against my widened eyeballs. "Ky—"

"Don't Abby. Just don't. I know how you feel. I see how you look at Crew." I shifted uncomfortably in my seat and refused to make eye contact with him.

"You look at Crew the way I look at you." I finally looked at him. He was staring at me.

"I'm sorry." It was all I could say.

He shrugged and put another fork full of pie into his mouth. Before he finished chewing, he said, "He's leaving, you know."

I nodded. "I know."

"Soon."

"I know, Ky."

"Maybe we can get to know each other better after he's gone and maybe this time next year we'll be preparing for our wedding."

"Ky. I cannot imagine knowing you any better than I already do. You're my best friend."

"I don't want to just be your best friend." He slapped the table with his open palm. The plates and silverware clang together. I was just as startled.

"I know."

"I love you, Abby Blue." He pushed back his chair and crossed the room, pulling the door closed behind him. He loved me. Why couldn't I bring myself to love him back? The way he needs it.

Chapter 15

MY FINGERS PRUNE QUICKLY IN the soapy dishwater. I was like a robot. I stoked the fire and extinguished the candles along the wall and mantle. I scrubbed my body as well as I could without actually bathing and pulled on my flannel pajama pants and a long sleeved light pink t-shirt that matched them. I pulled the covers on my bed up to my neck and drift off to sleep quickly despite the turmoil in my mind. This harvest season has been one that I'd like to forget but know I won't soon be able to any time soon.

I dreamed that a hand clasped over my mouth. My body thrashed and I tried to scream. Nothing worked. I tried to bite the hand smothering me but couldn't grasp hold of flesh. An arm held my body still as I was dragged from my bed, kicking. Muffled screams and sobs echoed out into the night, but no one was around to hear me. No one could help me. I begged for my mind to stop this assault, but then I heard it. The distinct sound of horses hooves pounding earth a few feet away. Parched dust assaults my nose and clogs my throat making me cough and gag. This was real. I twisted my head and made out the shiny slash of his scar. Norris. Norris was taking me from my home.

"Scream and I will kill you right here, right now," he gritted through clenched teeth. I felt sharp, cold metal pressing against my right side. I nodded.

"Get up on the horse." He lifted me up and I helped maneuver my leg over and sat in the saddle as he mounted, positioning himself behind me. He wrapped one arm around me, digging the knife blade under my rib, and grabbed the reins with his other hand, whipping them harshly. The animal grunted and took off into the night. With every gallop, I could feel the knife cut a little deeper. Cold, wetness seeped into the shirt on my stomach.

"Norris."

"Shut up! Didn't I tell you to keep quiet?" he hissed in my ear.

"You're cutting me." My voice was frantic and shrill. He looks down to where I pointed and grinned, but pulled the knife blade away from my skin.

"So I did."

He took me over a trail I'd never seen, far away from the village. He was going to kill me. I wondered this was what he'd done to Lulu. I fought tears back into my eyes, blinking rapidly. Norris would not get the satisfaction of seeing me cry. He would not see me cower. We traveled through woods, next to a small pond before coming to a clearing. I could see a small cabin ahead, lit candles twinkling in the windows. The glow of a fire within warmed the harsh, black night around it.

Norris hitched his black beast to a post in front of the house. Dread crept into my stomach. This was his cabin. It was so remote. No one would hear me here. No one would find me. As if reading my thoughts, he started to laugh and pulled me off the saddle.

"On the porch," he ordered.

I obeyed and watched him push a pail of water, and another of oats in front of his horse. "Welcome to my humble abode," he chuckled, pushing the front door open for me and sweeping his hand forward dramatically.

His cabin wasn't much different than ours in its layout. But his furnishings were plain and the entire place reeked of cigar smoke. He undoubtedly got those from his boss. No one but Councilmen could afford to smoke. No one else had the time to waste or goods to trade for the cigars or cigarettes.

The kitchen was bare, with the exception of a small wood burning stove and the dishes that were precariously piled in the sink. A small, rusty water pump sat idle beside the sink itself. A luxury. It was lucky to have placed the house so close to a well, or found one so close to the cabin itself. Most people had to carry water from the streams. Even the Preston's did. Lulu and I were constantly toting water home for drinking, washing laundry or dishes, cooking or cleaning up in the evenings when bathing wasn't an option.

Across from the small kitchen sat a small square table with two rickety wooden chairs. Coats and shirts were haphazardly thrown over the chair backs. A single wooden rocker was positioned in front of the small fireplace. "Sit."

Norris motioned toward it. I complied, causing the chair to rock forward and creak in protest. He took his time stacking firewood in the fireplace in front of me before adding the kindling, which consisted of some sort of paper. The cabin was completely silent except for his shuffling around. Even the horse was still. The strike of the match he held caused me to flinch as I wondered what was going to happen to me. I didn't fear death itself, just what I would have to endure to find the peace that only death could provide. No doubt, if Norris was in control, torture would be but a taste of what I could expect. I recalled the way his eyes lit up as he ripped the flesh off my back. It only took fifteen lashes for him to scrape bone.

He pushed himself up and turned toward me. "Get up."

His hair hung in greasy strings over his forehead. Chunks of dinner still dangled between his teeth, though I wasn't sure if it was from tonight's or one earlier in the week. He grabbed my elbow roughly and jerked me down the hallway. *No freaking way I'm going into his bedroom.*

"No." I planted my feet, but he jerked me forward another foot.

"Come. On," he grunted, jerking me again. I lost another foot to him.

"No!" I yelled. "I'm not going in there with you."

All of the sudden, he loosened his grip and laughed. "You could never satisfy the needs of a man like me. Don't flatter yourself, Abigail Kelley. You'll be staying in here tonight. My orders were simply to collect you. For now."

He jerked me into a bedroom. A dirty mattress lay on the floor beneath a candle holder on the wall. There was a small, white ceramic pitcher in the corner and a matching empty plate next to it. "Get on the mattress."

I sat down on the lumpy rectangle and crossed my legs. Norris clamped his big paw around my forearm and then clapped an iron manacle around my wrist. It was attached to a chain that had been drilled and affixed to the wall itself. It was just long enough that I could step a few feet away from the mattress itself, and so that I could reach the pitcher and plate. I noticed a small metal bucket in the other corner and it looked like I could reach it, too.

"Water is in the pitcher. I'll bring you bread at daybreak. You can use the bucket for your personal needs." He smirked at me and I wanted to rip the chain out of the wall, wrap it around his neck and squeeze the life out of his smug face.

He laughed as he stepped outside the room. I heard the distinct sound of a key turning the lock on my door. My cell.

SOMETIME IN THE NIGHT, OR morning, I'd fallen asleep on the dirty mattress. I sat up and stretched my back from the discomfort of that small lumpy mat. The smell of musk and mold wafted up from it, and now I realized that having slept on it, I smelled like that dirty mattress, too. Gross. Norris did not return at dawn. The biggest part of me was thankful. But, a small part was starving and scared.

The fear of the unknown was causing my mind to run wild.

Near midday, I heard him and his evil beast of a horse approach and rustle around outside the cabin. Then I heard another voice. Councilman Preston was here. The front door opened and closed again before two sets of footsteps echoed down the hall, pausing in front of my door. I could hear the key being inserted into and twisting in the lock. Slowly, the wooden door creaked open. I should have lay down and pretended to sleep. But, instead, stare wide eyed at the two pathetic excuses for men in front of me.

The Councilman's eyes were blue. Not as icy as Zander's, but not a deep blue either. They fixated on me. "You've caused quite a few problems for me lately, Abigail." He paced the dirty floor in front of me. "How dare you accuse me, speak to me, in public! Do you know the trouble you've caused?" His face contorted in rage and reddened with each harsh breath he drew. "You humiliated Zander. We welcomed you into our family with open arms and you repay me by dragging me in front of the Council?"

I kept quiet, damn near chewing my tongue to keep from letting loose on him.

"Bring it in," he yelled into the house. Someone else was here.

Mrs. Preston stepped into the room holding a white mass of fabric that bubbled up out of her arms. *Seriously? The wedding dress. Are they still going to try to make me marry their son?*

She smiled tightly.

"Clean her up. Get her dressed." He barked.

Mrs. Alyce Preston accepted a small key, nodded compliantly and watched as her husband stepped out of the room with Norris following behind like a lost pup.

She hung the gown on one of the wrought iron sconces and then moved forward. Without comment, she used the key to remove my restraint. Relief coursed through my wrist. I rubbed it, calming the itchy skin that had lay beneath. The iron was hard, tight, and unyielding and my skin screamed from the fresh air that assaulted it. Pitcher in hand, she stuck her hand in and pulled out a small cloth.

"Wash your face." Her voice cracked. I grabbed the cloth from her and scrub. "Now the rest of you." I washed my neck and chest, pushed my sleeves up and wash my arms. She nodded her approval and took the cloth back, throwing it into the pitcher again. Her hair was perfectly knotted at the nape of her neck, as usual. She pulled out a small comb from her pocket and motioned for me to turn around, before she began to comb my hair.

"Why are you dressing me up?"

Silence.

"Please. Why are you doing this? I don't want to marry Zander. He would be miserable, too. Don't you get it?"

"You won't be marrying Zander, today."

"Then why all of this?" Her eyes hardened.

"You've caused a lot of problems for my husband and family." She jerked the comb through my hair hard. Tears sprang into my eyes from the assault. She ignored my pleas and braided my hair, pinning it up in silence. Tears had streaked down my face and splashed onto the legs of my pajamas.

"Get up and undress."

I sat still. "Why should I?"

"Do it," she leaned in to face me. "Or, I'll see that Norris does it."

I undressed and stood in front of her covered only by my bra and panties. She released the gown from its hanger. It's tulle fabric stretched over only one shoulder, gathered tightly at the waist and then cascaded down the full skirt in a thick, rich flow of fabric so full, I couldn't imagine holding it up, much less walking in it. She lifted the gown and I folded my hands as though I was swan diving and sank into the fabric as it was pulled over my head. It was made to fit my every curve.

For a moment, I allowed myself to daydream. I thought of the Harvest Festival, of all of the beautifully adorned couples. The girls would wear dresses of every shade of the rainbow, hair curled or braided. The guys would be dressed sharply in crisp, dark suits, their hair slicked back. Music would pour from speakers and the couples would swirl and twirl in the evening air by the light of thousands of candles made for just this event.

I could see Crew walking toward me. I would be wearing this gown. Laney would have let me use some of her makeup and my skin would be glowing beautifully in the candlelight. His skin would be flawless and pale, contrasting with his dark hair. His jaw would be freshly shaven, and he would smell of spice and Crew. His hands would encircle my waist and pull me in as his lips closed in on mine...

Mrs. Preston slammed the door behind her as she exited, ripping me from my fantasy. A moment later, Norris entered and jerked me out of the room, down the hall and out onto the porch. A long piece of rope hung from the tree just out front to the right, its end formed into a noose. I shivered. *This is how it ends.* Zander stood on the porch facing me, his hands tucked into his suit pockets. His eyes were cold, icy as ever. His lips formed a snarl.

"Come on, girl." His dark eyes glittered as he led me over to the rope. Goosebumps spread over my skin and it wasn't because of the chill in the air. Leaves crunched underfoot with each step I took toward that serpent of rope that was waiting for me.

I thought of Crew's smile, of Kyan sticking his finger in my pie just last night, of Laney always trying to make me over into something beautiful. I remember the warmth of Lulu's eyes and arms. How she would kiss my boo-boos and comfort me with warm tea afterwards. I imagined her brave as she met her end. Lulu was strong. Always a rock beneath the soft façade.

I squared my shoulders and stepped forward with purpose. If this was how it ended, I would be dignified. I could be strong like Lulu. I stepped beneath the rope which was now swaying in the soft breeze. Norris grabbed my arms and tied the coarse, thin rope around my wrists. It cut my skin as it dug in tighter and tighter still. He grabbed my chin and pinched it as he slid the noose over my head and tightened it around my neck. The coarse fibers cut into my neck, while the rope that bound my hands behind me bit further into my wrists.

He moved toward the tree and motioned for Zander. "Pull this. Not too tight, but not too loose. Just make sure it doesn't fall off the branch."

Zander nodded, holding the end of my hanging rope. *Cocky bastard.* I could knock the smile right off of his...

Crack! *NO!* I twisted around. Norris stood behind me. The whip cracked loudly again as Councilman and Mrs. Preston looked on from the porch. "Wouldn't want to get your hands dirty, Councilman!" I screamed.

"We found some damning evidence in your cabin while we were searching for you the other night, Miss Kelley. You are being charged with Treason. Treason against our village and against the Greaters.

Crack! Searing pain shot across my back. "You're a liar! And a murderer. We all know what you're trying to cover up. Good luck with that. Don't you think people will wonder what happened? Don't you think it's obvious that you're getting rid of me for standing up to you? People aren't stupid, Councilman. They'll figure this out quick!"

Slash! "Why didn't you sell tickets? Set me up at the Harvest Festival?"

Another slash bit my left shoulder and tore its way down toward my right hip. "Want a turn, Mrs. Preston?" Another slice. I could feel blood seeping into the delicate fabric wrapped around me. The warmth of my lifeblood cooled when it met the evening air, comforting my skin until another crack of the whip lit it on fire again.

"You're cowards! You killed her! I know you did! You...AAAHHH!" My body slumped forward. My shoulder was on fire. I looked back toward Norris and he caught the back of my neck. I couldn't stand up. I tried to shuffle my feet, but he quickened his assault, slashing me from neck to buttocks. The delicate fabric of the gown, stained crimson, fluttered helplessly in the wind, like a wounded bird, trying to fly away. To escape.

Soon, my knees buckled. I felt the noose clench tight on my throat just before darkness swarmed into my eyes, clouding my vision.

Chapter 16

"ABBY BLUE!" LULU RUNS TOWARD me and throws her arms around me and tackles me to the ground. Leaves crunch beneath us. "Lulu?"

She nods excitedly. "Is it really you?"

"Of course, silly. Who else would it be?"

"But..."

"Shh. I had to come see you. When I heard you were coming, I wanted to make sure I was here."

"I miss you so much!" She hugs me tight.

"I miss you, too, Abigail."

I hold her for a long moment, savoring how she feels in my arms. She smells like she's been baking. Sugar and flour, and just sweet.

"Oh, sweetie. I wish you could stay with me."

"I want to stay with you, Lulu."

She pinches her lips into a smile. "You can't. It's not your time. You have to go back and finish this."

"Finish what?"

"You're going to have quite an adventure, Abby. Don't be stubborn or prideful. Follow your heart."

"My heart? What are you talking about?" She laughs.

She pulls me to my feet and hugs me again and kisses my cheek softly. "Follow your heart. Don't forget."

Suddenly, Lulu begins to fade away, becoming less and less against the brilliance of the fall backdrop around us. "Lulu?"

"Lulu!?" I scream frantically as she fades completely away.

∞

"OH, NO. OH, GOD. ABBY? Abby Blue, don't you leave me!" Kyan. What was he saying? Everything was so fuzzy.

"Cut her down." Crew?

Everything was black and cold. I wanted to go back to Lulu. It was so warm and nice with her. Something tasted funny. Bad. I remembered this taste. It was coppery and salty. Blood. My blood.

I heard a groan. *What is going on?*

"Bind them and lead them into town, now!" Councilman Ward? Bastard. Sided with the devil and didn't even know it. Or, maybe he did. I didn't know. Whatever.

I inhaled sharply. Pain washed over my body. I was dying. Or dead. I hurt. Pressure released from around my throat and neck. Someone was trying to lift me up and someone else was sawing at my wrists. No. *Are they cutting my hands off?*

"No!" I tried to scream, but it came out raspy and strange.

"Don't cut...hands...off... NO!!!"

"Shh. Abby, it's Ky. We aren't cutting your hands off. Your wrists are bound by a rope above your head. Crew is just trying to saw the rope in two. The bastards have some sort of knot that we can't loosen from the ground."

I groaned again. It hurt so damn bad. My wrists screamed. My back was on fire. My legs were jelly, they just wouldn't work. "Help me."

"Shh. Evelyn's coming." My wrists dropped and fell heavily down and relief washed for me for a moment. I heard footsteps rushing toward me. "Oh my..."

Evelyn. "Get her inside on a mattress now!"

"Evelyn?" I croaked.

"I'm here Abby. Be gentle, but hurry Kyan. She's lost a lot of blood."

"Just let me go back. Lulu..."

∞

"OHH." THAT WAS MY VOICE. My entire body hurt.

"Abby!" I felt a weight on the mattress beside me.

"Ky?"

"It's me. I'm here."

"Ky?" I whimpered. I was so afraid.

"Shh. I'm here. Crew's here, too. Laney just left to help her mom with something but she'll be back soon."

"Where am I?"

He cleared his throat. "You're at Norris's cabin."

"No!"

"Shh. He isn't here. It's just us. Crew's parents and Evelyn are in the kitchen.

"I need water." I felt like my tongue was made out of sandpaper. I tried to find moisture in my mouth, but come up dry.

I heard footsteps leave the room and two sets return.

"Abby?" Evelyn said.

"Water." I croaked.

"Okay. We can give you a drink." She positioned a small porcelain tea cup by my mouth and I managed a few drinks, though more fell onto the blanket below me than actually found purchase on my tongue.

"What happened?"

She felt my forehead. "No fever. Abby, do you re-member Norris bringing you here?"

What? Flashes filled my head. The black horse, the black night, the knife cutting into my stomach, being chained to the wall, Mrs. Preston braiding my hair and helping me get into the dress, Zander holding a rope, the noose I had been sure was meant for my neck, the rope biting into my wrists just before the whip did, the awful cracking noise, followed by that of my flesh being torn from my body, the hot pain, Lulu.

"Lulu. I saw her."

"Sweetie, do you remember what happened to you? Lulu is dead. You didn't see her. Mr. Preston had you beaten to within an inch of your life."

I nodded. "I remember it all. But, I saw her. I talked to her. Hugged her."

Evelyn crouched down so that I could see her face. Concern wrinkled the skin around eyes that found mine. "I did. I wanted to stay with her."

"Well, I'm glad you came back to us, Abigail."

I drifted off to sleep again, my last thought of hoping to find Lulu again.

∞

WHISPERED WORDS FLOATED INTO MY ears and at first, I thought I was dreaming. Then I heard Crew. Then his father.

"You need to make a decision. The harvest will happen."

Harvest? We finished. Didn't we?

"I know, Father."

"If she is your choice, you need to tell her. She won't like having been lied to. I doubt she will accept you when she finds out."

"I know." Crew said, sounding exasperated.

"Guthrie is here with the healing balm."

"Thank you. I don't know how to thank you, father." Silence.

"Make your decision final. That is how you can thank me. You must decide before she goes into the program, or you won't get the opportunity. If you do not select her, then she will go in anyway. Once she's in, it's final, though. No pulling her out of it. You understand?"

To whom is he lying? What decision does he need to make? What program?

"Very well. I will send Guthrie in now. She should be healed by week's end and we can proceed."

"Yes, Sir."

The door to my room opened and closed. I was so sore from having lain on my stomach so long. I wished I could stand and stretch, but Evelyn had advised against it. I turned my head and see Evelyn and a very rotund man, entered the room. His hair was stark white and he wore thin, eyeglasses made of silver wire, an intricate design situated at each corner. The man's cheeks were red and he used a small white cloth to wipe sweat from his brow, upper lip, and neck. His shirt was white and crisp, his pants creased perfectly down the center of each leg. Evelyn moved a chair to the side of my bed and the man seated himself in it and opened a small leather case, removing a metallic jar from inside.

Evelyn sat beside me on the bed and even the small change in position made my back scream in protest. She leaned down to my ear. "Sorry," she whispered.

"Abigail, this is Mr. Guthrie. He's here to help your wounds. He has come all the way from Olympus and just arrived by train this morning."

Olympus? Why would Olympus send someone to help me? I'm a Lesser. We were completely expendable to the Greaters. Weren't we?

Evelyn must have sensed my thoughts, because she continued. "Councilman Cole sent word to the Greater city about the events that unfolded regarding your injury and of the corruption of the former Councilman Preston. The city leaders sent Mr. Guthrie to remedy your injuries in an attempt to show its support of our village and encourage its healing as well."

She looked nervous. I was, too. I'd never seen a Greater before. The lenses in his glasses were dark, shrouding his eyes. I couldn't determine their color, and I loved to see people's eyes. Lulu always said that the eyes were the bearers of truth–the windows to the very soul of a person.

"Hold still, Abigail Kelley. This will be painful, but your back will heal very quickly."

"Okay."

He and Evelyn quickly unraveled the maze of bandages that crisscrossed my torso and soon, my back was bare.

"Gracious!" Mr. Guthrie exclaimed. "In all of my days I have never seen anything like this."

Well that makes me feel so much better. Evelyn squeezed my hand in confidence. At least that was what I thought, until the first swipe of the cool gel across the wounds on my back. Fire spread over my flesh and I literally panted in pain. I couldn't get enough breath in my lungs to scream. Evelyn positioned the handle of a wooden spoon at my lips. "Bite down."

I did. I tried to chomp the damn thing in half. He methodically swiped the strange gel onto my back, then went back over it again. Halfway through, I passed into unconsciousness. Thankfully.

∞

I WOKE AT NOON THE following day. Kyan sat beside me in a chair he had pulled next to the bed. His head was pillowed on his arms and he snored lightly. My back didn't hurt. I stretched slightly waiting for pain that never came. Then stretched, eagerly, languidly, and groaned in relief. Ky stirred and sat up, copying my motions.

"You're moving!" He leapt from his chair, overturning it behind him.

"I know. My back feels so much better!"

"Evelyn!" he yelled.

The door burst open. "What's the matter?" Evelyn looked disheveled. Has anyone slept around here lately?

Kyan smiled brightly and announced to her that I could actually move. "My back feels much better."

Mr. Guthrie entered the room and smiled lightly. "Feeling better, my dear?"

"Much."

"We need to check your back to ensure healing and ward off infection." I nodded and lay flat again. Bandages were peeled off slowly and when the last layer, a large square, was lifted, gasps sound out from Kyan and Evelyn. "What? Is it bad?"

Their eyes were wide. Evelyn covered her mouth with her hand. Kyan's mouth gaped open.

I looked to the other side where Mr. Guthrie smiled knowingly. "You are healed, my dear."

"Healed?"

"Healed," he affirmed.

"Evelyn, can you assist her with getting dressed. Her body will be stiff and sore from having lain in the same position for so long, but she's good as new."

Evelyn was silent. Mr. Guthrie and I both looked at her and she finally nodded. "Of course. I'll help her. Kyan.

Kyan," she nudged his shoulder. "Go. I'll help her get ready."

He shook his head. "I don't understand."

That made two of us. The men exited the room and closed the door behind them. Evelyn's feet hadn't moved. Nor had her hand. It was still clamped over her lips.

"Evelyn?"

Her eyes found mine. She moved over to the bed and grabbed hold of my shoulders and helped me up. I was so stiff. "Abigail. Your back is healed."

"He said it was. It feels better."

"No, baby girl. It's healed as in...flawless. It looks as if nothing happened. There are no scars on your back at all. Not from the prior whipping and not from this one."

"What?"

She nodded. "I don't understand. I know the Greaters have advanced medicine, but I've never seen anything like this." She moved toward the dresser and pulls out drawer after drawer, before moving on to the small table beside the bed. "Here!"

She pulled out a small hand mirror and then helped me up. The chest of drawers had a small mirror sitting atop it and she pointed it on my back. I held up the mirror and gasped. There was nothing on my skin. It was perfect. In fact, it wasn't even tan anymore. It was pale as the day I was born. My eyes found Evelyn's, tears springing into my eyes.

"How can this be?"

"I honestly don't know," she admitted, softly.

∞

KYAN WALKED ME HOME. OTHER than the stiffness of my joints and muscles, I felt amazing. The walk helped me work some of the soreness out of my body. The smell of the cut hay in the field next to my cabin fills the air and I sighed. I'd missed this so much. Missed the village and my home.

"What happened to them?"

"To whom?"

"Norris? The Preston's?"

He stopped and looked at me. Then with his eyes as soft as his voice, he said, "They can't hurt you anymore, Abs."

"I know, but what happened to them?"

"Cole took charge. They had Norris and the entire Preston family detained and placed in a rusty train car heading toward Olympus, where it was said the guard would be waiting for them. They will stand trial in the city. Not just for what the bastards did to you, either. I mean, that's one of the charges. But, I guess they're being charged with several things: abuse of their power and position, conduct against the Greaters, extortion, bribery, treason... The list goes on and on. I guess Councilman Cole learned a lot while staying with them the few weeks, and none of it was good."

"Cole seems well connected."

Ky nodded. "Very well connected. But, I'm glad. That Guthrie guy brought just what you needed and healed you right up. I've never seen anything like it in my life. But, I'm glad all the same. I thought I was going to lose you, Abby Blue." His voice cracked as he says my name.

I hugged him tight. "I'm fine."

He nodded into the crook of my neck and held me.

"God, I missed you. When you didn't show up to the festival, I knew something was wrong. I found Crew and when he hadn't seen you either, the dude went kind of crazy. We both did. He..." Kyan looked at me and then away toward the trees. His jaw clenched and his teeth clamped together.

"What? He what?"

"He pulled out some sort of device and punched a bunch of buttons and not a minute later, his Dad showed up, and we went looking for you. We checked the Preston house. It was empty, so we went to find Norris's cabin. That's when I saw you strung up to that tree limb. If someone hadn't have stopped me, I would have killed Norris. I nearly beat him to death for what he did to you. Arrogant jerk never even saw me coming."

"Thank you, Kyan."

He nodded. My mind was reeling. "Lulu had a communicator. She used it to order supplies and coordinate the shipments of apples to Olympus."

"I saw it once." He glanced at me. "Okay, more than once. I watch the tracks a lot."

"She never used it at the house, but when I was smaller, I would go to work with her sometimes and she always had it out while she worked. She would inventory the supply houses, interview planters about the crop and monitor growth in the orchards. It was all very detailed and intense from what I could tell."

189

"Why does a guy from Cotton have such technology? My bet is his father had one, too. That's how he reached us so quickly. That's who he was contacting."

"I don't know."

"Something's not right with him, Abby. I know...I know you don't want to hear it. I know you have feelings for him on some level, but something isn't right and I want you to be careful."

I nodded. He was right. Crew was hiding something. "I will. I promise."

"Good." He smiled and it nearly lit the sky. "Tonight, there's a celebration in your honor."

"What?"

"Well, the Harvest Festival sort of got interrupted, and you're all better so we're celebrating tonight. A do over. And, you," he put his arm around my shoulders and started walking toward my home. "You're the guest of honor."

I groaned dramatically causing Kyan to chuckle and drag me along.

Chapter 17

IT WAS EARLY EVENING WHEN Kyan left me to get ready. I washed my hair and was wrapping it in a towel when I noticed the small piece of paper on my unusually made bed.

LOOK ON LULU'S BED.
—YOURS, CREW

Crew's been here? I leaped up, still clenching the note and ran to Lulu's room. Stopping just before the threshold, I peered inside. Sure enough, a large rectangular box sat on the bed, tied in the middle with a thick, red ribbon.

I padded into the room, picked up the bulky package and rushed back to my bedroom. The box was heavy, the ribbon some sort of silky fabric, soft and smooth under my fingertips. Before I could pull on it, Laney yelled into the house. "Abby?"

"In here!"

She rushed into my room and pulled me into a hug, squeezing my neck tightly. "Can't breathe," I croaked.

"Oh! Sorry! I just was so worried and I missed you and I love you so much, Abby!" She hugged me quickly again and then let go.

"I love you, too, Laney."

Tears shimmered in her eyes as she took me in. "You look wonderful! The last time I saw you, you wouldn't even wake up! And your back... Oh, my goodness. Your back was mangled and I honestly didn't know if you were going to live or die or wake up or be in a coma forever...and I just love you and didn't want you to miss out on your life. I mean, it's just beginning. And tonight! Oh, Abs! Tonight is going to be so wonderful!"

She paused to take a breath, making me giggle. "Sorry. I just missed you!"

Her arms wrapped tight around me yet again and then she pushed me away. The red ribbon must have caught her eye. "What is this?" Her eyes widened and glittered mischievously. She bounced onto the bed landing on her knees. "Open it. Open it, please!"

"Okay." I blew out a breath and sat next to her. "It's from Crew."

"That guy worships you, Abs."

I tugged the richly colored ribbon, leaving it to fall limply onto the comforter below. The lid was suctioned to its other half, so I jerked harder. Laney's eyes widened and her mouth formed an "O."

My face mirrored hers. Folded delicately was a dress made in the most beautiful fabric I'd ever seen. It was teal.

I lifted it carefully out of the box and Laney smoothed her hand underneath it, and together, we laid it on the bed. It wasn't cotton or silk. The material was metallic looking but felt soft to the touch, like satin.

"There are no sleeves at all." How was I supposed to keep the thing from falling down and exposing myself to the world?

"It's strapless! Look! Here are the undergarments. Don't worry. With these, the dress won't move once it's on." Taking up the stiff white garment, I examined it closely. It looked painful and way too small for me. "It's a corset! The boning is exquisite. I've only read about these in the magazines Mother had Lulu order for the birthday celebration last year. Oh, my goodness!" She caressed the frightening piece of cloth reverently, its bones supporting it like a skeletal torture device. How was I supposed to get this on?

"I can tell what you're thinking and yes, I'll help you dress! You're going to look stunning for Crew."

For Crew? Yes. I wanted to look beautiful for him. I would look lovely for the last bit of time we could steal together. The thought made my heart clench. I would miss his smile, his eyes, and his rich, deep laughter. Laney's eyes narrowed at the fabric in her hands and then again at me. "Strip."

∞

LANEY LEFT ME TWENTY MINUTES ago to go her own house. She had to dress and get ready. But, the girl was a tornado, a bubbly whirlwind of energy and excitement, with a passion for all things fashionable. As much as we ever learned of such things in the village. And I knew that with her ability to sew and the fabric that I now knew her mother and Lulu managed to sneak in for her, she would no doubt look stunning as well.

Awkwardly, I sat on the sunken cushions of the old blue couch in my living room. The fine fabric, wrapped around my body like a second skin, stood apart from the threadbare tweed beneath it. If you looked carefully, in certain places, you could almost see a few of the pink flowers that once delicately dotted the country blue color beneath it. It was why Lulu loved the couch at first. I remembered sitting on it as a child, trying to count the tiny blossoms.

Two rapid knocks in succession sounded at the front door. *Kyan's early.* My palms were warm and sweaty. I was the guest of honor tonight. I prayed they don't ask me to speak in front of everyone. I crossed the room and opened the door to find Crew waiting for me. His eyes twinkled like the stars and his smile was so bright, it could chase away the need for moonlight. His gaze rakes slowly down the length of my body before making their way back up and meeting mine once again. I smiled.

"Wow."

He looked beautiful. If a man could be said to be beautiful, that man would be Crew. Especially on this night. His suit was black as the night sky, a color deep as the coal pulled out of the earth's belly. The shirt underneath was crisp and white. A small white rosebud was pinned to his lapel. His dark hair was slicked back and his jaw was clean shaven.

"Abigail. You look amazing." He emphasized the last word breathlessly.

"You look handsome, yourself," I teased, hoping he wouldn't notice my blushing cheeks.

"May I escort you to the festival?"

"Of course." He offered his elbow, which I greedily claimed, pulling the cabin door closed behind me with my free hand. The evening air was surprisingly warm. I mean, it was chilly. But, for this time of year, it was pleasant and perfect. I tried not to tug my dress up. It really hadn't moved, but I realized now how much of my flesh was exposed with this strapless gown, how much was heaved up by the corset. Crew had noticed, too.

Half way to town, Crew stopped abruptly. "I'm sorry. I didn't want to do this." His eyes flash to mine and somehow, they darken, like caramel.

"What's wrong?"

He leaned forward quickly and his lips crashed on mine. I bathed in the taste of his mouth and of the feel of his body against my own. Steel against softness. I wanted to stay wrapped up in him forever. Never leave this place. When we broke apart, we were still mostly molded together. "I didn't want to mess up your hair or dress or makeup. I'm sorry. I couldn't help myself. You look so beautiful. And that dress...it...I...wow."

"Thank you for it." I grinned up at him.

"Anything for you, Abby. We probably should go. People are no doubt waiting for the guest of honor." He grinned as I groaned. And we both began to climb up the final hill, with our fingers intertwined together, one last time.

When we approached the village square, I could see the torches. When this village was created by the Greaters, they installed the iron torch holders. We would pile firewood into the wrought iron baskets and with kindling, and light them. Soft flickering light and warmth flooded the square. The square was just that, a large patch of grass, lined with those torches. A few wooden picnic tables and benches normally dotted the landscape, which hosted a few beds of flowers that were now drying out and re-seeding the ground as the winter approached. But for this evening, the tables and benches had been moved aside and in the square, a wooden dance floor had been erected, just below a wooden stage. Musicians tuned their instruments. *Instruments?* I looked from the stage to Crew who smiled, blinked once heavily and nodded back toward them.

All four of the musicians were men, who wore shaded glasses over their eyes, just as Guthrie wore. Were they Greaters, too? How could they see at night through the dark lenses? How would they read the music in front of them? One dragged a long stringed stick across a curvy wooden instrument positioned at his throat. The sound was beautifully high-pitched, the note drawn out, like the cry of a lover to her match.

The second plucked strings on, what Crew explained, was a guitar. His fingers nimbly worked over the strings tickling them incessantly. A very tall man sitting on the outside of the group, pulled his bow, as Crew called it, across an enormous wooden instrument. A cello. I immediately fell in love with its sad, soulful sound. Its somber, haunting notes mirrored my own soul. I wanted to be happy, to enjoy this unique night with Crew, but deep down I was crying. I already missed him and he wasn't even gone yet. I missed Lulu, too. She would have loved to have seen live musicians.

Crew continued, listing the names of the other instruments, and I wanted to listen, but couldn't seem to drown out the sorrow bleeding from my own heart. Laney ran up to us and tackle-hugged me. I couldn't help but smile. She looked absolutely lovely in a light pink gown, overlaid with matching lace. The neckline was high and elegant and the hem of the skirt flirted with her calves. She'd pinned her hair up into an intricate twist upon her head.

Laney quickly and excitedly spewed comments about who was here with whom, who was to be wed at the ceremony at the end of the evening, about who she wanted to dance with. "May I dance one with *your* man, Abs?"

I looked from Crew back to her nervously. Crew smiled. *Thank goodness.* I knew he wasn't mine, but he didn't embarrass me by correcting her. "Of course," he answered.

The band stopped playing. Excited chatter filled the air as the festivities were about to begin. Laney pulled me and Crew through the crowd of well-dressed youth, past the parents, grandparents, children, and grandchildren who lined the square people-watching. The brides were easily distinguished. Each wore white. Each dress was unique and befitting. There were three this year. Dawn, Paige's best friend stood among them, along with two girls from the other Lesser villages. The latter appeared younger than I was and I wondered if these young women were truly ready for the responsibilities that come with being a man's wife. I definitely wasn't. Beyond the intimacies of the bedroom laid the hours of hard work, not only in their villages, but in keeping a house running.

We nodded to the featured brides as Laney dragged us past them to a rectangular table just to the left of the stage. A tented piece of white paper sat in the center of the table, backed against a beautiful vase of white roses, encircled by wildflowers. A burlap bow was sweetly tied around the glass. Candles twinkled from each side illuminating the words, "Reserved: Abigail Kelley, Guest of Honor."

I froze, but Laney pulled me forward while Crew pulled out one of the chairs on the long side of the table. There were only four chairs at the table, one on each end and two positioned next to each other so that the view was left open, and all seated at the dais could see the festivities.

I sat down, careful not to wrinkle my dress or pull it down further in the front. Crew settles next to me after offering Laney the chair to his right. The seat to my left was open and empty. The only person missing was... "May I have this seat?"

Kyan. "Of course." I motioned for him to sit down. He looked amazing in a dark gray suit, white shirt, un-buttoned at the top. His hair was wet and slicked back as well. Kyan was a very handsome young man on any given day, but he cleaned up well. He leaned in and placed a small kiss on my cheek. Crew stiffened beside me.

I pulled away from Ky and threaded my fingers through Crew's, hoping he understood my feelings. Kyan was my friend. I wished with all of my heart, body, and soul for Crew to be my forever. Once, Lulu told me that many stories had ended with the words... "And they lived happily ever after." I wanted that with Crew.

I wished that circumstances were different, but unfortunately had to live in reality. And the reality is that we were Lessers. We were not of the same village, or region, even. The Greaters never allowed village changes. We may as well have been from two different worlds. We cannot be together. It was nearly as impossible as it would be for a Lesser to fall in love with a Greater. The two worlds simply didn't mix. So, I squared my shoulders, determined to take this last glorious night with him and enjoy every second of it. It would be the closest I'll ever get to freedom, or to happiness.

∞

KYAN AND CREW EXCUSED THEMSELVES and walked to the far side of the square, gathering glasses of punch, and plates of exquisite fruits and pastries for the table. Laney squealed every time her eyes land on something different or exciting. "Can you believe it? Musicians! I can't believe this. I'm dreaming. Pinch me."

I laughed. "No, seriously. Pinch me." She begged giddily.

I pinched her lightly. "Not dreaming!" she squealed again.

The skirts of lovely white dresses spun happily around the dance floor. It was the bridal dance. All others had been asked to clear the floor in honor of the unions about to be made. Several people stopped by our table and spoke with me and Laney, as they made their way mingling around the square. Evelyn sat briefly with me. "I still don't know how Mr. Guthrie healed you, but the Greaters have more power than I ever realized, Abigail." She whispered conspiratorially, a genuine smile spread upon her lips. "But, I'm very glad that the Cole's requested help for you." She kissed my cheek, making my eyes fill up. I wished Lulu was here tonight. She should have been the one to help me get ready. "Shh. She's looking down on you, child. Always."

I nodded and swallowed the harsh knot of reality that had formed in my throat. "I'll see you in a little while. You look beautiful." With those parting words, she stood and blended back into the crowd, as if swallowed whole. Crew and Kyan arrived with refreshments and I was parched. I greedily drank the punch until only a tiny bit remained in my crystal flute.

Kyan leaned in and whispered, "Dance with me?" The bridal dance was over, and so I nodded and accepted the hand he offered. Crew watched as we stepped onto the dance floor. Kyan's hand rested on my waist and the other hands clasped together in midair, pointing to the heavens.

When the music began, Kyan swept me around the dance floor. With every turn and twirl the bottom of my dress flared out. I felt elegant. This dress even put the green dinner dress to shame. My normal clothes were old, dirty and torn. And with Crew watching, I felt almost ashamed. He'd dressed me up in the finest fabric I'd ever seen, let alone worn. I cringed imagining what he must think of our normal clothing. He has servants. New shoes. Uncalloused hands.

At the bonfires, couples would dance. People who'd been friends since infancy would dance and swayed back and forth to the beat of the music. This was the first formal dance I'd actually participated in. I'd attended the harvest festival every year since coming to live with Lulu, but had never been asked to dance.

Laney and Kyan tried to coax me onto the dance floor in years past. I always turned them down. Never felt confident enough to dance in front of everyone in the village. Never wanted to put myself out there. I'd been afraid of the snickers and chuckles that would have erupted at my expense, at the hands of Zander and his cronies. Crew changed all of that. He made me feel like more, for the first time in my life, made me feel good enough. Though he was leaving, I would have that part of him, the part of him that believed in me, with me forever. And for that, I was grateful.

The song ended and I looked for Crew, but didn't find him at the table. "He's not there," said Kyan coldly.

"What?"

"Crew. He's not at the table. That's who you're looking for, right?" He was mad.

"Ky."

"I know. I just hate it that it's not me, but I get it. I just hate to see him break your heart. He's leaving."

I nodded. "I'll be here for you, when he's gone. I'll help you pick up the pieces. I just hope one day... I hope one day it'll be me you look for."

Ky stalked away, leaving me standing on the dance floor alone. I was pretty sure my heart cracked a little more with my best friend's pain, and desertion. Maybe after Crew leaves, I could try to move on. Maybe, with Kyan. *Hurting him makes my heart ache.*

∞

THE TABLE WAS EMPTY. KYAN was gone. Crew was nowhere to be found. Laney was dancing with a guy a year younger than us, Wyatt MacGregor. The song was upbeat and the two were clearly out dancing everyone on the floor. Laney beamed with happiness. At one point, her eyes collided with mine and she mouthed, "He's so hot!" while she tried unsuccessfully to discreetly point toward her partner. I nodded back to her.

I spotted Crew only a few tables away speaking with his father and mother. The discussion seemed heated. Crew stiffened and clenched his jaw. "You're forcing my hand, Son. I told you to make a decision. If you won't do it, she won't go into the program, but she will marry him tonight," his father's deep voice overpowered the jovial music pouring into the night.

Crew shook his head furiously and then stalked away, leaving his father standing there staring at the spot he had been occupying only seconds before. Mrs. Cole patted her husband's shoulder and Mr. Cole's eyes found mine. He pressed out a small smile and nodded. I nodded back politely, before looking away quickly.

Back on the dance floor, Laney and Wyatt moved effortlessly together, as if they were of one body. I wondered if they were meant for each other. Love could certainly blossom there, it seemed.

The sound of a throat clearing behind me pulled me out of my reverie. Mr. Cole stood with his hands upon the back of my wooden chair. He was alone. Crew was still missing. Mrs. Cole stood, talking with a group of ladies, across the square. Every part of her long black dress glittered in the firelight as if it had been cut from the sparkling sky itself.

Kyan was at the refreshment table talking with Lucy Brown. Everyone knew her reputation. It was said she put the 'loose' in Lucy. Of course her dress was unbuttoned to reveal her assets. I guess I shouldn't talk, though. Mine were on display, too at this point.

"Mr. Cole." I stood and shook his hand. "I wanted to thank you for how you handled the Preston's and for calling for Mr. Guthrie to come and help me."

His eyes assessed me coolly. The warmth I could find so easily in Crew's was nowhere to be found in his father's. "You are welcome, dear. There is a way that you can repay me, if you are truly grateful."

"How's that?" I swallowed thickly.

"You are the town hero. The sweetheart, if you will. They credit you with ridding the village of Preston and Norris. In only a few moments, the marriage ceremonies will commence. If you want to repay me, you will join with Kyan during the ceremony, become his wife. He will take Preston's seat on the Council and your positions within this community will be solidified." The man didn't blink. And, did he really just ask me to marry Ky?

"I don't understand."

"We have to fill the vacancy in the Council. Kyan is a natural leader and would fit well. He would refresh the Council and the village would prosper from it. With you by his side, the villagers would be content again. Kyan would be happy. He's obviously smitten with you." The corner of his lips tilted upward. "You do want what is best for the village? For Kyan, don't you?"

"Yes."

"Then you will agree?"

"What does Crew think?"

He straightened, adding another inch to his height. "He didn't take it well."

"That explains his absence."

"It does," he affirmed. "But, you see. Crew is from a different world. One you could not possibly understand. The two of you will never happen. I believe that you have come to this realization on your own, but Crew..." He shook his head. "He's stubborn. He gets that from me, I'm afraid." His eyes twinkled with pride. They also coolly raked over me.

Kyan was retracting Lucy's claws from his arm and kept looking over toward me as he tried to disentangle. Concern was etched upon his brow. I searched for Crew. He was gone.

"Crew is on the train. He will not be returning to the village at all. You will not see him again. The train leaves this evening and I know my son. He is angry. He won't come back. Not now. I need your decision and will tell them to begin the ceremonies."

Kyan was striding toward me with a fierce determination. I knew that he loved me and would protect me. Crew was as gone now as he would be when the train pulled away for Cotton later tonight. I could grow to love Kyan. He was already a big part of my life and heart as my best friend. He would make a great leader and our village would benefit. How could I say no?

My heart protested, thrashing against my chest, but I squashed its argument like a bothersome gnat. *I'll do it. It'll probably happen anyway and we can get the village on the right track. I can learn to love him. Slowly. A bit more each day, until all of the sudden, Kyan would have taken hold of my entire heart.*

"You should know that I offered to let Crew stay here. He wanted to take you with him. It's simply not allowed, but if he stayed, I could have covered it up. He was already here. It wouldn't be as hard to disguise as if one a Lesser attempted to relocate from one village to another. With that, there are transport records that are nearly impossible to destroy. He could have stayed. But, he chose to leave the celebration and get on that train. He chose to leave, Abby." *What? He had the chance to stay with me and he left? He didn't want me.* I couldn't breathe. I tried to compose myself. Time seemed to slow, almost stop.

"Okay." I said quietly.

"Pardon?"

I locked eyes with Mr. Cole. "I'll marry Kyan."

He smiled genuinely. "I knew you would do what is best for everyone."

I tried to smile back, but I'm sure it looked as crushed as I feel inside.

Mr. Cole intercepted Kyan midstride just before he reached us. He clapped Ky on the shoulder and spoke briefly into his ear. Ky looked at me, his brows raised and then furrowed them. Then, his head ticks to the side. I nodded and smiled. A smile blossomed on his lips, but his brows refused to unravel. Mr. Cole led him to a small table near the stage. Kyan took a pen and quickly scratched something onto a piece of paper, given to him by Councilman Rileck. When finished, he stood, rubbed the back of his neck and tugged on his already loosened collar. His eyes met mine. I ignored the question in them.

Councilmen Rileck stood, his large belly protruding over the waistline of his pants. Thank goodness for the suspenders he wore. "Ladies and Gentlemen of Orchard Village!" The murmurs from the crowd faded slowly as the citizens fastened their attentions on the stage before them.

"It's time to begin the ceremony." He clapped his hands and again waited for the crowd's applause to settle. He then motioned for the betrothed couples. "Please stand upon the stage and join hands with your intended. We have a last-minute addition to the ceremony. Very exciting."

The three brides in their white dresses, rushed eagerly onto the stage, grooms in tow. I stood and slowly crossed the dance floor toward Kyan, my future husband. He extended his elbow for me. When I grasped it, I realized just how bad I was shaking. He looked over at me and bent down to my ear, "Are you sure about this?"

I nodded, not trusting my voice to betray me.

"About me?"

"I'm sure." Somehow it came out clear and almost confident sounding. I squeezed his arm and smiled. He led me to the wooden staircase. The smell of fresh cut wood wafted up from underfoot. Sawdust had gathered in the freshly built joints. When people in the crowd realized that Kyan and I were ascending the steps to the stage, gasps expelled from every corner of the square, from old and young alike.

It was hot. It was suddenly very hot out here. I tried to fan myself without drawing attention. Kyan laughed. "I'm not that bad a prospect am I?"

"No. It's freaking hot out here!" I squeaked.

"It's going to be okay, Abby Blue." I let his warm chocolate eyes calm me and then looked back out over the crowd that was now gathered in front of the stage.

Kyan turned me to face him, as all the brides were now doing. His hands clasped with mine and they were cool and comforting to my hot, sweaty ones. I smiled nervously at him. He just grinned, reveling in my discomfort. *Big jerk.* "Shut up, Ky," I whispered.

Councilmen Rileck began, "We are here to join these young people together. Marriage is a privilege and not to be entered into lightly. All of those on the stage about to be wed," he threw a look of warning my way, "have received guidance and instruction from the elders of the village. Marriage is something that must be nurtured, treasured. The binding cannot be dissolved unless one of the partners dies."

I looked away. Kyan squeezed my hand lightly. *Can he tell I feel like bolting?* Only my stubbornness anchored me to the ground, and it was not doing a very good job, either.

"If anyone has an objection to any of these unions, let them speak now or hold their tongues for eternity."

Silence filled the night air. Even the crickets hushed. I couldn't breathe. The weight of this vow was caving in on me, crushing me.

"I object!" Crew's voice broke through the thickness and I drew a breath.

"Son, don't do this..." Mr. Cole grabbed Crew by the arm. "You could ruin everything. You'd better be sure."

"I am sure." He jerked hard away from his father and strode toward the stage. "Abigail!"

Ky's hands tightened on mine. I could see the struggle in the taught muscles of his face. He ticked his head back toward the steps that Crew was now climbing. Mr. Cole's words haunted me. *Crew is from a different world. One you could not possibly understand. The two of you will never happen. He chose to leave.* But, he didn't leave. He was here. He came back for me.

Kyan's grip loosened, but I refused to let go. Crew stopped in front of us. Everyone in the village watched the exchange. Golden eyes locked on mine. "Don't do this!" he lowered his voice. "Don't do this." His eyes flashed to Kyan. "You don't love him. I know you love him as a friend, but not as a husband."

I closed my eyes. He was right, but it didn't matter. *Two different worlds.* "Crew. You have to leave tonight. We...can't be."

"I do have to leave. Come with me!"

"I can't. My life is here. My home and my friends, the only life I've ever known. Besides, it's not allowed."

"I can make this happen. Please. Come. You would be so happy. *We* would be happy"

"In Cotton? How can it be so different than Orchard? Anyway, I'll never be granted permission to leave. It's unheard of."

"Don't. Please, don't make me do this." His face contorted as though he was in pain. Fumbling around in his suit jacket's inside pocket, he pulled out a large circle of silver. It looked as if someone had bent a small, silver metal tube into a perfect circle.

"Make you do what? What is that?" It was completely smooth, about a quarter of an inch thick and looked large enough to almost fit on my head. *How did that fit in his pocket?*

"May I at least have one last hug?" he asked, somberly. "I have something for you. Something to remember me by."

I looked at Ky, who nodded, but kept his eyes trained on Crew. Releasing Ky's hands, I stepped toward him and he wrapped his arms around me and held me tightly. Before I could pull away, his breath brushed my ear. "I'm sorry it had to be this way." Before I knew it, he clamped the cold, polished metal around my neck. A loud sizzle sound came from the area of the back of my neck. I felt for the clasp but it disappeared under my fingertips, melting into the metal, making one smooth ring. I felt frantically for it again, but the cold ring was fused solid. I had no idea how to get it off. While searching, my fingertips could feel an etching. I tried to lift the metal and suck in my chin, but the ring sat flush against my skin and I couldn't see it. "Abigail Blue Kelley, I hereby claim you as my intended. My infinite. The right given to me by the glorious Greater Kingdom of Olympus."

"Olympus?" I mouthed.

"I am Crew Alexander Cole, Crown Prince of Olympus. And I claim this woman as my future bride."

I looked at Kyan who clenched his jaw and fists menacingly. His upper lip trembled in rage. I prayed he didn't hit Crew. Crew? The Crown Prince of Olympus? A Greater? I couldn't breathe. I pulled hard against the collar that now proclaimed me as his intended. I tugged and strained but there was no fault in this metal. No chink in the armor. The clasp had disappeared, somehow, by some Greater magic or technology. And, I had once again become a pawn in the Greater's game. As if I'd ever actually escaped it. I'd been a part of it since birth. All Lessers had.

Chapter 18

THREE SOLDIERS APPEARED FROM BEHIND the stage, wearing black from head to toe in nearly skintight uniforms. All wore the weird tinted glasses. Greater soldiers were in the village. This was bad. One positioned himself next to Kyan and immediately escorted him from the stage, none too gently. The other two, found my elbows and half-forced, half-helped me descend the steps and cross the village square.

Crew walked ahead with a fierce determination. The path was wide enough for four people and was the only one that led to the train depot. Tears bit at the back of my eyes. I hated crying. It showed weakness. But, that was exactly what I wanted to do right now. I wanted to run away from here. Put as much distance between myself and Crew as possible. He was a liar and a Greater. My enemy. And, I'd allowed myself to trust him, to love him. That was what hurt the most. I'd been such a fool.

Wrapping my arms around myself, I tried to keep up with the long strides and fast pace set by Crew and the Greater guards. I'd only seen them once. Two years ago, several guards came by train to collect information during a mandatory census. The Greaters wanted to know who owned each dwelling, how many adults and children resided in each one, current pregnancies, the number of males versus females in the village, their assigned jobs, etc. They asked all sorts of questions. Lulu had told me it was common and happened every ten years or so, but her forced smiles and knuckle cracking told a different tale.

We crested the large hill and began our descent. I gripped the strange fabric of my dress's skirt for dear life, hoping that it would somehow steady me; body and mind. My heart beat furiously and I felt sick, as if a millstone lay in my stomach, heavy and cold. Glancing behind me, the trees along the line of the forest waved in the wind, a macabre goodbye. Their bony, bare fingers mocked me.

I tripped over a rock and the guards who flanked me caught me and hauled me upright before I hit the ground.

"Put her in my car," Crew ordered harshly.

The two guards grabbed my elbows and all but dragged me around the back of the train and inside a shiny metal car, the insignia of Olympus proudly embossed upon the silver vessel. An "O" halfway filled with what looked like water or waves shone back at me. In the right upper corner, sat the sun, its beams striking the waves at the horizon below in various places. Two small birds flew happily off into the sunlight. Unfortunately, I was not one of those free, happy birds. I was being caged, a pet claimed to entertain a Greater. The guards exited and stood out-

REAP

side the doors. If I thought I'd been in prison in the village, I was wrong. Dead wrong.

I stepped into the car. Everything inside was white—walls, floor, ceiling, décor- everything. To the left, sat a small white circular table with two, short, unpigmented plastic chairs. The design of the furniture flowed in smooth lines. There were curves. No harsh lines to be found anywhere. If it had been made of wood, everything would have been angular. But this plastic flowed sensually, like the hips of a woman. There was a small couch to the right, upholstered in thick white fabric, over the back of which lay a white fur. The fur was soft and thick as I ran my hands over and under it. In front of the couch was an oval table, made of the same white plastic. It sat only a couple of feet off the ground.

A large bed took up the back half of the train car. The ghostly, ashen headboard had a symbol carved into it and the footboard was carved to match. Touching the footboard post, I found that it was made of wood. The bumpy wood grains dotted across my fingertips as I ran them over it. It'd been white washed. The symbol was an "O" much like the one on the outside of the train car, but it was what lay within that letter that scared me. An apple, stalk of wheat, twig with cotton on it, what looked like a chunk of coal, stalk of corn, bunch of grapes, and several other things fill the letter, all overflowing from a traditional weaved cornucopia. And, then I saw it. In small letters, stretched across the top curve read: "May the Harvest be Bountiful."

I knew the Greaters always took an interest in our production. They relied on us to produce their food and

213

raw materials, so I even understood their oversight. But, this was strange. Why was it carved on the head and foot boards of Crew's bed? On the bed of the Crown Prince of Olympus? Why did the crown prince have anything to do with the harvest of the Lesser villages? Why would he bother himself with us at all?

The door of the car opened automatically as Crew strode in. He stood rigidly on the other end of the car. His black suit and hair contrast dramatically with the stark, sterility surrounding him, surrounding us. I looked down at the teal dress that I was wearing. The dress he gave me. I thought he was a Lesser, someone who cared about me, if nothing more. My teeth ground together, the sound echoing into my ears. He stared at me, lips pressed into a tight grimace.

When he moved toward me, I flinched back. I didn't want him to touch me. Silently he put his hands out as if in defeat and moved toward the couch, taking a seat. Rubbing his palms along his thighs, he blew out a breath. Time stilled. *Is he ever going to speak?*

"You're a liar." There. I would start.

He looked at me. "That is fair."

I scoffed. "Are you really the *Crown Prince* of Olympus?"

"Yes."

"I didn't even know that they had a prince. Or a King. I thought they had a council, that the leadership in the Lesser villages mirrored those of the Greater cities." My hands were slick with sweat, which I tried to wipe off on the tainted gown.

"There is a council. My father consults them on all matters. He values their opinions. He's known and trusted most of them for years. But, my father is king and all decisions ultimately lie with him. Though he rarely goes against their advice."

"Why did you put this thing on me?" My fingers moved over the cool metal around my throat. "I feel like an animal."

"In Olympus, it is an honor to wear your husband, or intended's ring."

"This isn't a ring. It's a collar." My voice rises.

"It is a ring. It's just worn around the throat."

I moved it around, again searching for a clasp, some way to remove it. "Can I take it off?"

"No."

"Never?" I squeaked.

"It must stay on until we are joined. But most women display theirs proudly for the duration of the marriage."

Duration of the marriage? "How long do marriages last in Olympus?"

He laughed lightly and looked up at me. "Marriages last as long as the couples in them do. Same as they do here."

"Stop laughing at me. I don't want to wear this. I want you to take it off. Now!" ·

His smile faded. Blinking, he matter-of-fact answered, "I will not."

"You won't? You're going to force me to marry you? Do you think that forcing my hand and making me miserable will make for a happy marriage?"

"No. But I will *not* stand for the alternative."

"Kyan?"

He ticked his head back as if I'd slapped him. "Kyan? Kyan is a pawn and he doesn't even know it. My father is going to place him in the Council. He will nudge him and use him as he does all of the others."

"Your father said he couldn't be placed in the Council unless he was married."

Crew looked away from me and clears his throat.

"He is being married, as we speak."

"Excuse me!" I yelled.

He jumped to his feet, strode quickly across the car and stood in front of me. "You will remember who it is that you are addressing!"

"Oh, that's right! The Crown Prince, the liar who gained my trust so he could manipulate me. You speak of your father using people. You're no better." My hands shook uncontrollably, as did my voice now. "And Kyan won't be moved around like some piece in whatever sick game your father is playing. And, there is *no way* he'll marry Paige or anyone else right now." I stood my ground in front of him, praying that I didn't hit him or kick him in his junk.

"I am better. But here are the facts, Abigail. I love you," he raised his hand to stop me from interrupting and I snapped my mouth closed, huffing and crossing my arms. "I do. I love you. I think I fell in love with you the moment I saw you. You were being harassed by Zander. I wanted to have him dragged away and tortured, just for touching you, for intimidating you. I wanted...*I* wanted to kill him. With my bare hands." He looks down at his palms, which he held out facing him. "Kyan will be married tonight. My father will see to it. The ceremony is probably already over. Did Kyan ever want to marry Paige?"

His eyebrows raise, in expectation of my answer. "No."

"Don't you find it strange that Kyan accepted her as his betrothed for so long? It was all planned. You got in the way of those plans."

"I... Your father asked me to marry Ky just tonight at the Festival!"

"He wanted you out of the way." His voice rose.

"Whose way? What way?"

"Mine."

"I don't understand." I shook my head.

"Preston was his pawn for a long time. When he told my father about Zander's infatuation with you, my father told him to make it happen. That's why they came on so strong."

Oh my gosh. My stomach hit the floor. I grabbed hold of my abdomen. "Lulu?"

Crew slowly nodded. "She got in their way."

"But he saved me that day. And then he sent for Mr. Guthrie."

He shook his head. "He had to act like it was all Preston. Preston took the fall for everything. Then, to keep peace in the village, he called for Healer Guthrie to attend to you. If you had died, there would have been an uprising. I'm sure of it, and so was he. To stop that from happening, he saved you."

"Then, he asked me to marry Kyan to keep me away from you?"

"Yes. But also to calm the villagers. So much had happened that they were sure to rebel. I'm sorry."

I moved backwards until the post of the footboard brushed my back. *I get it.* "He didn't want his son to marry a Lesser."

Crew blew out a breath. "Yes. I was supposed to choose an intended upon my arrival back to Olympus, after the harvest. Although, I'm not sure—"

"Why did you stop the wedding? Why not just let me marry Kyan and go find a Greater, make daddy proud?"

"Because I love you. I want you to be my forever."

I blew out a pent up breath. "Crew, what's going to happen? Your father is not going to take what you did tonight in stride. You stood up to him in front of the entire village."

He laughed harshly. "You forgot the part where I exposed myself and him. But it won't matter now anyway." My eyes met his. "You aren't going to like what I have to say."

I rolled my eyes. "What else could you possibly say to surprise me?"

He shifted his feet and swallowed thickly. "We aren't here to harvest apples."

Chapter 19

My mind spun out of control, and I began to feel like a child who'd whirled around in one place for too long, dizzy and disoriented. "What *are* you here to harvest?"

Crew gently cupped my elbow and led me to the couch, where he settled down beside me. "We are here to harvest females of childbearing age."

"Excuse me?" My words barely left my lips as a whisper.

"The Greaters have prided themselves on eradicating a multitude of diseases that plagued humanity even just a couple of generations ago. As children, we are all given a battery of vaccinations against these illnesses." Crew shrugged off his jacket, and unbuttoned the cuff of his shirt sleeve at his wrist. He rolled up his sleeve one crisp, white fold of fabric at a time, until the muscles of his forearms, and then biceps were exposed. A one inch square filled with tiny white dots of raised flesh rested upon his right bicep. "See?"

"Yes." I look quickly at my arms, even underneath to make sure I don't have any marks like that.

He laughed, deep and hearty. "You don't have one." He recovered, "Only Greaters are inoculated."

"Oh." Well, I felt stupid. "Just making sure."

"With the vaccines, come side effects. We thought most were safe. There was swelling around the injection site, redness and soreness, as well. Some individuals would be feverish for a few days; others would experience nausea or vomiting, sometimes both." He searched my eyes.

"Okay."

"Over time, all Greater children were vaccinated and it became mandatory to do so. There were no long term complications or side effects, or so we thought. When the first round of children came into adulthood, about half had trouble conceiving after reaching adulthood. Testing revealed that the problem lay within the reproductive system of the female population. Greater males were not sterile. However, the females were barren. At first, no one understood what was happening. But after more and more of the female population became sterile, and fewer and fewer Greater children were born, the problem was tracked to the series of vaccines given to the females as children."

He continued, "We've since stopped giving the vaccines to female children, until we can isolate which specific one or combination is causing the infertility. But, all Greater women of childbearing age right now are barren. No more Greaters will be born in this generation, maybe for several."

"So, you want Greater males to take Lesser females as wives? Breed them like cattle? What?"

"The scientists want to harvest eggs from Lesser women, inseminate them, and place them into the wombs of Greaters so that the Greater females may have children of their own. Information about this issue isn't widely known. The procedures are mostly painless and can be done in doctor's offices discreetly, so as not to cause a panic."

"So the Greater women don't know they're having Lesser babies."

He swallowed and nodded. "Yes." Rolling his sleeves back down, Crew buttoned the cuff and looked back over at me. "Look, I know you don't understand all of this and probably think it's wrong, but—"

"Oh, I understand it all very well. And, it *is* wrong. What you're doing is deceitful, to the Lesser and Greater women, and the population of Olympus itself. Your father is a master manipulator and your standing by his side tells me a lot about your character, Crew. And, I don't like what's been brought to light."

He lowered his eyes and turned his head away, then stood, grabbed his jacket and stalked silently out the door.

∞

WHAT FELT LIKE AN HOUR later, while still sitting on the blanched couch in the ghostly car, I heard the unmistakable sound of screaming erupted outside the train car. All of the girls who'd been helping Orchard Village with its harvest were being rounded up like cattle. I could see the girls from Wheat and Coal, from Vineyard and Maise. Then came the ones from my own village. Girls I'd known my entire life, were being dragged toward the trains by an army of guards, clad solely in black, like thieves in the night. The car roughly rocked to and fro as they were loaded into the cars attached to Crew's.

Laney! Two guards dragged Laney down the hill. She dug her heels into the dirt, causing a two-foot high dust trail to follow in her wake. She thrashed and pulled, scratching and clawing for a freedom that would never be hers. I banged on the glass panes of the windows. "Laney! Laney! Let her go! Please! Laney!"

I moved toward the front of the car watching as she disappeared into the train car in front of me. What are they going to do to them? To us?

Would the Greaters let them come home after they strip their ovaries? The thought left a sour taste in my mouth. Bile burned my throat and tears stung my eyes, before spilling onto the flesh of my chest. And I cried. Sobbed. For my friends. For what would be stolen from them, ripped out and given to someone else. I seethed with hatred for the Greaters and Crew was very lucky he wasn't in my presence right now.

∞

I LOOKED LIKE A BIG stain of color in a room of nothing, dirt upon perfection. For twenty minutes, I cried, sitting by the window looking out at the only home I'd ever

55

known. Unable to escape this prison. Two angry, deep voices boomed just outside the door of my car: Crew and his father.

"I told you to leave her alone. What part of that did you not understand?"

"She *is* a Lesser. You also said I could choose from among the eligible females. The only stipulation you gave me was not to bother with those who were betrothed. That was it, Father!"

"Do you not have eyes, Son?" Exasperation laced his voice.

"What are you talking about?"

"She may have been raised a Lesser, but look at her eyes." Silence. "Ahh, now you get it. She was born Greater. She may have been inoculated. She may be infertile. And, you...you have to give Olympus an heir." His voice raised with each word.

"What about Cam?"

"You *are* my firstborn. It is your responsibility."

"That is archaic, Father."

"Perhaps, but it's just the way things are. Does she even know of the ring?" Silence. "I didn't think so. The mirrors here are aged. At best, most are tarnished and warped."

"I love her."

"I know you do, Son. But, you have a duty to your people. I'll have her tested. If she is fertile, you can have her."

They were speaking of me like I was a possession. Have me? And why would they think I was born a Greater? How would a Greater come to be a Lesser? And what freaking ring?! They weren't talking about the one around my neck.

The door of the car opened with a whoosh of air and Crew climbed the three steps and then walked down the narrow aisle way decreasing the physical distance between him and me. "I know you probably heard part of that."

I nodded, not having anything to say to him. Most of what left his lips was a lie and I was worn out and tired of his lying tongue. The mouth he'd used to love me with had cut me in two.

"We are about to depart. This train is on a designated Greater track and is state-of-the-art, amazingly fast."

I stared at him.

"You'll need to rest. We will arrive in Olympus in only a few hours." He looked at me and I looked away, out the window. The leaves had begun fallen off of the trees. Stragglers clung for dear life to the knobby, awkward limbs that birthed them just months ago, like toddling children to the legs of their parents. The full harvest moon stood proud in the sky spilling light over the landscape.

I realized that I now sat on the same train that Kyan had dragged me up the hill to look at just after those from the other Lesser villages had arrived. We had climbed the hill just up there, on the hill beyond the depot and took it all in. The sleek styling of the car seemed new and awesome as we stared, taking in the unusual shape and curve of the metal that night. I had no idea then that it would be a prison, a hound dragging me back to hell with it.

"I'll sleep on the couch. You take the bed."

He walked to the bedside, tugged down several stark blankets and then the pale sheet. He stepped back and dragged his hand down his face before approaching me on the couch. "Please?" He extended his hand to me. Ignoring it, I rose and stepped around him, collapsing upon the plush bed before covering myself completely. I imagined the charcoal tracks of my tears staining his spotless pillow and a grim satisfaction bloomed in my chest.

I had to do something. I couldn't let the Greaters get away with this. They had to be stopped. Perhaps Olympus should know about the secrets their King has made. Perhaps I could learn to lie, too—at least until the truth needed to come out.

The muffled sounds of him shrugging off his jacket, unlacing his shoes and kicking them off, and then settling on the couch filled my ears. I wondered if he pulled the fur blanket over himself. He blew out a tense breath. The blankets that covered me sealed me in their warmth, cocooning me, while the sheets and featherbed below me softly cradled my body. After a while, I heard his soft, even breaths. Peeking out at him, I leaned forward to see him better. Crew lay on his back on the couch, one arm beneath his head and the other draped over his eyes. Sleep did not claim me during the train ride. I lay curled up on my side, clutching the blankets and watching my region slip away from me.

Chapter 20

THE TRAIN BEGAN TO SLOW steadily a few hours later, just as Crew said it would. It was still dark outside, but the full moon created a sickly pale blue glow over the landscape. It was desolate. Silhouettes of bare trees scattered along what look like marshes stretch on as far as the eye could see. There were no houses. No buildings or signs of human beings anywhere.

I threw my covers off and padded to the window, taking a seat at the small table across from Crew, who still snored lightly. We slowed more and then passed between enormous gates made of concrete. Two halves of the Olympian insignia was carved on either side of the entrance, illuminated by bright lights. I watched out the window in awe of the enormous concrete and metal structure.

It was taller than I could stretch to see out the window. As we were riding in the last train car, we had a panoramic view out the very back window. After we passed through the gate, I could see an enormous shiny, silver door slide closed and seal itself behind us. We were in the city. The City of Greaters.

Great towering metal and brick stacks stretched to the sky pouring steam and black smoke into the air. One skinny, tall tower even spewed flames into the atmosphere. Tiny lights flickered throughout the area. I scrambled to see it again, but it was already out of sight. "Factories," Crew said, sleep clouding his voice. He yawned widely and stretched his back out like a cat. Factories. I'd heard of them. They were where the Greaters took the things we grew and turned them into other things: wheat into flour, apples into applesauce, sliced apples, etc.

What I didn't imagine was how enormous and widespread these structures were. Some seemed tall enough to brush the sky. The train crawled along until the factories were completely behind us. More forest surrounded us for a time until finally, the trees thinned. "Here." Crew stepped behind me and leaned over my head, fiddling with the window, until it dropped down. "What do you smell?"

I sniffed the air. A faint smell of smoke filled the air. "Smoke?"

Crew laughed. "It lingers from the factories, but what else do you smell?"

I stood up and stuck my head out the window. The wind whipped my hair across my face. I could smell the lavender soap that I used to wash it with just last evening. But, that wasn't it. Something else hung heavy in the air. I closed my eyes. Salt. *That's strange.*

"I smell...salt."

Crew sat in the seat across from me and smiled proudly. "Yes. You smell the ocean. The salt water."

"The ocean?"

"Yes. Olympus is settled near the ocean."

The sky was no longer the deep sapphire of the dead of night. It faded to cerulean and lighter still to the east. The train seemed to be circling to the left, in a wide arc. "If you want the best view of Olympus, come here." Crew crossed the train car and stood silently on the opposite side of the car, at the windows near the couch. He ticked his head for me to come.

I stood and slowly walked over. "Look." His eyes tracked to the right and mine followed suit. The trees that surrounded us disappeared suddenly, and plush lawns surrounding stark white buildings, at least six stories high lined up one after the other, one behind the other, in a matrix of green and white. "What are those buildings?"

"Housing. Every Greater male is assigned housing based upon how many family members reside with him. With the current...situation, our housing for couples is currently overflowing."

Of course it was. If housing was assigned based upon the number of family members and no Greaters were currently able to conceive, it would definitely be overcrowded. Didn't they understand what that meant? Or were there bigger factors playing out here? Were the Greaters afraid to question their King? Perhaps being a Greater wasn't so wonderful after all.

The housing buildings, or complexes, as Crew called them, grew larger, the buildings taller. All were white. The train slowed. Its wheels grated and squealed. "Almost there."

"Where?"

"City Center." I looked for him for clarification. He ticked his head to the right again. In the distance, enormous structures burst forth from the ground. I lowered the window and stuck my head out to see the tops of them as we began to pass by.

"Oh my gosh! What are these? Are these houses?"

Crew chuckled. "No. Well, not exactly. Some are apartment buildings, where a family lives on each floor. Some are offices, where people work. Business is conducted."

"Greaters work?" My mouth hung open and I shut it quickly, feeling my cheeks warm.

"It's okay. Some do work. It takes a lot of organization to keep a city clean and functioning properly. To keep food distributed fairly, for example."

"Do Greaters work in the factories?" I marveled at the passing structures that were tall as the clouds and painted to mirror the same, craning my neck to see their tops. They must have been a thousand feet tall. Maybe more.

After clearing his throat, Crew answered, "No. We have Lessers that work in that district. They work in the factories. Their housing is also within the district walls. They live and work just outside the city, separated from the Greaters, but still within its walls. They receive food and goods for their role in helping the City of Olympus."

I nodded. The train wheels screamed, slowed, and jerked to a stop. I was jerked forward, but steadied myself on the window sill. Immediately, the warmth from Crew's hands upon my waist registered with my brain. For a split second, I wanted to wrap my arms around him and press my lips to his. But, then I remembered that this is all some sick game to him and pushed his hands away.

"Abby." His eyes clenched shut.

"Look, I'm not happy and I'm not going to pretend like I am. You forced me to come here. You put this...thing on me and claimed me like some piece of property." I spat. "You cannot expect things to be the same after lying to me, earning my trust, and then treating me like the Lesser I am. If you had been honest with me from the beginning, we wouldn't be here right now. Blame yourself." His eyes of molten gold met mine.

"And what did your Father mean about me being born a Greater? I've been a lesser all my life."

He shook his head and walked to a five drawer dresser next to the bed, removing something from the top of it and returning to me. A mirror. Glass framed in smooth, cool silver. "Look at your eyes, Abby."

He extended the mirror and I grabbed hold of it, but not before rolling my eyes at him for good measure. My eyes were blue. Always have been. Lulu said that's why my father named me Abigail Blue Kelley. I held the heavy oval in front of me. It was so clear, I gasped when I saw myself.

The mirrors at home were dark and distorted the images they reflected. If you were lucky, you'd be able to tell if your clothes matched and were crooked, but in this orb, I could see every pore in the flesh of my face. My lips were still pink from Laney's ministrations last night. My nose was small and slightly upturned.

The brows that guarded my eyes matched my dark, auburn hair. Black tracks stretched from beneath my eyes, fading away as they trailed down my cheeks before fading away, making the skin of my face feel tight, stretched. My eyes *were* blue. Very blue. A deep, blue, not so dark as the sapphire of last night, but not like the daytime sky either. A blue settled somewhere in between. Lighter blue streaks radiated from the black pupils in the center. I looked at one and then the other. Then I saw it. I gasped. *Oh my God.*

Moving the mirror closer, it brushed my nose. The pupil of my eye was encircled by a small, golden ring. The ring? It must be what Mr. Cole was talking about last night. "You see it." It wasn't a question.

"Yes," I whispered.

"Do you understand?"

"No."

"After the first vaccinations were given out, changes in the iris of the eyeball of recipients were noted. Usually a small, golden ring appeared around the pupil. Within a couple of generations, the rings became almost a genetic trait. Do you know what that is?"

He wasn't condescending when he asked. "No, and what is an iris. I know what the pupil of the eye is. It's the black ball in the center."

"Yes. The iris is the colored portion of the eye. Genetic traits are passed down from parents to their children, generation to generation. Like hair color, for instance, or the ability to roll the tongue, like this..." He demonstrated, twisting his tongue to the side. I mimicked his motions. I could roll mine, too! "Yes. You got that ability from one or both of your parents. The stronger the trait, the more often it is passed down in the family line."

"I understand."

"So, all Greaters are born with a golden ring, even if it's small, like yours. After the person is vaccinated, the medicines within cause the ring to spread. My ring was quite large, so after my inoculation, the gold spread almost all the way to the edges, erasing most of the brown that had been there. Scientists aren't sure why this happens, but it isn't something harmful to the individual or detrimental to society, like the infertility of the Greater women. So, it is accepted and ignored. Eventually all Greaters will have completely golden irises."

"Couldn't some Lessers have a ring?"

"No." His fingers brushed my eyelashes gently. My breath hitched. "You said your parents gave you to Lulu, that they couldn't raise you?"

I nodded. "Can I suggest something and can you please not get angry at me for it?" I nodded again, looking into his eyes. "Perhaps, they sent you a way to keep you safe. So that you wouldn't receive the vaccines. Wouldn't be barren later in life."

Chapter 21

WE WERE STOPPED OUTSIDE AN enormous three story building. Its sparkling glass facade glistened in the moonlight. The large panes were settled in between pieces of white metal. *What is with this preoccupation with white?* Screams of the girls in the other cars echoed through the metal and glass of the train car, and out into the early morning air.

They were herded into the sterile building like cattle. Guards, dressed in head-to-toe black, armed with large black guns slung across their shoulders escorted the women and stood guard outside of our car. Crew raised the windows, but his eyes took in the scene unfolding around us. We couldn't see all of the cars, but could clearly see the three ahead of us and what was happening to them. Some were being dragged by arms and hair into the building where they disappeared behind heavy wooden doors, silence and sterility swallowing them whole.

Laney stepped off of the car that was just ahead of us. She planted her feet and raised her hands. I'd never known her to be much of a fighter, but I understood her primal need to protect herself.

My eyes were torn away from her when a sucking sound of air filled the cabin and a tall guard stepped up into it. His hair was black and short around the sides. The top half of his hair was longer and it fell lazily into his eyes. The signature golden rings of his eyes were surrounded by a strange brown-orange color. "She has to be processed, Sir." He addressed Crew, glancing briefly at me and then back at him.

"No."

"Your father sent me. She must be cleaned and processed. The King has ordered it."

"Tell my father that she will be cleaned by our staff, not here. Not like this." Crew positioned himself between the guard and me. He was protecting me. I couldn't help but feel grateful and at the same time wonder if this was another act, another manipulation.

"I can go with him."

"No," his eyes pierced mine. "No." He shook his head almost imperceptibly.

The guard looked outside the door. "He refuses," he shouted to someone below.

More footsteps. Two more guards stepped into the small space.

"Crew." I tried again.

"No, Abby."

"Crew, just let me go."

"No!" he roared, causing me to jerk backward from his harshness.

One of the guards pointed a small device at Crew. Crew looked haughtily at him until the man pushed a series of buttons. Immediately, Crew grasped the back of his neck. He dropped like a stone to his knees, and then collapsed face-first onto the floor.

"Come with me, now." The guard who aimed that strange device at Crew and his partner, exited the train car. The guard with black hair and strange eyes, stood before me extending his hand. "Easy way or hard way, Lesser. It's your choice."

I looked at Crew beside me and back at his large hand. His skin was tan, unlike Crew's and his family's. "What did you do to him?"

"He was immobilized. He'll wake up shortly, so we need to hurry."

"Will he be okay?"

He snorted. "He'll have a headache, but don't worry. Can't kill the Crown Prince."

I huffed and gathered my skirts. "Fine." Ignoring his hand, I stepped away from Crew. His chest moved up and down rhythmically. He was still alive.

The guard chuckled at my blatant refusal. "That's a first. Most of the other girls are terrified. A couple of them even tried to climb me."

"I'm not like the other girls." I stomped around him, down the steps and out into the cool dawn.

∞

I MOVED TOWARD THE BUILDING where the other girls had been shoved into, with the guard following close behind. My hands shook violently as I lifted the skirt of the gown to ascend the few stone steps leading to that dreadful wooden door. I turned to look back at the train car before I grasped the handle. Strange eyes looked at me. "What happens in here?" I gulped down my nervousness.

"You will be cleaned, evaluated medically, and screened for disease," he answered automatically.

"Then why are they screaming?" His jaw clenched as I opened the door and we were assaulted with the sounds of terror and the harsh smell of disinfectant.

"I don't know," he muttered.

I stopped before gathering a deep breath of fresh air.

"Go on." He poked me in the back with his gun.

"Not necessary. I'll walk in of my own accord. My dignity is the last thing I will allow you Greaters to take from me." And with that, I gathered my skirt and walked inside, shoulders back, confidence fueling my steps forward.

The scene in front of me was more horrible than I had imagined from the opposite side of the door. The women were being lined up, forcibly stripped of their clothing, shoved into strange white paper dresses, and herded from one station to another.

Greaters wearing the strange glasses were examining their heads and hair, before ushering them into tiny stalls from which huge billows of steam erupted. Others were having lights shone into their eyes and ears, flat wooden sticks shoved on their tongues.

Their bodies were being poked and prodded. Machines were squeezing their arms and then beeping frantically. One was lying flat while a doctor scanned her stomach with some sort of wand. A square on the wall projected a grainy black and white image of what the strange wand saw inside the girl's stomach, my guard explained.

A skinny, middle-aged woman with sharp cheekbones and a matching nose approached me. "Take her to the first line," she ordered the guard behind me, refusing to address me. The look in her beady eyes said that I'd been found wanting. I watched as her dark pony tail swished away behind her. Before he could poke me in the back again, I turned sharply. His hand was already moving his gun forward. I pushed my finger into his face. "Don't poke me with that thing again. I'm not fighting you."

He nodded toward the furthest line and moved the gun back closer to his chest. I walked across the room and settled in at the back of the line. Laney stepped out of the steam closet and gasped when she saw me. "Abby!" she yelled. "Abby!" She tried to run toward me. I shook my head, tried to motion for her to be quiet but she refused. She was frantic. Two guards seized either of her arms and a Greater male stepped forward and quickly injected her with something.

She fell limp and they dragged her to the table where they proceeded to scan her stomach. After Laney's outburst, the other girls turned their attention on me. I kept my head up, held high and waited patiently. Soon, a calm seemed to fall over the others.

Some who had been in other lines first, fell in behind me and I was ushered into a seat. A Greater combed and separated my hair several times, raking my scalp in different places as if looking for something. Before he allowed me to get up, I saw my name on a communicator.

Abigail B. Kelley—negative for lice. *Lice? What is a lice?* Whatever it was, I was pretty sure it was a good thing that I didn't have one. I was ushered into another line, the one waiting for the steam closets, my guard only one step behind.

"Is it really necessary that you're here?" I asked. "It's not like I'm going anywhere." I motion to all of the Greaters around us.

"Following orders."

"Of course you are." I grumbled. "Looks like you always do as you're told regardless of whether or not it's right."

"I—"

"Abigail Kelley, move forward," barked another faceless Greater. She shoved me into the small box, instructed me to undress and stand still, closing my eyes tight. Pushing down the gown, I stepped out of it and then my undergarments and shoes, throwing each over the top of the stall at her. I hoped she lost an eyeball from the point of my heel, but knowing those freakish glasses, they would protect her.

No sooner than I closed my eyes, my entire body felt like it was being fried or steamed rather. I was being scalded. When it finally stopped pouring into the small compartment, I peeked out and saw that my hair was wet and my skin was tinged pink. The compartment door flew open. Covering my intimate parts as best as I could, I looked up to see a raging bull where the Greater woman had stood. The Greater that I'd tried to assault with my wardrobe stood there with a look of rage on her face. Her lips shook. "Lesser, get dressed. Now!" she roared, shoving me backwards with one of the white paper gowns.

I put on the strange garment, which left my rear end exposed. Clamping the paper closed at my derriere, I stepped out of the box. Her face was still red. She looked like she'd gone a round in the steam box. I smirked at her and looked over her shoulder at my guard whose shoulders shook in restrained laughter. Smiling sweetly, I stepped toward him. He would protect me from her, right?

I clenched the back of my gown closed. It was barely long enough to hit my upper thigh and cut low enough in front to nearly show my breasts. Settling on one hand on my behind and one on my chest, I inched through the line. My guard laughed. "You haven't got anything I haven't seen before, Lesser."

"You know, I really wish you'd stop calling me that. You Greaters have no manners at all. It's disgusting."

He smirked. "What would you have me call you, if not Lesser?"

"Abigail is my name. You could start with that. And, what should I call you? Guard?"

The line moved ahead and I was next for the stomach scan. "Guard is fine. I probably won't be with you much longer. My orders were just to see to it that you were processed with the others and then taken to the palace."

"Palace?"

"Where the President and his family reside." He looked at me as if I were dense.

"Great." I deadpanned.

"Next!" barked the man standing beside the table holding the strange wand. He motioned me over and I climbed up onto the table. The man tugged a scratchy sheet up to cover my bottom half, and then raised my short paper dress. I clenched it under my breasts, holding it tight to my body. Sweat began to bead on my head and chest and I found it difficult to breathe all of a sudden.

"What are you doing to me? What is this for?"

"Do not speak unless spoken to, Lesser." I opened my mouth to argue, but he squeezed some sort of blue gel like goo onto my lower stomach and began to smoosh it around with the wand. Stopping occasionally, he would punch something into a communicator and begin digging into my flesh again. Nothing about it was gentle. Though the probe glided over my skin and flesh easily with the gel lubricant, the man dug it deeper and deeper across my stomach, bruising my skin.

When finished, he wiped the goo off of my skin and gave me permission to go with his sharp dismissal as he screamed for the next in line to step forward. I pulled down my gown and then carefully moved my legs together and off the table, trying to remain as modest as possible under the circumstances.

Guard refused to make eye contact with me. He led me by the elbow to the next station where three Greater women used strange devices to scan my hands and fingers, and then my eye. A retinal scan, they called it. When the scanner wouldn't work, one woman banged it on the table. When it refused to scan my eye again, they called for a male Greater from another section to help. He couldn't get it to scan me either and became very irate.

"What kind of trick is this? It's worked all day." The portly man jammed the machine at my eye causing me to yell out in pain.

"That's enough," Guard told the evil man. "It's broken. Get it fixed. If you need to scan her later, she will be at the Palace."

"Let me just try one more time." He tried to thrust the small rectangle at me again, but Guard caught his arm, stopping the assault about an inch away from my eyeball. My eyelashes nearly brushed the cold, metal contraption.

"I don't think so. You've damn near blacked her eye already. I have to deliver her and I prefer her to be unscathed. Unless you want to answer to the King himself, back off," he warned.

The evil man backed away and held up his hands in surrender. "Just doing my job." He slapped the device back into the palm of the woman who'd summoned him to help. The girl behind me stepped forward, tears streaking her face, nose red and swollen. She peeked at me from behind now stringy blonde hair and sniffed. The woman held the retinal scanner up to her and it worked fine.

The Greater woman pinned me with an incredulous look and shooed me and Guard away. *Maybe she thought I was a witch. If only that were true. I would poof myself out of here in an instant and take my Lesser friends with me.* I flashed what I hoped was a freakish smile at her. Maybe if I scared them, they'd leave me alone.

Guard moved toward the door, his hand still positioned on his weapon. "Let's go."

"I need clothes."

"You'll get clothes—at the Palace."

I shook my head. "No way I'm leaving in this. My hind end is all but hanging out. It doesn't even close in the back and you can see all of my legs. I need clothes. Please."

He blew out a breath, and then spoke slowly to me, as if I were a child. "Look, I don't have them. These girls are going to be placed in housing for now. They'll all be together and given clothes there. You are to be taken to the Palace. Your clothes are there."

"Fine."

"Fine. Follow me." He opened the door and we descended the stone staircase. He led me down a small sidewalk to another platform where several individual train cars were awaiting passengers. "Your chariot, my lady." He swiped his hand dramatically and the train's door opened automatically with a loud whoosh of air.

I stepped inside with him and it closed behind us and then took off into the city so fast that I rocked backward and nearly fell over. Guard caught me by the elbows and stood me upright again, but not before I caught him looking down my shirt. I jerked my arms away from him. "Hey! Stop ogling me."

"As if I would need to ogle a Lesser."

"Well, you just were. I saw you!"

He smirked and snorted leading the way onto the white pod. *Jerk guard.*

In no time at all, our tiny white train car zipped between several enormous buildings and then was slowing. It stopped smoothly in front of a tall stone gate. When we exited, the train's doors snapped closed and it sped away quickly making a strange, high-pitched zipping noise as it left. "Weird little trains," I remarked.

"They aren't trains. They're PerTs."

"Perts?"

"Personal Transporters."

I nodded. Whatever they were, they were weird and fast. The whole city was on rails and the tiny white cars zipped along the tracks like busy little bugs, rushing from stop to stop, happily zipping this way and that. The stone wall was tall—taller than the trees in the forest at home, tall. Guard led me to a gate. It was wooden, white washed and intricately engraved with the Olympian insignia, which stretched across both doors. "The Palace," he said.

He punched something in to his small communicator machine thing and the doors opened for us. The sight behind those doors was more than I could have ever imagined. Perfectly manicured grass led to immaculately sculpted hedges that swirled and wound around the grounds in intricate patterns all pointing toward a large fountain in the center of a brick lined courtyard. Amazed by the water shooting high into the air, I almost missed it.

The Palace stood ominously in the background. It was constructed of stones larger than the old rusty pickup trucks at home. Large windows with arched panes stretched toward the heavens. The main structure was huge, but the towers and turrets that pointed toward the clouds were even more intricate and beautiful. It was like one of the stories that Lulu used to tell me—of a princess trapped in a tower. I could almost picture the girl she had described in such detail sitting on one of the window sills that towered above us.

"Close your mouth, Lesser." Guard teased.

"Huh?"

"You act as if you've never seen a building before."

"Well, we don't have buildings like this in our village. Most structures are made out of wood and are small. My house is tiny. There are only three rooms."

His brows knitted together. "Seriously?"

"Yes. There's nothing wrong with it, either." I huffed.

"No. There's not. I just...I just can't imagine you there. In the dress you were wearing, you almost looked the part of Greater."

"Well, don't let the fancy clothes fool you, Mister. I'm as Lesser as they come."

He chuckled. "I doubt that. You obviously caught the eye of the Crown Prince during his visit."

"Unfortunately, yes. I did. He pretended that he was a Lesser from another village, helping with our harvest. He's a liar and perhaps you Greaters shouldn't trust him either."

Leaving him with his mouth gaping open, I clenched the paper dress tight to cover my bottom and started carving a path directly to the Palace.

Guard caught up with me a moment later and we ascended the massive stone staircase side by side. The stairs led to an enormous wooden door. He punched more buttons on his communicator and then pinned me with his dark orange eyes. Opening his mouth as if to say something, he was interrupted.

The door opened and I was ushered into the Palace by a rotund middle-aged woman covered head-to-toe in black. "Hurry!" she squawked. I almost lost hold of my gown as she grabbed my arm and yanked me forward. "I'm to prepare you for dinner." She led me past enormous shiny wooden tables that held equally huge vases of freshly arranged flowers, closed doors, enormous crystal structures that hung precariously from the ceiling, up a staircase that curved along with the walls that it skirted and down a long hallway. Doors mirrored one another all the way down its length.

I followed along quickly. Guard's footsteps fell heavy on the stone stairs and richly carpeted floors. The woman's graying brown hair flowed behind her as she led us up a tightly spiraled staircase, to a locked door at the top. "Your room," she said, out of breathe. From her apron, she fished out a set of iron keys. She picked through the keys until she found the one to unlock my door and then pushed it open.

The walls were stone. A fireplace sat cozily in the far corner of the rounded room. A turret. I was in a turret. The woman scared me by abruptly turning on her heel. I nearly ran into her. "Guard! Start a fire quickly!"

"That's not—"

Pinning him with a no-nonsense stare, she reiterated slowly, "I said, start a fire. Quickly!" He grumbled but complied and began piling logs and kindling into the hearth. A long white piece of furniture sat across from the fire. It sort of looked like a couch on one side, and then stretched down into a bed, or something. The woman must have noticed my gaze. "It's a lounger. A chaise."

I nodded. *Okay.* A large bed sat on the opposite side of the room as the fireplace. Its posts nearly hit the ceiling and delicate swaths of gauzy white fabric canopied the top of the frame and cascaded delicately to the floor. It was beautiful. Plush blankets and more pillows than I could count were piled upon the mattress. A large wooden armoire sat next to the bed next to the window.

A window! I rushed over to it and looked down. Wow! I was really high up. I'd never been so high. Climbing up the trees in the orchard, or even in the woods had never scared me. This was frighteningly high. I slowly backed away from the sill.

The woman rushed around frantically, grabbing towels, cloths and what looked like soap. "Come on, dear. Time to get you cleaned up and dressed for dinner." She ushered me toward a small door. Stepping in behind her, I gasped. A large porcelain tub stared back at me, along with a sink. She turned some sort of knob and water began pouring into the tub automatically. Steam wafted up into the air. It was water. Running water. Hot water. Guard stood behind me. The woman pinned him with a stare. "You stay out there."

Red filled his cheeks and I giggled. He looked angrily at me and then turned and strode back toward the fire. She moved around me and slammed the door after him and then took a deep breath.

"Alright, dear. I'm Gretchen. I'll be your servant here at the Palace. I didn't get a chance to introduce myself because we're in a real hurry. I know you don't know me and I know you're probably overwhelmed, but we have to do this quickly, so just let me take care of you. Okay?"

"Okay."

She released a pent-up breath and said, "Let's get you out of this hideous excuse for a garment. Shall we?" The skin around her eyes crinkled when she smiled and helped me into the tub. Into perfection. Pure bliss.

I let Gretchen work her magic. She scrubbed my skin with purple soap that smelled like flowers that were even more fragrant than the lavender soap we had at home. She washed my hair twice and then helped me out of the cloudy water and into a plush robe. I snuggled into its comfort while she combed my hair out quickly and efficiently.

She powdered my face and spread light pink lipstick on my lips. She weaved my hair into intricate braids and then knotted them to the side at the nape of my neck, before inserting a yellow lily into my hair. The flower's center was brown and speckled. It was beautiful. It made me beautiful and its sweet smell baptized me in complex floral notes. I could only enjoy the scent for a moment.

"Follow me." She jerked me up from the chair and led me back into the main bedroom where guard looked up in surprise at us. His gaze fell over my hair and face, and then lower. He'd seen me in the tiny paper gown, but by the look in his eyes, you'd never have known it. It was as if he'd seen me for the first time. I clutched the robe tight across my chest and ran along after her, out of his scrutinizing gaze.

"You get out," Gretchen told him. "She has to get dressed. Wait outside the door." This time, he didn't even put up a fight. He just grabbed his gun and quickly exited the room, slamming the door shut behind him.

Rummaging around in the wardrobe, she pulled out a beautiful gown. It had only one shoulder and was stark white at the top, gradually fading into pale and then bright yellow at the bottom. She held it up to me and nodded. "This is it. Right now, since you're still not technically a member of the royal family, you can wear some color. Don't get used to it, though. Royalty wears white. Nothing else is permitted. So this will be the best of both worlds, I think."

She helped me cinch a tight white corset after I pulled on my undergarments. Then, Gretchen held the dress up while I dove into it, careful not to mess up my hair. It fit perfectly, as if it had been made for my body alone. She smoothed and tugged it into place, stuffed my feet into some bright yellow heels and then looked me over from top to bottom. A bright smile stretched over her face and she nodded in approval, crossing her arms over her chest.

"Time for dinner. Ready to meet your Prince?"

My prince? My fingers found purchase on the cool steel ring still clinging to my throat. "Let's get you to the dining hall, sweetie." She led me to the door and instructted Guard to escort me to dinner immediately, before turning around, winking at me and pushing me forward. Guard was perched on one of the stone steps, his mouth open as if he was about to say something, but no sound ever came out.

I stepped forward and began down the staircase, holding onto the stone walls for support. Heels weren't something I was used to at all. They'd never been practical in the village. My feet teetered dangerously as I made my way to guard.

His gun was slung across his shoulders by the wide black strap. He gripped it for dear life. "Is everything okay?" I paused, looking at how he held his weapon.

"What? Oh, yeah." He relaxed and released the gun, which fell to his side and collided with the wall behind him. "Do you need a hand?" He extended his hand to me and I took it, thankful to have something else to steady me. His sunset eyes watched me until I stepped onto the stair just above the one he was standing on.

"Hmmm."

"What?" He asked.

"The ring around your eyes. It's not very pronounced like the others I've seen. It's barely visible."

He shifted on his feet and looked away and then back up to me. "Some rings are larger than others."

I laughed out loud. "Do you have ring envy?"

"No." He grumped. "I do not have ring envy, as you put it." A lazy smirk surfaced, his smile lopsided and ornery. "Besides, the size of a man's ring has nothing to do with the size of his—"

"Guard! Take me to dinner. Now!"

He chuckled. "Let's go, Princess."

"Stop calling me that."

He laughed again.

Chapter 22

We traced the steps we'd taken to my room, back down the staircases to the main floor and then headed deeper into the palace. I kept hold of Guard's hand, teetering precariously with each step. I was going to break my ankles if I kept this up. Luckily, he didn't protest or make any more embarrassing remarks. I meant to tease him. But, boy had he turned the tables on me.

I'd joked around with Kyan my whole life, but something about Guard was different. My heart began to jump erratically. I would be coming face to face with Crew and his parents, the Royal Family of Olympus, rulers of the Greaters and Lessers alike, in only a matter of minutes. Guard stopped outside of a large wooden door. *Make that seconds.* A long creak sounded as he pushed the door inward and motioned for me to go ahead.

I made eye contact with him one last time, taking comfort in the burnt color for a moment. Though, I wasn't sure why it was comforting.

Harrison and Alyce Cole sat opposite one another, Mr. Cole positioned at the table's head. Mr. Cole's suit was completely devoid of color, matching Alyce's evening gown, adorned with matching ivory feathers that jutted out here and there all over the bodice and skirt. She looked like a regal white peacock. My heels clacked my arrival with each step I took closer to the royal family.

Crew was seated in between his parents with his back to me, but turned once he heard my approach. His eyes lit up, as if they could become molten gold, they began to roil like a gilded storm cloud. He quickly rose and walked to me, offering his elbow, which I gladly clung on to. Leaning in to me, his warm breath brushed my ear and his stubble grazed my jaw. "You look stunning, Abby." I could feel my cheeks warm. Nervous moisture coated my palms.

I smiled in response but couldn't bring myself to look at him directly. He walked me around the ornate wooden table and pulled out my chair. Seated, I finally grabbed hold of the napkin in front of me and placed it in my lap, twisting it into a cloth spiral, strangling it with each squeeze. Mr. and Mrs. Cole were now seated again as well. Both had stood when I was seated and waited for Crew to seat himself before settling into their own chairs again.

The table wasn't large, but the decor was elaborate. Plates sat beneath other plates. I had more forks and spoons than I knew what to do with. I even had three glasses. One held water with ice in it. The other two sat empty. I raised my glass and sipped the cool water greedily, before I looked up and saw three pairs of eyes fixated on me. I slowly lowered the water and looked back at the napkin in my lap. "Sorry," I muttered.

Several servants spun in and out of the room, around the table, filling our plates with food, our empty glasses with white and red wine. One even filled my water glass again. When everyone had a full plate of food in front of them, Mr. Cole clinked his fork against his glass of white wine. "To young love. May your union be prosperous and fruitful." With the last word, he pinned his eyes on me.

Alyce raised her glass, as did Crew, so I took mine up as well. "Well said, darling," she cooed before sipping daintily from her glass. Crew's eyes locked with mine. He smiled slightly, but I could tell it was forced. I recalled the conversation they had about me outside the train car. Crew could have me, if I was fertile.

"Crew, you should try the new salts that we've been given to try." Mr. Cole waited until Crew picked up the tiny shaker and shook it onto his food generously.

My thoughts ran rampant as I watched him. I didn't know what I wanted. I didn't want to be infertile. It had been my dream to settle down with someone I loved, have babies and raise them in the village together, as I had been raised, surrounded by love and friendship. And, as much as I had grown to like Crew while he was in the village, and as much as I thought I loved him, things had changed. He had lied. Deceived me and then claimed me as his own possession in front of the village and his parents. He was a Greater Prince. I was a Lesser. End of story.

Now, I just wanted to find a way out of this Olympian nightmare. I wanted to go home and go back to normal.

And, I wanted to take the Lesser girls that had been stolen from their homes, back with me. Something in my gut told me that was never going to be an option now. Something said I would never see my home again. I'd never see Kyan again, either. Crew's eyes met mine. He took a gulp from his glass and looked down at my neck. My fingers flew to the ring.

Dinner was quiet. No one spoke at all after the toast offered by Mr. Cole. The only sounds were the scurrying of the servant's feet, the clink of a glass, or ting of a fork against the porcelain upon which it lay. Crew's parents seemed to be having a silent conversation with each other, making eye contact periodically along with frowns of disapproval. Those were probably aimed at me.

After a while, I just chewed, sipped and avoided eye contact. It was more than clear that I wasn't welcome at this table. Crew's jaw flexed and tightened. He shifted in his seat more and more as the evening wore on. When the servants had taken away our plates of rich cheesecake, drizzled with cherries, the silence became deafening. Guard stood in the corner toward the door. My gaze found his more than a few times. I wished he could get me out of here.

Crew followed my line of sight and turned around to look at Guard. His parent's followed suit. "You. Guard," said Mr. Cole.

Guard walked swiftly to his side. "Yes, Sir."

"You were assigned to Miss Kelley?"

"Yes, Sir."

"Has she left your sight?"

"Only while in the steam bath, Sir."

Harrison Cole chuckled. "Very good. You are assigned as her personal guard until further notice. You will not let her out of your sight—even when she must bathe. You are to be with her constantly. Plaster yourself by her side. Understood?"

Guard's face looked completely unemotional, but I could see his fingers flex into balled up fists at his side. "Yes, Sir. I understand. She will not leave my sight, Sir."

"Even while she is with my son, you are to be present. Do not allow him to dismiss you."

"Yes, Sir."

"Escort Miss Kelley back to her room. Dinner is over."

"Sir." Guard pulled the back of my chair out and grabbed my elbow to help me up. The moment that his hand touched me, Crew stood.

"Let go of her, *now*." He growled.

"Crew, he's just helping me up." I pleaded with him with words and eyes.

His lip snarled up and eyes hardened. "No one touches what is mine." He pointed a finger at his father. "And you!" He glared at his father. "How dare you say that she can*not* be in my presence without an escort? Never mind supervision or impropriety. I am her intended."

His father did not blink. "You are her intended. And until she is found fit," he emphasized the last word. "You will not be married. She will remain chaste. The guard will see to it. Do not test me on this, Son. You will not succeed."

Crew circled the table and grabbed my elbow, jerking me toward the door. "Crew, stop!"

But he didn't stop. He all but dragged me all the way to my room. I had lost one of my shoes on the first staircase and the second on the narrow spiral leading to my room. He unlocked it and shoved me inside, entering just behind me. Guard wedged his boot inside the sliver of space and pushed his way into the room before Crew could slam the door on him.

"I have orders." He gritted, as Crew's hand found his throat.

I grabbed crew's forearm. "Please, Crew. Don't. This isn't you!"

He turned his eyes toward me. I'd never been afraid of him until that moment. They were hard and lifeless. His breaths were heavy and uneven. His entire chest heaved, veins in his neck bulged out as his teeth clenched together. He released Guard, who fell back against the wall beside the open door, and then turned his attention to me.

I began to back away, around the bed and toward the window. My hands trembled as I gathered my dress, which was now a bit too long without my heels. He stalked slowly toward me, meeting my retreat step for step.

"Don't touch her!" Guard rasped, still trying to catch his breath, scooting himself up with is heels and trying to lean over to get himself up.

This was a Crew that I'd never seen before. Even when everything happened with the Preston's back in the village, he'd never frightened or threatened me before. My back bumped the wall beside me. The window was just to my right. Night had fallen during dinner.

I turned my face to the side just as he stepped up to me, wincing, expecting the worse. The warmth of his breath fanned my cheek. If I turned my head, my nose would have collided with his. His fingers wound into my braids while those on his other hand grabbed my collar.

"You. Are. Mine. I claimed you. I love you. No other man touches you. Understand?" I didn't dare nod. He was too close and his fingers inside the collar around my neck were choking me.

"I understand," I squeaked. My voice trembled.

"Good." He moved my head to face him and when my eyes met his, his lips fell on mine. They weren't gentle and loving, not sensual as the kisses we stole in the village. No. This kiss was possessive and demanding. When his hand jerked my collar to get me closer to him, I whimpered and opened my eyes.

Guard had stood up and was watching from his position near the door. His body was coiled tight, ready to strike. I could tell he wanted to help me, but was conflicted. Crew was his Prince. His superior. Though Mr. Cole had ordered that Guard stay with me, Guard didn't want to upset Crew. And what could he do to him anyway? Crew was the Prince.

Guard stepped toward me. I shook my head. No. He stopped and looked at me as Crew's mouth claimed my own. When he finally pulled back and let go of my hair and collar, my lips were bruised and swollen. Tears formed in my eyes, and I blinked them back.

Crew turned without even looking at me and fixed his eyes on Guard. "If I find out you've laid even a finger on her, even to help her out of a seat, I'll have you beheaded, *friend*."

Guard nodded once, his jaw muscles flexing in rage.

Crew stalked past him, out the door, slamming it closed and locking it behind him before I heard his footsteps retreat down the spiral staircase below. When I could no longer hear him, I released the breath I'd been holding, along with the tears that I hadn't let Crew see.

I ran to the bathroom and began to sob. I sat on the edge of the large sink and wrapped my arms around myself and cried. After a time, I heard the doorknob turn. Looking up, Guard's eyes collided with my own.

"You should go. You heard him."

"I won't touch you. I just wanted to make sure you were alright."

"I'm fine." I sniffed and wiped the tears from my cheeks.

"No, you aren't."

"That's not how he acted in the village. He was so sweet and seemed like any other Lesser. I thought he was one. Except for his pale skin, he seemed to have fun and acted like he liked me, maybe even loved me. Until he put this thing around my neck and confessed who he really was. I don't even think I ever really knew him. That," I motioned out the door, "was not the Crew I knew in the village. That was a freaking monster!" I began sobbing again.

"That stupid—"

"Guard!" Gretchen pushed the door open behind him. Her eyes widened as she took us in. "What happened to her?" She ran to my side and hugged me, pushing my head into her shoulder. She shushed me and told me all would be well. I doubted it.

"Did you do this?" Gretchen was scary when she was mad. She was like a big, angry mother hen.

Guard threw up his hands in surrender. "It wasn't me. It was her intended." He said the last word as if it tasted bad on his tongue.

Gretchen felt around my neck and then began unpinning my hair. When I turned to the mirror, I could see the angry red and purple marks encircling the sides of my neck made by the collar. Made by Crew.

Gretchen buzzed around the bathroom as angry as a hornet, her voluminous black skirts swishing to and fro as she went. Before I even knew it, my hair had been taken down and brushed, my face had been scrubbed, and my dress and all of the uncomfortable undergarments had been removed and I'd been stuffed into a soft, floor-length night gown in a purple so soft, I almost thought I'd imagined it.

When she pulled me out of the bathroom, Guard was crouched near the fire. A fire that he'd built, without even receiving direction from Gretchen. She'd been too busy attending me. My eyes were swollen and stung from all of the tears that I'd spilled that evening.

I just wanted to crawl into bed, cover my head and pretend for a minute that I wasn't here. I would pretend that I was safe in my bed, Lulu in the next room. Kyan would come for me in the morning and we would go to the orchard together. Laney would greet me on her ladder with a smile, or maybe she would have already climbed into the tallest portion of the tree she could reach. She and I wouldn't be in Olympus, wouldn't be violated by the Greaters. I wondered where she was tonight, if she had a warm bed, or slept upon cold floor. Tears flooded my eyes again and I just let them leak out slowly on their own volition.

Gretchen pulled back my covers. "Thank you, Gretchen. For everything you've done for me today." She nodded slightly and fidgeted with the folds in her skirt, before finally muttering something and pulling me in for a hug. I hugged her back, while my tears soaked into the fabric on her shoulder.

"You've had quite a day. I can't even imagine what you've experienced in the past twenty-four hours."

"Guard needs something for dinner, Gretchen. Can you take him to get something to eat?"

His smooth, deep voice sounded from behind me. "I'm not allowed to leave you, Abigail."

"I'll have someone bring your dinner, soon, dear." She hugged me again and headed out the door, locking it behind her.

Guard stood, still as a tree, behind me. "You called me Abigail."

"What?"

"You called me Abigail. Not Lesser or Princess." I laughed and sniffed.

"Yeah. I guess so."

"You're going to be hanging around for a while, huh?"

He shifted on his feet. "Looks like it, from what King Cole said."

I started laughing and couldn't catch my breath. I doubled over with giggles. The tears now clouding my vision were happy ones. Or, at least, funny ones. Guard looked at me and quirked a dark eyebrow, a small smile lifting on one side. "What's so funny?"

"King Cole." I giggled.

"Yeah." He drew out.

"Get it? King Cole." I emphasized between laughs and attempts to recover oxygen. "Have you never heard the nursery rhyme? Lulu, my aunt, used to tell me all sorts of them when I was a child. I recited the rhyme for him and he began to laugh, too, deeply and heartily.

"I've never heard that," he admitted. "It *is* funny."

"Will you please tell me your name? Calling you Guard is just weird."

He smiled lightly. "You are strange, Lesser."

I feigned heart pain, clutching my chest. "And I thought we'd made progress. You called me Abigail!"

"Ha. Ha."

"Abigail," he emphasized, "my name is Gray."

"Gray? Like the color?"

He nodded. "Yep. Like the color."

"I like it. What's your last name, Gray?"

"Wilken."

"Gray Wilken. It suits you."

"Thank you."

I nodded once. "You're welcome." Gray stared at me for a long moment. A loud knock sounded at the door. His dinner had arrived. He tore his eyes away and unlocked the door for the servant boy who brought a large tray of food and a pitcher of water for him to drink.

Gray ate his dinner quickly. I wondered if his food had even been chewed, he was finished so fast. I guess when you're a guard, you have to eat quickly and get back to work.

"What do you do? You know, when you aren't ordered to guard a Lesser?"

"Different things. Guards patrol inside the city walls and keep things peaceful. We serve the Royal Family. I was assigned to the factories when I first started. Things are more tense with the Lessers there. None of them want to be there. I'm a Greater. They definitely didn't want me anywhere near them. The working conditions are, um....less than ideal." Gray's eyes flickered toward mine. "There are often fights, and disturbances in the Lesser sections."

"Is that why you hate Lessers?"

He paused for a moment, his last piece of bread caught midway between his plate and mouth. "It wasn't easy. Left a bad taste in my mouth." He took the bite and began chewing. "But, in all honesty, you're different from any other Lesser I've ever seen. You haven't caused any trouble. Not that it hasn't found you anyway." He ground the last sentence, motioning to my neck. I feathered my fingertips over the tender skin on the sides and back of my neck and head.

"I'm sorry about everything that happened today." I couldn't even look at him.

The metal fork he'd been holding clanged loudly on the plate below him. "You're sorry? You have nothing for which to apologize, Abigail. Your intended was way out of line. I know that I could be hanged for speaking about the prince in such a way, but it's the truth. You did nothing to provoke him. I've only seen him a handful of times, but this evening's behavior seemed way out of character from what I have seen."

"It was. I've never seen him like that. He's never been anything but gentle and sweet to me. Until today, anyway..."

Gray kept chewing his food and looking at me sporadically. I settled on the bed and pulled the covers up to my chin, blowing out a tense breath.

"Where will you sleep?"

He glanced up at me. "I've got a bed roll in my pack."

Pack? I didn't even realize that he had one with him. But, sure enough, next to the fireplace sat his weapon and something that looked like a small rolled up blanket with a strap around it. He would be uncomfortable on the floor, but there wasn't much I could do about it.

"Help yourself to the extra pillow. I can spare a blanket, if you want." I sat up and started to fold the top blanket up. The bed had two, so I definitely could spare one. Looking over at Gray, he sat still, just staring at me with the strangest expression on his face.

"What?" I asked.

"I'll be fine."

"You'll freeze. Come on. I have plenty."

"No. It's not that cold out yet, and I have a blanket and will sleep near the fire."

I huffed. "Well, at least take the pillow." He seemed to be mulling over it. "Please, Gray."

"Okay. I'll take the pillow." He had finished his meal and pushed away his plate. Standing, he stretched, crossed the room and took the pillow I extended to him. "Thanks," he muttered, eyeing me as if I were some puzzle.

"You're welcome." I lay back down and pulled the covers back over me, the warmth of them enveloping me immediately. I sighed as he unrolled his small blanket and settled in front of the fire, his hands clasped on the pillow behind his head. When all was still, I leaned over.

"Goodnight, Gray."

He turned his head to look at me again, with brows pinched together. "Goodnight, Abigail."

As I lay back down, memories of the harsh way that Crew treated me surfaced and silent tears fell once again, this time caught in the soft linen pillowcase beneath my head.

Chapter 23

THE NEXT WEEK, I DIDN'T see Crew at all. And, I wasn't allowed out of my room. Gretchen and Gray were the only two people I saw during that time. I was literally pacing the floor, about to climb the stone walls one evening when a key turned in the rusty door lock, squeaking loudly. Crew ducked his head in and gave me a tentative smile. "Abigail, would you please accompany me on a walk around the grounds?"

"Sure." I started walking toward him.

"It's cold. Best to grab a coat at this point. Winter seems to be making an early appearance."

"Oh, okay." I scurried to the armoire and shoved things to and fro, finally finding a deep blue wool coat that cinched with a tie around my waist. Crew, as usual, was clad in head to toe blanched garments. He held out his hand for me to take and I hesitated, but slipped my fingers into his, reveling in the way his eyes smiled. The smile was short-lived when he saw Gray behind me pulling his black coat on.

"I apologize for his intrusion, Abby. I'll speak with my father about having him removed."

"Gray doesn't bother me, Crew."

"Gray?" His fingers tightened around mine.

"Um, that's his name. I couldn't call him Guard forever, it sounded stupid. So I asked him what his name was." And I was rambling.

"Well, Gray, perhaps you will be able to pack your things after our stroll."

Gray nodded once, his eyes flickering from me to Crew. "Perhaps, Highness."

Crew didn't answer. He just began walking out of the room with me in tow, before barking at Gray to lock the door behind us. Only he didn't address him by his name. He called him Guard.

As we neared the front door of the Palace, I could feel the temperature change. It was frigid outside. The long skirt of my dress would do little to keep my legs from freezing. What was with these people and dresses? I longed for my jeans and a warm zip up hoodie. All dress here in the Palace was formal. All the time. The only exception was our nightgowns. Those were the only simple things I'd worn since arriving.

Crew pulled open the enormous door and the cold air hit me in the face and then in the legs, blowing my skirts flush against my skin. I shivered in response. Crew smiled. It looked genuine.

Gretchen appeared behind us and told us not to be too long outside, due to the cold. She pinned Crew with stern, motherly expression that told him not to cross her and I loved her for it. She bent into Gray's ear and whispered something. His eyes hardened and jaw clenched. He nodded once and locked eyes with my own. *What was that all about?*

Crew's voice boomed over my shoulder. "Don't look at her, Guard."

Gretchen looked at Crew. "Go for a walk, Prince. Clear your mind. You're imagining things that simply aren't there." Crew looked at Gretchen for a moment, then to me and smiled. It was forced, but he took my hand and led me down the steps and into the gardens.

Green still clung to the leaves on the bushes, but the trees were releasing leaves in the cold breeze. Gold, orange, and rust colored leaves swirled around in tiny dust devils around the courtyard. It was beautiful. I imagined how beautiful the village was in the fall and winter and how I was missing the change of the seasons. Nothing in Olympus was truly beautiful. It was too sterile and contrived. The Greaters strived too hard for the illusion of perfection. It certainly made me appreciate the natural beauty of Orchard.

Crew and I walked side by side toward the fountain that I'd passed on the way into this compound. He broke the silence. "You will report to the medical center tomorrow for testing. Your *guard* will escort you there and back."

"What kind of testing?"

"Fertility."

"I don't want to be tested."

"I didn't ask you what you wanted, Abigail."

I felt as though he'd smacked me. "No. You certainly slapped this baby on my neck without my permission." I motioned toward the collar. The bruises had faded to yellow now and I wondered if he even noticed or was aware of what he'd done.

"I couldn't let you marry Kyan. You didn't love him. You love me."

"First of all, I didn't love him. At least not in the way a woman should love her husband. Secondly, I loved the Crew who was sweet and loved my lips. The Crew who talked to me and held my hand. I loved the Crew who was a Lesser like me and never tried to make me feel bad about myself—the Crew who saved me from the Preston's. I do *not* love the Crew who claimed me as his intended in front of my entire village, *without* my permission, or the Crew who lied about being the crown *freaking* prince of Olympus. I do *not* love the Crew who is a Greater! And, I could *never* love someone who kidnapped every young, fertile female Lesser they could get their *grubby* little hands on because of a Greater vaccination screw-up!"

Crew's eyes widened in surprise before narrowing in anger. "Shut your mouth! Do you have a death wish?" His beautiful face contorted with rage. "I screwed up. I went about this all wrong. I admit it. But, I do love you, Abby Blue. And I want you to be mine. The only way my father will let that happen, is if you can produce an heir. Maybe several. So he is demanding that your fertility be tested. He's demanding that the tests be performed tomorrow. And, you will obey the order of the King!"

His eyes were blood shot as he raged closer and closer. "Fine." I crossed my arms, guarding myself from more than just cold outside. Small snowflakes began to fall delicately around us. Winter had arrived.

Once again I was marched back and locked into my room with Gray standing guard. A very pissed off Gray. I couldn't figure out why he was so angry though. He looked at me disgustedly. I guess now he knew the Greater secret, the reason the Lesser women were brought here. And it looked like he didn't like it or me anymore, not that he probably like a Lesser like me anyway.

WITH HIS HANDS ON HIS assault rifle, Gray motioned for me to enter the medical center. The building was enormous, silver and glistening in the sun. I couldn't even tell how many stories it held and its facade was completely covered in glass. I could see my reflection in the door, but was unable to see inside the building. It was like a mirage, every mirrored panel reflecting the other buildings and scenery around it, making the building itself almost seem to disappear. The door made a sucking noise and slid open by itself when I stepped toward it. I grabbed my chest and sucked in a breath. I thought the building was caving in until Gray laughed and motioned me forward. I felt like slapping his arm, but he was still acting standoffish. A petite Greater woman with bright red hair was positioned at a small desk just inside the door. I stepped forward when Gray's eyes jerked toward her quickly and then landed back on mine.

"You must be Abigail Blue Kelley. We've been expecting your arrival." She smiled sweetly. I must scan your retina. She grabbed the same machine that had malfunctioned on me during our initial intake into the Greater city. I flinched when she positioned the device, remembering how the last man had shoved it into my eyeball without remorse or emotion, and then tried to repeat the process again. "It's okay. This won't hurt." Her voice was sweet and lilted as she tried to reassure me, but if there was one thing I'd learned: you can't trust a Greater.

The machine beeped three times and then let out a honk. She looked at me and then at it and said, "Let's try that again, shall we?" She held the machine back up to me and the same series of sounds were emitted. "Huh. It seems to be malfunctioning. I apologize. I will inform your physician and they can administer the test during your evaluation."

I nodded, afraid to tell her that I'd failed every retinal scan the Greaters had given me. "Follow me," she chirped and stepped around the desk with a stack of papers in her arms. She led us down a short hallway and pushed a small, round button on the wall. It lit up immediately, revealing an upward pointing arrow. Several dings sounded before another set of doors opened automatically. She stepped into the tall box and motioned for me to join, holding the doors open with her free arm. I looked back at Gray, hoping that he would say I didn't have to get in that metal box. "Go, Abigail. Get in the elevator."

"Elevator?"

The Greater woman smiled. "It's okay. It will take us to your doctor. It lifts us up to the right floor. It's perfectly safe." I looked to Gray, who nodded.

I gingerly stepped into the box and tensed when I could feel it move ever so slightly with my footsteps and then even more with Gray's. I grasped the metal bar lining the box until my fingers grew numb and knuckles turned white with desperation. "Twelve." The woman said.

Gray punched a round button with the number twelve on it and it lit up. In another second, we were being rushed upward. My breaths were ragged as the box raced toward the sky. Gray must have sensed my unease because his hand fell on mine. Shocked, I looked up at him in question, and then I saw that the Greater woman's mouth was hanging open, her gaze fixated on his hand upon mine.

He quickly removed his hand and turned to face the outside of the box, staring at the doors that had closed behind him—the same ones that opened once the elevator finally slowed down. Gray was the first to exit and he did so quickly, rocking the mechanism and scaring the crap out of me. I leaped from the elevator onto what I hoped was more solid ground. Again, the décor was sterile. I'd grown tired of the color white. Should I ever get married, I'd decided that I wanted a colorful gown. I didn't even want to look at sugar, or flour, or even bread anymore. The Greater woman stepped in front of us and cleared her throat. She pushed her strange glasses up onto her nose and mumbled for us to follow her. Her heels and mine clacked down the tile hallway.

Long light fixtures flickered frantically as we walked beneath them. No pictures lined the walls. The only break in the monotony was the white doors with brass handles affixed to them. All were closed and I could hear nothing but our footfalls and a faint buzzing from the lights above. At the end of the hall, she opened a door on the right.

I followed her in to find a small cot, cabinets that hung off the wall, and a counter that contained a small sink. The woman rifled through some drawers and began removing various items and placing them on a tray that sat on the countertop. I gulped looking at all of the strange looking items and groaned when she handed me the familiar white paper sorry excuse for a gown.

"You need to undress completely and wear this gown to cover yourself. Here is a paper sheet to cover your bottom half with, sweetie." She shoved the thick, folded sheet at me and nearly leapt out the door. I looked over at Gray, who swallowed thickly.

"Can you step outside for a minute?"

He paused. I rolled my eyes. "Oh, come on, Gray! There is no other exit. Just stand guard at the door. I am not undressing in front of you."

He blew out a breath. "Fine. I'll give you two minutes and then I'm coming in. Understood?"

"Yes. Now get out," I pointed at the door. He smirked and sauntered out the door. I heard a muffled, "Two minutes!" from outside.

"Yeah. Yeah."

True to his word, as is unusual for his kind, Gray entered the room two minutes later. I had undressed at record speed, thrown on the hideous gown, sat on the cot and covered up as well as I could with the fragile paper sheet, which I managed to tear at my knee somehow.

The metal around my neck felt cold as cool air filtered into the room through a small vent or fan in the ceiling. A small ribbon had been tied around the grate and was flapping wildly in the airflow. I crossed my arms and legs in front of me and hoped Gray didn't notice that the cold was pebbling my skin, among other things.

A tall, thin Greater man walked into the room after knocking twice on the door. His glasses hid his eyes, as was the custom here. "I'm your physician, Abigail Kelley. My name is Doctor Fredrick." His smile was friendly and he shook my hand. His was warm and moist, where mine was cool and dry. "You're freezing."

I nodded. "I'll be quick. I promise. We need to perform a sonogram on your womb and ovaries. It will be similar to the one that you received when you arrived. Do you recall having your abdomen scanned?"

"Yes," I croaked.

"Good. I'll also have to examine your female anatomy." I tensed up. "Don't worry. It will only take a moment and you won't feel any pain, only perhaps a bit of discomfort. Okay?"

I nodded. "I need you to place this on your tongue, dear." He held out what looked like a small, gray square of paper.

I looked at Gray, who was staring at the wall across from him. The square was thin, almost transparent. Opening my mouth, I placed it on my tongue, feeling it immediately dissolve. I began to feel warm and happy. My body felt lighter somehow, as though I were floating above the bed upon which I lay. I could almost feel the cot beneath me when I sank down onto it, the world swirling away into a peaceful blackness. Before I lost all touch, I heard a familiar voice roaring, "What the hell did you do to her?"

Gray.

Chapter 24

EVERYTHING WAS DARK AND SOMEONE was trying to pound their way out of my skull from the inside. Lying flat on my back, I blinked until my eyes finally focused on the ceiling above me. Exposed wooden beams crossed one another in an intricate pattern. Dingy gray walls stretched to dirty wooden floors. *Where am I?* My neck was stiff and I wondered how long I'd been lying on my back.

My abdominal muscles were stiff. No, that wasn't it. My entire stomach was sore. I tried to sit up twice without success. It felt as if someone had repeatedly kicked me in the abdomen from just above my belly button down. Using my arms, I finally pulled myself up, panting from the effort it took just to sit up. Sweat beaded on my head, but I shook with cold chills. Not normal.

A frosty gust of wind rattled the warped window panes that were settled in wood that had long since turned gray. The breeze entered the room and fluttered a few pieces of my hair. Goosebumps pebbled my arms. I grabbed the blanket behind me and pulled it around myself as carefully as possible.

My stomach throbbed. Pressing my fingers into my lower abdomen, I could tell I was bruised, sore inside and out. A small oil lamp sat beside the bed on a small wooden table, providing a little bit of warm light in the tiny space. Focusing on trying to regain the strength in my legs, I tried to put a little weight on them every so often to get them used to holding me up again. It felt strange that they wouldn't work. Shuffling outside the door frightened me and I clutched the blanket to my neck, hiding the loose white nightgown into which I'd been placed.

The doorknob slowly turned. Inch by inch and then the door crept toward me revealing a large, dark shadow. Burnt orange eyes met mine. "Gray?" My voice was raspy and strange and I was sure the desert had taken up root in my throat and on my tongue.

"Oh, hey. I didn't think you'd be awake yet. They said it would be awhile." He looked at me from the corner of his eyes.

"Where am I? Are we still in Olympus?"

"Yes. We're in the Lesser section of the city. You probably saw it from the train."

"Where the factories are?"

"Yep."

"Why are we here?"

"Do you remember what happened at the physician?" He sat down on the bed beside me, making the soreness in my stomach bite at me. I winced. "Sorry. I know you're sore."

"I'm okay. I remember the doctor and the paper he made me eat, and then I don't remember anything. It's all black."

Gray muttered a curse. "They drugged you. Hell, they drugged me. Then, when we were both out, they performed some sort of test on you, on your...um, lady parts."

My eyebrows lifted in unison. Hearing Gray say the words 'lady parts' any other day would have me in a fit of giggles, but the gravity of the situation weighed me down. "What did they do? Did they take my eggs? Will I still be able to have children one day? Why did they send me here?"

"Shhh. I think they tested them. They sent you here because of the results."

I gasped. "Does this mean what I think it means?" My fingertips searched for the collar. It was still there. "I don't understand."

"Only Crew can release you. His fingerprint sealed the ring. But, I was told that your test revealed that you are infertile. President Cole ordered that you be brought here with the other Lessers and announced that you are no longer Crew's intended. The union was dissolved. Officially, I guess. I'm sorry."

Tears flooded into my eyes. To say that I was overwhelmed was an understatement. "Can I go home?"

Gray's hand fell upon mine and held them with their warmth. "I don't think so, but I really don't know what they plan to do at this point."

"I just want to go home and pretend that this nightmare never happened." I sobbed and Gray pulled me into his shoulder and then into a tentative embrace. "Why are you still with me?"

"Because I want to be. I didn't want you to wake up alone and afraid."

I shook my head. "But you're in the Lesser section. You hate Lessers. Especially here."

He smiled crookedly. "Not everything is always as it appears on the surface."

Sniffing, I asked, "What does that mean?" My eyes search his. His hands softly fell on either side of my face, pulling me close. At first I wondered if he intended to kiss me, but he held me still, his smile fading quickly away.

"Abigail."

"What?"

"I never noticed before."

"Never noticed what, Gray? You're freaking me out."

"You're not a Lesser. Your eyes...the pupil is ringed in gold. It's such a tiny ring, but it's there."

"I know. Crew showed me in a mirror on the train." I told him about my parents, about how they couldn't raise me and sent me to Lulu. Pouring my heart out to him, I explained how she raised me, about my childhood and of the village in which I grew up. We laughed and a look of wonder and amazement never left Gray's face.

"Why did they send you here? You don't belong with the Lessers. You *are* most definitely a Greater. I don't understand."

"I've never received the vaccinations. That's why the ring isn't very noticeable. The medicines didn't make it spread."

"This makes no sense. They said you were infertile."

I shrugged. "Maybe it's a natural occurrence."

Shaking his head and pinching the bridge of his nose, Gray said, "No. I think it was a ploy, a way to get you away from Crew. I wouldn't put it past the President. He always gets his way."

My stomach dropped and I tensed all over, making deep pain radiate through my abdomen. "He told Crew he could have me if I was fertile."

"Maybe he lied."

"Maybe." I conceded. I knew he was trying to be sweet and supportive, but I wondered if I really were infertile. Barren.

"Thanks for being here for me. I know you don't have to be."

"I want to be. Besides, you need someone to be with you when Crew shows up. He's... Gretchen said something to me the other day before your stroll around the palace grounds." His eyes locked onto mine. "The President ordered that the cooks sprinkle a substance on Crew's food. They've also put the mixture in the salt shakers that he uses. President Cole told them it was a vitamin mineral mixture to help promote virility, but Gretchen thinks it might explain his mood changes and aggression. She thinks it may be a steroidal drug."

I must have looked lost. "It makes a person much more moody, hostile, and more violent. Men become quick-tempered and sometimes angered to the point of harming another."

It made sense. That was exactly how Crew had acted. Perhaps he *was* being drugged. If that was the case, I was glad that Gray had chosen to stay with me.

"You don't think Crew would hurt me, do you?"

"I don't know." He stood and paced the floor. "If Gretchen is right, he could be angry about your infertility—that you were taken from him. He could act out. I just want to be here when he comes—just in case."

I spent the rest of the evening napping on and off. Gray brought me some sort of chicken broth and made-from-scratch bread. It was both salty and sweet, delicious.

Chapter 25

TWO DAYS LATER AS I dressed in the stained dove gray dress begrudgingly borrowed from another Lesser, a ruckus began outside the small house at which I'd been staying. Gray's voice and then Crew's bounced back and forth outside the rickety front door. I opened it and peered outside at the two men, who were now nose to nose and boot to boot, spitting venom at one another like two coiled snakes, both ready to strike. Easing out onto the tiny porch, I tried to decide how to diffuse the situation. Better to dive in now and beg forgiveness later.

"Crew."

He turned his attention to me. "Abby!" Running at me, he caught me by the waist and lifted me, spinning me in a half-circle. "I was so worried about you!" I cried out in pain. The soreness had worsened, not subsided. He must not have noticed, so I didn't say anything.

"Worried?" The old Crew was back.

"Of course. I love you, Abby. Look, I know what my father said about you, but I don't care. We don't have to have kids. I just want us to be together." His eyes darted back and forth searching my own, squeezing my hands with his.

"Crew, your dad will never let us happen. He sent me away. It's more than clear that he doesn't approve."

"I don't care. It's my life. I'm sick of him telling me what to do," He raged, and then began pacing, chest heaving.

"I want to go home. I want to go back to the village."

"You don't want to be with me."

"I want to go home. Please, help me get home."

Crew's face contorted in rage. His golden eyes smoldered. "I can't believe you, Abigail. After all I've done for you!"

"All you've done for me? What? Take me from my home? Claim me in front of everyone with this," I motioned toward my neck, "ring! Lock me in a room! Have physicians run a battery of tests so horrible that I can still barely walk days after the procedure! What have you done for me, Crew?"

He ticked his head back. "What are you talking about? Is this more of your lies? Father said you would lie. He said you would want to avoid embarrassment of having been found wanting, infertile—no better than the other women who have been subject to this plague. He said you would say anything to get out of the Greater city. He told me that you'd threatened to expose the vaccination program to the citizens. He said that you chose your guard, over me!"

Crew glared at Gray, his nostrils flaring and face red with rage.

"Your father is a liar and I guess the apple didn't fall far from the tree. He taught you well, huh, Crew? How dare you accuse me of lying when that's all you've done since the first time we met! Does this look like I'm lying!" I pulled up my skirts and yanked down my undergarments so that he could see the purple, brown, black, and green that mingled together on my lower stomach. He took it in, his mouth dropping slowly open.

Gray's warmth radiated from behind me. "Shh. It's okay, Abby," he said. "He sees it now."

I looked to Crew. His eyes were wide and moist. "Abby. My God, I'm so sorry."

I couldn't even speak, so I just nodded and sniffed. "I'm not lying."

His arms folded around me. "I know. I should have believed you. I'm so sorry, Abby Blue. I feel like I'm losing my mind. What the hell is wrong with me?"

I sobbed into his chest. "What did they do to me?"

"I don't know," he said into my temple. "I don't know, but I'll find out. Okay?" He pulled back and his eyes found mine. They were filled with determination, with resolve and an amount of well suppressed anger.

To Gray, he said, "You'll go with her."

I looked behind me. Gray nodded. "Go where?" *I'm confused.* Crew nudged my chin back toward him before placing a soft kiss on my lips. I was taken aback. His hand slid around my neck and into my hair. He kissed me again, pinching his eyes closed. His thumb moved down the back of my neck and brushed my collar, my ring. I could hear the moment the metal separated and a piece of my heart broke along with it. This was goodbye. He was letting me go.

Chapter 26

GRAY USHERED CREW, THE GREATER prince of Olympus, into the dilapidated shack that we'd been calling home. We took turns explaining the events of late. Gray told Crew what Gretchen said about his food being tainted and that he'd since spoken with her. She had taken the containers and emptied them, replacing them with simple table salt. The effects might linger for a short time, but would not intensify and would ultimately fade away, along with his abnormal feelings of rage.

I was certain that a part of him would remain angry for a long time. Crew knew who his father was. He knew how he ran the country, how corrupt and dirty he was. He just hadn't expected his own father to drug him, or for him to take what he had from me.

"I have to find out."

"Find out what?" I asked him.

"I have to find out what they did to you, Abby. What they are going to do with the others. What my father is truly capable of."

Gray cleared his throat. He was leaning against a small wooden dresser. "I think I have someone who can help us, at least with respect to the Lesser girls."

"Who?" Crew and I said in unison. I smiled slightly, making eye contact with him, before turning my attention back to Gray.

"Gretchen."

Crew looked taken aback. "Gretchen?"

"Yeah. She's been checking on them at night. The guards love her. She already has an in. I can talk to her about everything."

Crew nodded his head. "Do it. See what she can learn. Have her befriend Laney. She will help. Tell her Abby said for her to help. Is that okay, Abs?"

"Yes. Laney can tell Gretchen what is going on and Gretchen can report to you, Crew."

Crew sat on the bed next to me, elbows on his knees, rubbing his temples. "This is so messed up."

Gray and I agreed. It was.

"I'm going to have a friend hack into your medical records. I'll find out what's going on Abby. I promise. I'm so sorry to have dragged you into all this. And, I...." His voice broke. "I am so sorry for how I've acted. I hurt you. I swear I would never hurt you on purpose. I love you."

I hugged him tight. "I know. It's okay."

"No. It's not okay. But, I promise you, I will make it okay, even if it means taking down my own father. I will make this right."

I clung tight to him and nodded into his neck.

He exhaled and said, "God, I'm going to miss you. Wait for me?"

I nodded again, a tear slipping down my face. "Of course. You're my forever."

He chuckled and wiped the tear away. "And you are mine."

∞

GRAY AND I EACH CARRIED a small pack with one change of clothes, food and a couple of bottles of water that we managed to sneak away. Crew had arranged everything with Gray via messengers over the past few days. He didn't trust the security of the communicators. We made our way, as instructed, toward the main train depot in the Lesser section of the Greater City of Olympus.

It was very early in the morning and a heavy fog cloaked our movements. Had he known this dense cover would descend? With the technology found here, anything was possible. The freight train sat empty on the tracks. We climbed into the ninth car from the rear and found the bag that had been promised, behind several stacks of empty wooden crates. Gray pulled from the bag two blankets, more water and food and a heavy white envelope. Scrawled in beautiful penned letters was 'Abby Blue."

Gray cleared his throat and stepped away giving me some space. I opened the large square and found a familiar circle. My ring stared back at me. Etched with the symbol of eternity. Infinity, Crew had called it. A letter was tucked in behind it. It read:

My Dearest Abby Blue,

I want to apologize to you with every fiber of my being, with all that I am. I lied to you about a great many things. I pretended to be someone I wasn't. But you saw through my facade and found the real me. I forced you to become my intended, claimed you, tried to possess you. I was wrong. You're like a thunderstorm, a wildflower. You cannot be possessed. You can't be tamed, for if you were, you would wilt and wither. You would die. The light I see within you would dim and then fade away and I couldn't live with myself if I were the one who had extinguished everything that is you.

You have every reason to doubt me, but do not doubt me when I say sincerely that I love you, Abby Blue. I've loved you since I first saw you. And for me, you will always be my forever.

Your Infinite,
Crew

Warm tears cooled against the skin on my cheek as I fingered the parchment and the ring that I once detested. I was jerked out of my reverie quickly as the train jerked forward, its great wheels squealing and groaning against their tracks. Gray and I settled behind the crates. Crew had mentioned that the freight trains took longer to travel. They weren't as high tech as the Olympian passenger trains. For once, I was glad. I was content to enjoy the journey.

"What are you thinking?" Gray asked.

"I'm just enjoying the present. I've always been so focused on the past, or worried about the future, that I've never just been still and enjoyed what's right now."

He laughed heartily. "What?" I asked.

"The present doesn't exist."

"What do you mean?" I cocked my head to the side. His orange eyes glittered happily.

"Think about it. The present is a myth. It's just what we try to call the split second that our past collides with our future."

"Hmmm. I never thought about it that way."

"The moment you were trying so hard to enjoy a second ago is already gone." I looked at him. "What? It's true."

I laughed. "I guess I never figured you for a philosopher."

Gray threw his arm around my shoulders. "Me either, Abs. Me either." I snuggled into him and the stubble on his chin grazed my forehead lightly as we rocked to and fro over the land, toward Orchard village. Toward home.

∞

IT WAS NIGHT WHEN WE arrived in Orchard. On the depot's platform, a few fiery torches were lit, but provided little resistance against the blackness that surrounded it. Gray pulled me to standing and we moved stealthily toward the heavy steel door, which he opened just enough for us to squeeze through.

Looking back and forth and declaring it clear and safe, he grabbed my hand and pulled me out the door. We ran quickly toward the shadows lurking in the tree line just beyond the small wooden building. I was focused on trying to be fast and trying not to fall. A hand grabbed me around the stomach and another clasped down on my mouth before more than a squeak of the scream I tried to let loose was uttered. "Shh. It's me, Abs."

My heart thundered in my chest. I could feel my entire body shaking. "Ky?"

"Yes."

Gray pulled me away from Kyan. "Get off her, now," he warned, with a cold concern that I'd never heard from him before. Kyan released me and stepped back. Looking from Gray to me and back.

"I got a comm that you would be on the train. I was coming to help you. I didn't realize you weren't coming alone."

The two sized each other up. Rolling my eyes, I stepped forward and hugged Kyan with everything I had. "I missed you."

"Missed you, too, Abby Blue." His muffled words sounded into my hair.

"Ky, this is Gray. Gray, Kyan's my best friend." The two stayed rooted to the ground until I gave both a stern "be nice" look. Reluctantly, they shook hands quickly and then fixed their eyes back on me.

"Abs, I came to warn you, too. A lot's changed since you've been gone. The Greater guards never left. More

CASEY L. BOND

have come and things have gotten very difficult here in Orchard." He swallowed thickly.

"Why?"

"They're here to prevent rebellion. Everyone went sort of crazy after they rounded all of you up and took you away. They're here to make sure we don't step out of line. Punishments have been hard and frequent. There's a curfew now. The Greaters have everyone working, even the elderly and children. It's....well, it's rough, Abs. I just wanted you to know so that you would keep your mouth shut." He pinned me with a pleading, yet stern gaze and I nodded.

"I'll try."

"You'll do. Norris had nothing on their punishments, Abs. It's bad. Really bad."

My heart sank. What had happened to Orchard? I was supposed to escape Olympus to return to my home, to my normal. But, it seemed as if the Greaters had even taken that away from me.

"What do we do?" I asked.

"We'll figure it out, but until we do, please keep your head down and do as you're told. Okay?"

"Okay."

"You're house is being used by guard members right now, so you two can stay with me."

"Kyan, your parents don't have room for us."

He laughed heartily. "I don't live with my parents anymore."

"Oh, right. How is Paige?" I felt my entire body stiffen as her name spit from my mouth.

"Paige? I guess she's okay. She's married to Council-men Stephens. The wedding took place the day after they took you away."

"But Crew said..."

"What did he say?" Kyan asked, brows raised.

"He said you two had been married and that you were now on the Council, as was promised."

He shrugged, "I declined their offer. They did make me supply coordinator, though. It's how I knew you were coming."

"You have Lulu's job?" Tears flooded my eyes.

"Yeah. Sorry, Abs."

I shook my head. "Don't be. I'm happy for you."

"Well, with the job came my own place, so I have plenty of room for you both. It looks like you might want to clean up and rest. Tomorrow is sure to be interesting."

Kyan led us through the night, down the well-worn familiar path toward town before veering off onto an obviously new one. His cabin appeared in the distance. It looked like my old home—small, wooden, with a little porch attached to the front. Candles flickered happily in each of the windows and a sliver of smoke poured from the chimney. I covered my nose with my sleeve, trying to warm it as we drew near.

We had to make a plan, figure out how to rescue the girls that had been stolen away. I need to see if Lulu left any clue as to who my parents were and how I could find them. We needed to rid the village of the Greaters that now occupied and ruled over it with heavy hands our freedom, our future was worth fighting for and had now become my cause, my obsession.

Chapter 27

CREW

THE FIRST THING I DID after arranging for Abby and Gray to leave Olympus, was contact Senn. He was brilliant—a master of all things technological. He seemed to think it would be a challenge to hack into the city's mainframe and obtain Abby's medical records, but smiled, and accepted the task, along with my money. He tried to refuse it, but I had insisted. What he was doing wasn't easy or without dangerous.

I arrived back home at the palace and realized that it wasn't even my home anymore. My home was with Abby, as was my heart. It hurt now that she was gone. But, I had to get her out of here. I felt like burning the entire city down when I saw her bruises—bruises that my father had mandated that she receive. I passed by his office on the way to my quarters. He was in heavy conversation with someone.

A deep voice boomed. "You shouldn't have sent her to the Lesser section. What if she talks? Spreads rumors? It wouldn't take long for the Lessers to spread it around to the Greater guards and for them to spread it to their families. Rumors can take off like wildfire."

"She won't talk."

"How can you be sure?"

"I have her friends here. I control the council in Orchard, too. I can eradicate everyone she loves. I can make her life Hell on Earth if I choose. She is intelligent. She knows what she faces should she wag her tongue."

"Perhaps you should cut it out."

"Her tongue?"

"Yes."

Father seemed to mull it over. "Perhaps. But for now, she will stay in the Lesser section. Greater or not, she doesn't belong in our great city."

"Agreed."

I heard chair legs scoot across the wooden floor and hurried to my room, disgusted that I had come from such a vile human being. I only wished I could see his face when he learns that Abby is gone. I hoped Kyan and the villagers would conceal her. She believed they would, but I wasn't sure. Of course, she'd grown up there. She knew the political dynamics better than I ever would, and with the Preston's gone, Dad had no crony to call up for information. If I knew my father, he would find another soon.

I hoped Senn hurried. I needed her records.

I'd secured everything with Gretchen. Laney was on board. Everything was falling into place. And, if everything went as planned, Abby would leave with Gray for Orchard

Village tomorrow. I'd offered to send her to another village. She refused saying, "Better the devil you know, than the devil you don't." I just wished I could go with her, return the girls who'd been taken, make things right. It's funny how loving her had opened my eyes to so many things. I'd been raised thinking that the Lessers were only alive to serve the Greaters, that we had been merciful in allowing them to do so. I came to Orchard on a train, prepared to harvest the women that our city needed to right itself from our self-inflicted calamity. I left with an entirely different perspective and feeling more alive with her by my side than I'd ever felt in my life.

She completed me. She challenged me to be better, to see things anew. She loved me when I'm not sure anyone in my life had ever truly and unconditionally done so. And, I would not let her down. She truly was my forever and I would damn sure protect our future.

Chapter 28

KYAN

Comm Alert from Anonymous:
   Abigail Blue Kelley, 17 years of age, Fertility confirmed.
   Harvesting and implantation successful.
   Tracking device successfully planted in utero.
   Current Location: Lesser Village of Orchard.

I stared at the palm-sized communicator in my hand. It had buzzed urgently. When I realized what it was, I memorized every word as fast as I could, before erasing it from the device. Who had sent it? Crew's comms always came from someone named Senn.

The second thing that crossed my mind was the fact that she was fertile. They had taken Abby's eggs and put a tracking device in her womb. What the hell was implanttation? The last sentence made me shake with pure, unadulterated hatred. They knew where she was. I had no idea how to fix this mess, how to keep her safe, how to make her love me. But, I would go down fighting for it all if that's what had to happen. The Greaters would never touch her again, and I would somehow work on winning her heart. Now that Crew was gone, I had hope.

amazing readers:

Thank you so much for taking the time to read what I wrote. If you'd like to help other readers decide whether or not to read this book, you could leave a review on Amazon.com, Barnes & Noble.com or Goodreads.com.

Connect with author Casey L. Bond!

Facebook: www.facebook.com/authorcaseybond
Twitter: @authorcaseybond
Website: http://caseybond.tateauthor.com
Goodreads: Goodreads.com/goodreadscomcaseylbond

Other books by Casey L. Bond.

Winter Shadows
Devil Creek
Pariah
Shady Bay (Releasing in the Summer 2014)

READ ON FOR A SNEAK PEEK OF

WINTER SHADOWS

LASHED IN DIFFERING DIRECTIONS, THE sky bled bright orange, contrasting against the pale blue behind it. White paint peeled up from the worn sill and curled toward my fingers. I could feel the cool draft flowing in from around the window, sneaking into the room around me. Dad threw open my door, which ricocheted off the wall behind it. Taking a deep breath, he calmly but directly said, "It's time. Get your things." The deep-set lines on his furrowed brow and the urgency in his warm brown eyes indicated the seriousness of the situation. Would this really happen today? My nineteenth birthday?

Months ago, he made me pack a bag just for this occasion. Reluctantly and with both eyes rolling in defiance, I succumbed, and tossed some clothes into my black duffel and threw it in the bottom of my closet. Discarded clothing now heaped on top of it. Shirts and jeans flew over my shoulders as I tried to unearth the bag before Dad returned. I could almost hear him sigh in disappointment at my reluctance to take his warning seriously.

I ran into my bathroom and began to stuff the side pockets with toiletries and make-up. Dad would disapprove of anything unnecessary. But, I didn't care. I just wanted the familiar to travel with me to the unfamiliar. The reflection in the mirror stared back at me, revealing an empty shell of a person that I no longer even recognized.

"Claire!" his voice, agitated, urged me to hurry. My hand grasped the cold doorknob. I turned and glanced over my shoulder for just a moment. My eye caught the dark purple down comforter my mother had sewn for me. The headboard was barely visible through the mound of mismatched pillows. A red rose, beaded with dew hung on the wall, above my bed. The last photograph my mother took from her garden.

A tear carved its way over the fissures of my skin, slowly slinking toward my jaw line. I wiped it away with the help of my sleeve and bounded down the stairs, the front door wide open revealing my father standing near his truck. Rusted and old, the tractor-trailer was a dinosaur, craving for extinction. Somehow through all of the turmoil thus far, Dad had kept his job, probably due to his fierce mechanical skills more than his reputation. The corruption of the government made good men fall out of fashion and favor.

"Get in the truck, Claire." Glancing back at the house, I remembered my father and uncle hammering the wooden beams into submission when the hair on their heads was brown and thick. The black shudders and fixtures clung to the rusty brick. White wooden chairs, worn by weather and humidity, softly rocked forward and back in the persuasive breeze, waving goodbye. I jumped at the sound of rusted, squeaky metal as he pulled the trailer's tall doors apart. Pulling myself up into the empty vessel, my hands awkwardly caught hold of the bunched bag Dad launched at me.

Familiar faces jogged across the yard, toward the truck, mists from their breath quickly expelled as they climbed up dragging the belongings they could carry with them. Dad stiffly and slowly climbed up into the trailer behind us, walked to its wooden wall, carefully eased out a small, stubborn door. A false door—revealing a space only a few feet deep and wide as the trailer. It concealed the refugees and the only remnants of our lives that we could carry.

Motioning for the other family to enter first, one by one they ducked into the small door and shuffled into the space, situating their bags as they took their seats. Last to duck in, I caught a last glimpse Dad's face disappeared as he repositioned the panel. Muffled, but discernable, Dad yelled that we would be passing through three or four checkpoints on the way to our destination and instructed us to be quiet during the inspections. Would the guards find us?

The false door, constructed brilliantly, with varying lengths of wood, as if it were a piece of a perfect puzzle was the only thing separating us from them. My heart beat rang fast in my ears, and my breath quickened. *Calm down. We haven't even left yet.* The similarity of Anne and her family, hidden behind a false wall trying to elude the Gestapo flashed into my mind.

I tightly squeezed my eyes closed, in a feeble attempt to forget the fact that they were ultimately apprehended. *In America?* The truck's engine roared to life. The grumbling rattled the trailer violently, as its wood and metal retaliated. Regretting that I hadn't taken Dad seriously when he told me we may have to run, I realized that I had no idea where we were going.

How long would we be cramped in the back of this trailer? I closed my eyes and leaned my head back against the vibrating metal, its reverberations echoing down the length of my spine. I didn't even want to look at the others cramped in here with me. It was too much to take in at once.

After driving for a while, the brakes squealed and the truck violently jerked to a stop, forcing my eyes open in fear.

The faces of the others were sober and intense. Their eyes flashed back and forth in silent but understood conversation. *The first checkpoint.*

We could hear Dad talking to another man—undoubtedly a member of the guard and I imagined him tall and muscular, clean cut and shaved, armed and leery, even of my dad who had a government I.D. and truck. After his examination of my father, he asked Dad to exit the cab for inspection of the trailer. "Are you hauling anything?" he asked my father, flatly but sternly, his voice very deep.

"Not yet. I'm going down to pick up some medical supplies for the Kentucky camp. Here's a copy of my instructions," said Dad. I heard the doors squeal open and the floor shift right then left as he climbed up. Heavy footsteps fell on the old wooden floorboards causing them to creek and protest with each progression he made. He walked slowly, which seemed strange.

The trailer was empty, except for us. *What is he looking for? It's empty. Does he suspect something?* We were all as still as possible as he paused and walked, and paused again. My chest was still as I held my breath, but my heart felt as if it would leap from my chest and run as fast as possible into the hills. *Exhale.* Relief swept over me as I heard him jump down and tell Dad he could secure the door.

We all looked at each other, and I felt a slight release from the tension that had built up in my shoulders and abdomen. We weren't out of the woods yet. The engine revved back to life and we jerked forward, passed the checkpoint's speed bumps and began to accelerate toward our destination.

The next section of roadways was much more curvy and hilly. Though, it was no surprise. It was nearly impossible to find a straight, flat road in West Virginia. Unfortunately, I began to feel bile rise in my throat. I had always gotten sick in vehicles when I couldn't see out the front windshield. Today made no exception.

Dad's best friend, Michael Jones, was somewhere in the neighborhood of 50 years old. He was at least 6'5" tall and lanky. On his head, silver clung to the few brown remnants of his youth. He was quiet and serious, and sometimes avoided eye contact when he spoke with others, which really bugged me for some reason. He and Dad were deacons in our small, country Church and very devout men. Michael's wife, Trish, was his polar opposite. She was short, maybe 5 feet tall in heels, round and shapely. Her hair was completely gray now, and soft curls escaped her bun, and framed her round face. She had a beautiful, toothy smile and her dark brown eyes danced when she laughed. And apart from right now, she was always laughing.

The two sat directly across from me. One of his arms squeezed around her shoulders and the other was cradled in both of her hands. She leaned her head lovingly against his chest. Ethan and Helen looked at one another and rolled their eyes at their parental display of affection.

Ethan was a year older than me. Like his dad, he was quiet and tall, though not lanky at all. Having been on the football and basketball teams of Arcana High, he was muscular and athletic. His dark brown hair parted in the middle, slightly longer than his father approved, gently grazed over his coffee brown eyes as he stared forward past Helen. We three grew up together in a sense. They lived three houses away and we attended the same school and Church. Though Ethan was older than me he always made a point to say hello, or at least waved and acknowledged my presence. Most people didn't even know that I existed.

Helen was a lovely sixteen year old. Her curly black hair grazed her waist. Ebony eyes glittered hovered over cheeks always the perfect shade of peach. Whenever I saw her with friends, she was bubbly and talkative. Though sometimes, she would sit alone and scribble away in a little notebook, furiously as if whatever she was writing would disappear if it was not placed on the page immediately. I always wondered what she was scribbling.

Of one thing I was certain, if we did make it to our destination we would all get to know each other very well, very soon. Crossing my arms over my knees, I laid my heavy head down, only moving when mandated by a sharp curve. The truck again slowed and then squealed to a stop. *The second checkpoint.*

I heard another man ask for Dad's I.D. and paperwork, both of which my Dad immediately produced. Again, he asked Dad to exit the truck and open the rear trailer door for inspection. His footsteps resounded quickly through the seemingly empty trailer and then disappeared altogether. Again, I exhaled, after the trailer door slammed closed. My father and the guard exchanged a few other niceties and the truck and trailer slightly rocked side to side as Dad climbed back into the cab and started the engine.

We lurched forward and began to slowly accelerate, as the gears ground and groaned in protest. I just hoped this old truck would make it, to wherever we were headed. I tried to rearrange my bag to get more comfortable, sitting cross-legged with the duffle in my lap. I knew it was not an option to stop, but I really needed to use the bathroom. My bladder was getting angry. I wondered if the others felt the same or worse.

It sounded like the truck went over some train tracks or a bridge and then it stopped. *The third checkpoint.* I was wrong. The engine never stopped and we started forward again, making a sharp left turn that slung us all to the right, and the metal behind me ground into the flesh of my back. Gravel popped and crunched under the wheels of the huge machine. We went a short distance again and then every-thing sounded strange. The roaring of the truck was amplified, and yet muffled. *A tunnel.*

The hollow roar ended and the truck ground to a stop. *Now the third checkpoint?* No, I realized Dad didn't speak with anyone. He was alone. I snapped back to reality as Dad's footsteps approached the false door and slowly it was pried open. Dad looked in at me, sweat beaded on his nose and upper lip and dripped from his forehead. He dragged the white handkerchief across his face and said, "Get your things and hurry."

The pins and needles in my feet pricked as I shimmied from the small space. My joints popped and cracked as I exit, stood and finally was able to stand erect. The others threw their bags out into the trailer and climbed out behind them. Then, we were off. Dad slammed the door of the trailer closed, locked it and then turned around to us. His voice was gruff and jaw stern, as he spoke.

"Michael, take them half a mile to the west. You'll come to a small creek. Stay near it and I'll find you. I've got to lose the truck," he ordered. Michael nodded his head in agreement and immediately began hiking off to the west toward a large looming mountain. My dad climbed back into the truck cab and started the engine once more. He waved to me as he drove away, disappearing around a curve, leaving a slithering trail of black smoke in his wake.

I rushed to catch up to Michael. It was the fifth of December and the leaves had already fallen from all of the deciduous trees. The thick brown carpet crunched and crumbled beneath our footsteps. The evergreens were the only remaining hints of color. Clouds hovered in the gray sky above as if to mock our attempted escape.

I was never a follower. After Mom died, I tried to "grow up" and left my dad little to worry about. I guess most teenagers would have caused problems out of some primal rebellious instinct. But, I wasn't like most other teenagers. My mom always said I had an "old soul." She was right.

The noon sun peeked through the spotted gray clouds. I didn't know if this trek through the woods would lead us to our destination or to another means of transportation. We walked up and down three or four more hills, before we could see the small creek at the bottom of the hollow below. Water trickled over rock and land in nature's soft symphony composed by God himself; far more beautiful from the music of my soul. Smoke hung thick and heavy in the afternoon air, filling them with its acrid scent. *What is on fire?*

About twenty minutes later, the sound of crunching echoed from just down the creek. "Just a bit further," he yelled back, leading us down the creek in the direction from which he had just come. We walked along the creek bank for about five minutes and then came to a rocky cliff in the landscape. Enormous, jagged boulders, draped with bright green moss, dotted the valley along the creek's edge. These megaliths loomed down even on the tallest member of their group. *Thwump!* Dad's bag struck the ground.

"Home sweet home," he said sarcastically. I searched around to find shelter anywhere. My gut wrenched when I saw the dark black void creeping out from under the rock face. How would we fit inside? *Oh, Crap. Surely, this isn't our sanctuary.* "Don't worry, Claire. Looks can be deceiving," said Dad, with his lips upturned in an almost smile. Crouching down, he stiffly ducked and shifted his body down under the lip of the mountain. His voice emanating from the rock, "Come on. You've all gotta see this."

I looked around at the others, shrugged my shoulders and stooped under the lip of the rock myself. The rock opened up into a large cavernous room. My eyes adjusted to the darkness and took in the majesty of the vaulted space. Limestone. All caves around here were carved by millions of years of eroding water, not fast and powerful, but patient and diligent in its task.

Trickling water caught my attention in the damp, darkness. The stream from outside entered into the cave and continued its path deep into the abyss. The sound of the water echoed all around me, filling my ears with its serene notes. The others apparently brought in all of the bags because mine ended up next to my feet somehow and I sure hadn't placed it there. "There's much more to see," laughed my father. He grinned at me, and I saw hope in his expression. Hope that I would find this shelter suitable. Hope that we would all be safe here.

Reaching into a red backpack, he pulled out flashlights for each of us. The cool humidity flooded my nose as he led us down a narrow pathway, deeper into the cave. *Our new home.* The pathway curved back and forth, weaving its way into the mountain, revealing room after room, beautifully adorned with rugged formations of the dripping minerals that flowed from the Earth itself. Dad had been preparing this place for quite a while. *How long?*

Wrought iron sconces with new white candles lined the rocky pathway that gently curved along with the small stream. The flashlight beam stretched out in front of us illuminating a fairly large opening, jars and cans of various food and jugs and bottles of drinking water stared back at us—the front supply room, he called it. How long would these provisions last and what we would do when they were gone?

Traversing deeper into the cave, my flashlight beam shook at the sight of small furry brown bats that clung to the wall, tucked and asleep, occasionally stretching or writhing to implore the light to extinguish itself. In one crevice to my right, the wall of the cave became fluid as the bugs and spiders writhed and scaled, one on top of another, moving in every direction, their legs and antennae twitching. Goose-bumps spread up my arms. The cave opened up into a enormous towering room whose ceiling was strewn with dripping amber formations that defied gravity itself.

Spaced carefully apart, were several mattresses each with a folded blanket and pillow neatly piled on top of it. Sconces clung to the cave wall over each waiting to provide light to its claimant. Paths emerged and snaked through the terrain in different directions. Getting lost in this labyrinth would be easy. Everyone was silent as we delved deeper into the earth through stone-scattered, winding paths. *Crap!* I tripped over a rock and crashed into the cool water, my shoes filling up. Would it be possible for the stream to flood the cave?

"Can I ask a question, John?" Trish asked, her tiny voice amplified by the hollow acoustics.

"Of course," my father answered. We encircled the two, both to listen to her concern and hear his answer.

"There appear to be more mattresses than people present" she stated as a question.

"Well..." he paused, "two other families will be joining us. They're traveling here today as well, but will use a different manner of travel and will come from a different direction. We thought it best to split up, number one because there wouldn't be enough room in my truck's hidden compartment, and number two because if any government agents or guards caught up with one group, the other might be able continue to safety," said Dad. How carefully he planned for our escape. His meticulous attention to detail impressed me, as at home he seemed to barely even notice me at times. My father continued, "Michael is aware of this as well. We thought it necessary to keep it secret until we all were able to meet here at the cave together in case someone was captured. If no one knows the secret location, no one can give it away."

"I see," Trish said, raising one eyebrow to her husband and cocking her head to one side.

"The last thing I want to show you is as deep into the cave as we'll be able to go—and what may be the most important room in this place, at times, at least," said Dad with a wry smile. Passing more storage areas loaded with garden tools, more food and water provisions, fishing poles, bows and arrows, and guns, we finally came to a small room where the stream became quite wide.

"This," he said, "is the bathtub." We followed him a bit further into another small room. The stream in this room got smaller, but the water ran faster and then disappeared down a hole into some deeper place. "This is the toilet facility—at least while we're in the cave," he said. "Eventually, when things calm down, we should be able to move more freely outside, especially at night. The caves are constantly cool and damp. The temperature never goes above or below 55-60 degrees, so sweaters or jackets should suffice year round as long as we're in here. I'm sure we'll all grow accustomed to the environment very soon," he said. *I highly doubt that.*

After surveying the "facilities," Ethan and Helen followed their mother back out of the room and I assumed they were heading back toward the entrance of the cave. That journey would take a while, as we were very deep into the cave.

"Hold on a minute," said Dad. Trish, Ethan and Helen returned. "Please don't forget to use your flashlights in the cave or a candle, at least. It is extremely dark and there is *no* way to find your way out without a light source. I've been in here a lot so I know my way around in the dark, but it can be disorienting at first. Turn your flashlights off," he instructed. Click.

The light faded from my flashlight's filament as the others followed suit. In a few seconds, all lights were off and we were standing in the middle of the Earth in complete and total darkness. Obsidian. Funny how moments can define your innermost feelings—cold and empty and dark. Three years ago, I would never have imagined that I would end up in this hole.

Everyone turned their lights back on and chattered about the darkness absolute. So consuming, it encompassed you entirely and squeezed the breath from your lungs. Without light, I felt claustrophobic and trapped and yet was in a spacious room. I made up my mind to never be without some sort of light—just in case.

I hated that feeling. It was truly miserable. And, I imagined it would be difficult, if not impossible for one to navigate the narrow, rocky paths in complete darkness. The acoustics made even simple sounds echo as if to seem they were coming from every direction, all around you. It was truly disorienting to say the least. It was as if the cave were a large beast, swallowing you whole, leaving you to hear the gargling of its hollow stomach while you were still lucid.

Trish, Helen and Ethan again turned and began their journey back to the main room. I followed. Michael and my father walked slowly behind me and began to discuss the arrival of the other families. No doubt they would be friends and members of the Church, but who? I wondered. I overheard Michael tell Dad that they would arrive close to dusk if all went well. *Four or five more hours,* I thought. I didn't ask questions on the way back to the front of the cave. I just listened and hoped they would reveal some hint as to who was coming. They didn't. I would have to wait and see like everyone else. Hopefully, they would make it.

Back at entrance of the cave, Dad announced, "you can go claim any room you like. Just be sure to take your flashlights. We'll deal with the candles later." Helen and Ethan wasted no time in grabbing their bags and lights and setting off into the darkness. They disappeared quickly. I hoped I would, too. Grabbing my duffel, I headed off behind them as well. Dad would probably wait until the other families arrived and let them choose their spaces first. He was a true gentleman and I'd always admired that personality trait.

Ethan and Helen began to explore the "rooms" in the first large section of the cave toward the entrance. I decided to adventure to the deeper portion of the caves and take a room there. I liked the limestone formations there. The stalactites and stalagmites met one another in large, cascading columns throughout one portion of this area. There was a mattress in a little alcove nearby where I would have a perfect view of them. I decided to stake claim to this piece of cave, threw my bag down and flopped down on the mattress beside it.

I tried to remember Mom's face. She died when I was sixteen. I missed her terribly. Dad was great, but Mom and I just had a connection. It was special. We could complete one another's sentences and would laugh hysterically at the same stupid things. Dad would just smile at us and roll his eyes. We were happy. We were happy even after she got sick.

When I was fourteen when she had a cancerous mole removed and underwent chemotherapy and radiation and was told she was free of cancer at that point. The next year, she felt a lump in her right armpit. She saw her oncologist about it and was told that her melanoma had returned, and with a vengeance. She fought hard to stay alive and underwent extensive radiation and chemo treatments again, but some things couldn't be fought against. My biggest fear was forgetting what she looked like.

She was always bright and glowing and vibrant. Her hair was dark blonde, the exact same color that mine was now. Her eyes were crystal blue and sparkled even when she was mad. There was always a spark about her. She lit up a room, regardless of who else occupied it. She had beautiful, naturally-red lips. I always wished my lips would look like hers. She didn't even need lipstick.

She said the strangest thing to me before she died. It was like she had been given a glimpse into the future in which I now lived. She was in bed with her quilts pulled up around her neck. I was sitting beside her rambling on about my day at school. She grabbed my hand and said, "Claire, a lot of bad things are going to happen very soon in this world. Listen to your father and follow him without question. It is really important that you do exactly as your father says. He will take care of you and make sure you are safe."

Of course, at that point, I had no idea what she was talking about and assumed that she didn't have long at that point. I agreed to appease her, smiling and blinking back tears. My heart was torn out after she passed away. She had been my other half, my best friend and sometimes my only ally in this world. I felt that she understood me on a deeper level than any other human being on the planet. When she died, I felt empty and alone. Much the same as the feeling I got in this stupid cave when we all turned our lights out earlier.

I quickly snapped back into reality, as I heard some footsteps coming toward me. I could tell there was more than one person coming toward me. I saw two lights emerge from the darkness. Helen and Ethan's faces emerged from the shadows.

"Our rooms are in the big space near the cave entrance," she said excitedly. I couldn't believe she was actually excited to be here. "Great," I said. "You chose this one, so deep in the cave. Why?" she asked perkily. Ethan just stood behind her, quietly looking around with his flashlight.

"Yeah," I said, "I like the cave formations in here. Plus, someone else might want to be closer to the entrance."

"Can I look around?" she asked excitedly.

"Sure," I answered. Helen started walking toward the other side of the cave and crossed the stream beginning her exploration. Ethan stood still and kept his light on Helen as she walked around looking in every crevice. He seemed quietly protective of Helen. I guess because this was quite a change and adjustment for her, as it was for us all. Keeping her in his line of sight, Ethan said, "Your father wanted me to warn you that a thunderstorm is rolling in and to watch the level of the stream. If it rises, you should really make your way toward the cave entrance to be safe. He said it can rise quickly with enough rainfall."

"Thanks. I'll keep my eye on it," I replied. Then, without saying another word, he started off in Helen's direction, looking around the cave himself. He paused for a moment at the area of my favorite formation, where the cave formed draperies that cascaded from the ceiling. I wondered if he found it to be as beautiful as I did. They continued until out of my sight. I hadn't yet taken the time to explore the cave and wasn't sure how long its winding pathways and rooms extended. It must have been quite extensive because their footsteps faded and then were gone and I didn't see them again for quite a while.

While a part of me wanted to explore the cave as well, another didn't want any part of it at all. Heat surged through my face and I clenched my teeth. I was livid that it had all come down to this—my family and our closest friends, cowering in a hole.

Made in the USA
Charleston, SC
19 March 2014